AFRICAN WRITERS SERIES

Stories from Central & Southern Africa

Stories from
Central & Southern Africa

Edited and introduced by
PAUL A. SCANLON

Professor of English
University College of Bahrain

HEINEMANN .

Heinemann International Literature and Textbooks
a division of Heinemann Educational Books Ltd
Halley Court, Jordan Hill, Oxford OX2 8EJ

Heinemann Educational Books Inc
361 Hanover Street, Portsmouth, New Hampshire, 03801, USA

Heinemann Educational Books (Nigeria) Ltd
PMB 5205, Ibadan
Heinemann Educational Boleswa
PO Box 10103, Village Post Office, Gaborone, Botswana

LONDON EDINBURGH MELBOURNE SYDNEY
AUCKLAND SINGAPORE MADRID
ATHENS PARIS BOLOGNA TOKYO

British Library Cataloguing in Publication Data

Stories from Central and Southern Africa—
(African writers series)
1. African fiction (English)
I. Scanlon, Paul   II. Series
823′.008   PR9347.5

ISBN 0-435-90254-7

Set in 10/11pt Plantin by Castlefield Press of Northampton
Printed in Great Britain by
Cox & Wyman Ltd, Reading, Berkshire

92 93 94 95 10 9 8 7 6 5

For my parents

Contents

Acknowledgements	xi
Introduction	1
Notes on Contributors	13
Beggar My Neighbour: Dan Jacobson	17
Kwashiorkor: Can Themba	28
About a Girl Who Met a Dimo: Susheela Curtis	40
Hajji Musa and the Hindu Fire-Walker: Ahmed Essop	42
The Sisters: Pauline Smith	53
Tselane and the Giant: B.L. Leshoai	58
Johannesburg, Johannesburg: Nathaniel (Nat) Nakasa	67
Coming of the Dry Season: Charles Mungoshi	73
A Soldier's Embrace: Nadine Gordimer	78
Witchcraft: Bessie Head	92
The Old Woman: Luis B. Honwana	102
Dopper and Papist: Herman C. Bosman	108
The Dishonest Chief: Ellis Singano and A.A. Roscoe	114
The Soweto Bride: Mbulelo Mzamane	117
A Sunrise on the Veld: Doris Lessing	133
The Soldier without an Ear: Paul Zeleza	141
Riva: Richard Rive	150
Sunlight in Trebizond Street: Alan Paton	161
The Christmas Reunion: Dambudzo Marechera	169
The King of the Waters: A.C. Jordan	173
Power: Jack Cope	184
In Corner B: Es'kia (Zeke) Mphahlele	194

Acknowledgements

The editor and publisher would like to thank the following for permission to reproduce copyright material:

Jonathan Cape Ltd, London and Viking Penguin Inc, New York for 'A Soldier's Embrace' by Nadine Gordimer for *A Soldier's Embrace*.

East African Publishing House, Nairobi for 'In Corner B' by Ezekiel Mphahlele from *In Corner B*.

Heinemann Educational Books, London for 'Kwashiorkor' by Can Themba from *The Will to Die*; 'The Christmas Reunion' by Dambudzo Marechera from *The House of Hunger* and 'Witchcraft' by Bessie Head from *The Collector of Treasures*.

William Heinemann Ltd, London for 'Power' by Jack Cope from *The Man Who Doubted and Other Stories*.

Luis B. Honwana and A. P. Watt Ltd, London for 'The Old Woman' by Luis B. Honwana from *We Killed Mangy-Dog and Other Stories*

Dan Jacobson and A. M. Heath & Co. Ltd, London for 'Beggar My Neighbour' by Dan Jacobson from *Beggar My Neighbour*.

Helena Lake and Human & Rousseau Publishers (Pty.) Ltd, Cape Town for 'Dopper and Papist' by Herman C. Bosman from *Unto Dust*.

Doris Lessing © 1951 and Curtis Brown Ltd, London for 'A Sunrise on the Veld' by Doris Lessing from *This Was the Old Chief's Country*.

Longman, Harlow for 'Tselane and the Giant' by B. L. Leshoai from *Masilo's Adventures and Other Stories*.

Mbulelo Mzamane © 1975 and Inpra, Long Ditton for 'The Soweto Bride' by Mbulelo Mzamane.

Alan Paton © 1975 and Charles Scribner's Sons, New York for 'Sunlight in Trebizond Street' by Alan Paton from *Knocking on the Door* (ed.) C. O. Gardner.

Popular Publications, 'Malawian Writers Series', Limbe for 'The Dishonest Chief' by Ellis Singano & A. A. Roscoe from *Tales of Old Malawi* and 'The Soldier Without an Ear' by Paul Zeleza from *Night of Darkness and Other Stories*.

Ravan Press (Pty.) Ltd, Johannesburg for 'Hajji Musa and the Hindu Fire-Walker' by Ahmed Essop from *The Hajji and Other Stories* and 'Johannesburg, Johannesburg' by Nathaniel Nakasa from *The World of Nat Nakasa*.

Richard Rive for 'Riva' by Richard Rive.

Pauline Smith © 1952 and Tessa Sayle, London for 'The Sisters' by Pauline Smith from *The Little Karoo*.

University of California Press, Berkeley for 'The King of the Waters' by A. C. Jordan from *Tales from Southern Africa*.

Zimbabwe Publishing House, Harare for 'Coming of the Dry Season' by Charles Mungoshi from *The Coming of the Dry Season*.

Introduction

Some explanation, I believe, is needed concerning the precise nature of the present collection of short prose narrative. All the writers, in the first place, either by birth or adoption, are from the southern part of Africa, and most of the stories are intimately bound up with their experiences there. Secondly, despite the fact that English is the medium of expression, it is not necessarily the authors' mother tongue. Indeed, this is so in the majority of cases, with some works being in translation—from Portuguese and local African languages.[1] Furthermore, as might be expected in this day and age, a large proportion are short stories, a form of immense popularity in Africa generally amongst almost all ethnic groups. Other kinds of narrative, however, are also included here, whose antecedents lie in various areas of literature. The most distinctive of these, certainly, with its markedly different origins and properties, is the African tale. Unlike the short story, which appeared in the region towards the end of the nineteenth century, it is an integral part of the oral legacy of the continent. Although threatened during colonial times and eclipsed by western influences, it has remained a living tradition and is currently the subject of much interest, viewed by many as vital to the African social and cultural resurgence.

In considering the boundaries of the area, I have taken 'central and southern Africa' to comprise the following countries: Zambia, Malawi, Zimbabwe, Mozambique, Namibia, Swaziland, Lesotho, Botswana and South Africa. With the exception of Mozambique, the influence of Britain is considerable and English has played a crucial role in the shaping of their modern literatures. South Africa, as well, has laid its hands over the entire territory, socially, politically and economically, and its racial policies have provoked a flood of writing. There are also deeper African ties, formed over generations of continuous, interracial contact, both friendly and otherwise, witnessed by the common store of folk tales found throughout the region.

An attempt has been made in this collection, accordingly, to represent the diversity of peoples who live and write in this part of the continent: black, white, coloured; Indian, Jew, English, Afrikaner, Portuguese and the different African groups that compose the vast majority of the population. Each writer, from his own particular culture and background, and in terms of his own identity, expresses himself in these pages on a range of issues by means of a variety of literary methods. The South African obsession, naturally enough, and one which is also quite apparent in Zimbabwean fiction, is with race—apartheid. A good number of these stories, among both black and white, with the exception of course of those of folkloric interest, are of protest, expressing the physical and psychical dislocation, the misery and degradation, caused by such an inequitable system. While the black writers, usually with unflinching, graphic realism, seek to portray their feelings of resentment, humiliation and, finally, of hostility, the white writers, from their quite different position, concern themselves as well with the whole emotional-moral sphere of guilt and sin.

As one moves somewhat beyond the reach of apartheid, however, especially to Zambia and Malawi, racial issues—while by no means forgotten—give way to more familiar African preoccupations, namely, of coming to terms with a much altered, contemporary society. It is generally agreed among the writers that a process of rehabilitation is necessary, an indigenizing through the rediscovery and recovery of the past. Hence, again, the indispensable role to be performed by the entire oral heritage, myth-dominated and yet firmly rooted in the soil of Africa. But most are able to find their material more immediately at hand, in the activities of life about them: the rites and customs of marriage; the relationship between husband and wife, parents and children; the intricate bond uniting the spirit and human worlds; the role of the individual in the family and community at large—such is the regular fare of these modern stories.

What is patently obvious, nonetheless, is the fact that these themes have remained essentially the same over the years. Only the emphasis has changed, and a far greater sense of uncertainty, conflict and urgency has emerged. In the sphere of marriage, the concerns are fairly predictable and commonplace: women's rights in a male orientated society; the opposing attractions of love, duty and ambition; extramarital sex and male prowess; polygamy versus monogamy. With religion, in the running encounter between Christianity and traditional practices, a reassertion of the latter is quite definitely to be seen, centring on the particular activities of witch-doctors and the manifest powers of the spirit realm. But the overriding issue, certainly, is the plight of the individual as he strives to find his bearings in an unfamiliar environment. Detached from his roots by alien attitudes and values, he is usually depicted as a rather pathetic figure, ceaselessly struggling to re-establish his moral identity in the new society. It is significant that the most prevalent title in southern African short fiction is 'homecoming'.

No matter what the stage of struggle and change, whether of the condition of South Africa, Zimbabwe or of the other countries, the main pursuit is for a more truly African emphasis. In addition to providing entertainment, despite certain statements to the contrary,[2] the old tales endeavoured to inculcate a system of values, spiritual and material, to offer a comprehensible and cohesive approach to life. And so it is with their modern counterparts, though with them there are probably more questions posed than answers given. One which is of keen interest to the writers themselves, and highly controversial in nature, deals with that of language. Basically, can English (and other European languages elsewhere in Africa) effectively express black aspirations? Can a literature develop properly in a tongue which is not deeply rooted in the culture, a language which is not indigenous? Is English, finally, to be regarded rather as an impediment to the African quest? While Oswald Mtshali and others have turned back to the vernacular in their search, a good number, following the lead of Gabriel Okara, have attempted to forge a new, more African English, especially suited to their own outlook and aims. In this anthology it is evident that a wide range of English is used, from the highly poetic style of Dambudzo Marechera to the township argot of Mbulelo Mzamane. Perhaps out of such experimentation will evolve a language that will more completely meet the needs of modern African literature.

Jacobson's 'Beggar My Neighbour', the first piece in the collection, involving the relationship between children of two races, is a study of apartheid in miniature. The author-narrator, while centring on the young teenage white boy, Michael, maintains a careful objectivity as he depicts the series of encounters between the youths. From the beginning the racial norms of the society are well understood; and yet they are not so deeply ingrained as to negate certain feelings of common humanity. Michael, for instance, is especially indignant when their cook-girl complains about feeding 'every little beggar in town ...' Nevertheless, underlying his little acts of kindness is a conditioned attitude of patronage, at once recognized by the brother and sister.

'What do you say?' Michael asked.
They replied in high, clear voices, 'Thank you, baas.'

While dismissing closer contact with the two ragged black children, in his fantasies Michael plays out various games with them, which both mirror and magnify the changing relationship: at first, in their passive subservience, he behaves with nobility, performing acts of generosity and courage; but as they become more persistent, in anger he has them banished or executed as traitors. A child's fantasy is a striking way of making scenes of a pedestrian nature vivid, of intensifying more routine actions and behaviour. But Jacobson goes a stage further by having Michael fall ill, driven first of all in his feverish dreams to flee the childrens' increasing demands and then, in fear and desperation, to commit acts of great cruelty against them.

Apartheid has thereby run its course, ending in hatred, violence and death. But Michael's dreams continue, taking on visionary qualities. Rising from bed, he walks from the house into the symbolic, golden glare of the sun in search of the two children. In confronting them, their hands interlinked as usual, the true situation occurs to him:

.... that they came to him not in hope or appeal or even in reproach, but in hatred. What he felt towards them, they felt towards him; what he had done to them in his dreams, they did to him in theirs.

The only solution, implies the author, the essentially human one, is now enacted, as Michael takes the brother and sister into his world—and into his heart. It is only afterwards, however, to his grief, that he realizes he has never left his bed. And so, though the answer has been found, his search is just beginning.

But for many writers apartheid is viewed in quite a different light, with other sets of problems emphasized and with solutions generally not so readily available. Can Themba ('Kwashiorkor') and Nat Nakasa ('Johannesburg, Johannesburg') are much alike in that both wrote from personal experience, directly, intensely, spontaneously. Both were reporters, not attempting to produce carefully crafted stories but—in journalistic fashion—to document the truth about the dreaded infant disease of kwashiorkor and to describe (with surprising good will and humour) the problems of being young and black in Johannesburg. There is a definite note of insistence, and perhaps of innocence and vulnerability which, to my mind at least, distinguishes these two works from the rest in the anthology.

Alan Paton, too, and Nadine Gordimer are both directly concerned in their stories with aspects of apartheid. But the perspective has shifted to the position of the white 'liberal'. In 'A Soldier's Embrace' Gordimer opens during the heady days of black independence in a southern African country, as the soldiers of both armies, the freedom fighters and the colonial forces, mix with the jubilant throngs of people at the cease-fire. It is a brief moment of intimate contact, which is lingered over afterwards by the central figure and becomes the dominant symbol of the narrative.

> There were two soldiers in front of her, blocking her off by their clumsy embrace (how do you do it, how do you do what you've never done before) and the embrace opened like a door and took her in—a pink hand with bitten nails grasping her right arm, a black hand with a big-dialled watch and thong bracelet pulling at her left elbow.

Almost as if the lawyer's wife is presenting the story, the unobtrusive narrator moves through the next number of months, giving glimpses of the new order as it struggles to establish itself. New alignments must be forged, old images (particularly of white élitism) overcome. Corruption is resisted but cannot be controlled; suspicion breeds factionalism, and violence constantly threatens. The initial euphoria and high aspirations seem to be as quickly discarded as are the lawyer and his wife, who—to their own

surprise as much as to others — suddenly decide to follow the white
drift to South Africa.

> A friend over the border telephoned and offered a place in a
> lawyers' firm of highest repute there, and some prestige in the
> world at large, since the team had defended individuals fighting
> for freedom of the press and militant churchmen upholding
> freedom of conscience on political issues.

The final question, undoubtedly, is concerned not so much with
the problems of the newly independent black state as with the role
of the white liberal in it.

Unlike Gordimer's short story, Paton's 'Sunlight in Trebizond
Street' deals with a white revolutionary, imprisoned for his
political beliefs. Subjected to continual interrogation over a period
of months, the doctor-hero is driven in on himself in order to
preserve his sanity and silence. It is from this position that the story
is presented, the style of the work closely mirroring the responses
of the prisoner as his sense of time and place breaks down in the
void of his cell. 'Only one thing mattered,' he believed, 'and that
was to give them no access to my private self.' Nevertheless, under
these remorseless conditions, with his mind reluctantly straying
back to earlier times, he lives in constant fear of being tricked into a
confession, an inadvertent word. Others better than himself had
been broken. How much longer could he last? Would he crack
under physical torture? Assailed by such doubts and questions, in a
form which might be described as a modified interior dialogue, he
is first told that they have taken his friend, then his lover and finally
his boss, and that he has been blamed for the final act of betrayal.
His release, into noisy, sunlit Trebizond Street, is in marked
contrast to his former twilight existence. But it is clearly pointed
out that: 'There is [only] an illusion of freedom in the air.'

While the previous prose pieces are chiefly concerned with
apartheid, the next two stories include themes which, in quite
different ways, succeed in transcending it. To be sure, the central
figures in Honwana's 'The Old Woman' and Marechera's 'The
Christmas Reunion' are both victims of the system. But it is not so
much the system which is of primary importance as the individual
reactions to it and the personal effects of it. The youth in
Honwana's work, after being humiliated in a fight with a white
man, returns to his family in the country for solace, and there

unburdens himself to his mother. It is a poignant scene as the son, hesitating to express his mortification, bitterness and frustration before his young brothers and sisters, embraces his mother and gives vent to his feelings. Set within the framework of a monologue and written in a simple, colloquial style, it is the moving childlike nature of the boy and the tender relationship between mother and son which are memorable. Distinctly different in nature is the main character in 'The Christmas Reunion', a young university lecturer, who has returned after seven years to celebrate Christmas with his sister, Ruth. Unwilling to kill the traditional goat, he spins out a series of philosophical justifications for his refusal, which are at once lighthearted and in deadly earnest. Taking the form of a dramatic monologue, with both Ruth and the goat directly shaping the movement of his thoughts, he repeatedly protests against man's brutality, wondering if it is not part of some larger, more cosmic, scheme.

> What I mean is, my mind is in such a mess because every step eats up the step before it and where will this grand staircase of everything eating everything else lead us to? Who wants to be the first step and who will be the last all-eating step? God?

With such ideas and images undergoing continuous metamorphosis throughout, the work ends with the happy escape of the goat and the speaker's revelation that dinner has already been arranged, leading to a further reunion between his sister and his wife.

Similar to Honwana's narrative approach in 'The Old Woman', Rive writes in the first-person, to some degree associating the coloured narrator, Paul, with himself. But in making Riva, a Jewish woman, his titular heroine, he purposely provokes questions of a somewhat different racial order. From the beginning of the story, in a club house on Table Mountain, Cape Town, Paul is rudely interrupted by the sudden appearance of Riva. He finds her airs ludicrous, her laughter offensive, her appearance objectionable. And yet, months later, wandering rather aimlessly in her vicinity of the city, he seeks her out and ends up visiting her flat. She knew he would, she said. But why, he asks himself, has he bothered? And what does it matter anyway? Unlike most of the other stories in the collection, 'Riva' is basically in the interrogative mood. Mainly due to the introspective nature of the narrator, the strength of the story, it seems to me, lies not in the answers given, but in the questions raised.

In turning to Mphahlele's 'In Corner B' and Mzamane's 'The Soweto Bride', preoccupations with individual characters and personal traits have almost completely given way to larger social matters. Surprisingly enough, however, neither story is very directly concerned with the issues of apartheid: it is an essential part of society's fabric, unquestionably, but it is not of primary importance. Both writers are more interested in representing life in the black townships: the births, marriages and deaths of people; the preservation of old customs; the adaptation to new ways; the different modes of language and the behaviour of the community generally. Mzamane, with great gusto and humour, centres his story on the marriage festivities of a friend to an American black woman, and concludes that:

> To me the 'back-to-Africa call' would always remain a black American myth, at best a rallying slogan and an emotional focus. A political weapon and little besides.

Mphahlele, on the other hand, uses a funeral ceremony as a means of bringing together a fairly broad cross-section of black people. While concentrating on the thoughts and feelings of the widow, he is able to introduce a range of conversations and activities that provide important insights into township living.

Mphahlele, to a greater extent than Dan Jacobson for example, exploits his omniscient powers as narrator in order to probe into the world of his characters. Mzamane, rather, is closer to Honwana in that, as a principal figure, he virtually *speaks* his story, giving personal impressions, describing observed events, relating passages of dialogue and making judgements on people and things. There is, nevertheless, one main difference: whereas Honwana is the primary character in his story, central to its action, Mzamane is both participant and observer. As such, whatever else it might signify, his access to the main material and basic issues is more limited. Essop, in 'Hajji Musa and the Hindu Fire-Walker', employs the same point of view, but takes it somewhat further, for the story-teller, identified only as Ahmed (the author's first name), is almost totally relegated to the role of observer. In his episodic presentation of the affairs of the fraudulent Hajji Musa, we learn virtually nothing of his personality or of his views about the Asian community in which he lives. No event is interpreted, no character is appraised. Yet by means of this technique of naïve narrator, Essop has not only managed to create a hilarious portrait of the main figure but to give a sympathetically critical account of his own culture and society.

In the short fiction considered so far, there has been a progressive distancing from the effects of apartheid, to the extent that in 'Hajji Musa and the Hindu Fire-Walker' no direct evidence of it remains. And so it is with the rest of the stories, which tend to move further from the centres of contemporary urban society and more into the traditional past. Cope's 'Power' and Lessing's 'A Sunrise on the Veld' are set in rural conditions, within large expanses of nature. In the former, though, there is a town ten miles away, where the boy's father works, and a powerline which passes directly overhead, providing energy to the outside world. In the latter narrative, containing one son as well, the veld spreads out endlessly beyond the isolated farm. Perhaps it is this difference which has considerably shaped the respective outlooks of the two boys, one dreaming of distant places and the other steeped in the immediate life of nature around him. Whatever it is, in each case a natural accident occurs which deeply affects them and contributes significantly to their growing up. The use of interlinking major symbols in 'Power', with its lovely wide-angle descriptions and its joyous ending offers an interesting contrast to Lessing's intense focus on her Wordsworthian youth, in his close identification with nature at a moment of death.

With Herman C. Bosman and Pauline Smith, a step is taken back into the Afrikaner past. Bosman, in 'Dopper and Papist', lets the reader know immediately that his story is as it was directly told to him by one of the actual characters, Oom Schalk Lourens, about an incident in his life when he was a young man. Certainly it takes little time to realize what a consummate story-teller the old fellow is, leisurely in pace and yet economical of language, constantly underplaying his role to the best advantage. The humorous incident, involving the 'old-fashioned method of overcoming fatigue in draught animals' by blowing into their nostrils, is surely a case in point, achieving a delicate balance between naïveté and knowledge, while at the same time contributing to character and plot. In certain ways Bosman may be associated with Essop in his narrative aims and methods; but a much more important kinship exists between him and Pauline Smith, not only due to the nature of the subject but because of their simple profundity. 'The Sisters', set in the Karoo, under much sterner conditions, offers a story almost biblical in character—in essence, a parable. It is of a girl, Sukey, the younger of two sisters, who in order to save her sister from a disastrous marriage, tries to make a pact with God. When the marriage takes place, Sukey turns against God. But by the selfless behaviour of her sister, who gradually dies from grief and shame, Sukey is afterwards able to repeat her words: 'Who am I that I should judge you?'

In considering narratives of a more traditional kind, there are several in the anthology which express the problems arising from the clash of cultures or the dangers inherent in the encounter between the old and new ways. The son in Honwana's 'The Old Woman', as we have seen, after his punishment in the world of apartheid, wants to go home. He finds something there, at least temporarily, that he has lost. Moab Gwati, in Mungoshi's 'Coming of the Dry Season', is not as fortunate. He, too, has left home for the city, and after a period of time manages to find work. But as his mother's demands increase, so in turn does his guilt. The more she complains, the more trapped he feels—and the more of himself he squanders, until he does not go home at all. She becomes increasingly the microcosm of his existence, and his relationship with her reflects itself in his treatment of other women. With the news of her death, near the end of the story, isolated in his misery and despair, he feels like one of the damned. Brutally he turns out a lonely prostitute, after taking money from her, and 'cried for something that was not the death of his mother'.

Zeleza's 'The Soldier without an Ear', presumably told by the author himself, is about an interview he had conducted many years before, as a university student. In 'trying to find out the reaction of the people of the country to the two World Wars', he had visited a number of villages, including the house of one Baba Fule's. This old man was half-blind and his memory was failing, yet his warmth of character, wealth of experience and philosophical mind led the young interviewer well beyond his immediate topic, beyond the discussion about the nature of wars and into such things as the virtue of large families and the importance of traditional values. Perhaps more than anything else, however, remains the image of the old soldier, reviewing with cheerfulness, candour and humour, his rich and satisfying life.

While Zeleza speaks out in favour of the old customs, Bessie Head believes that witchcraft (the title of her work) has become 'one of the most potent evils in the society and people afflicted by it often suffered a kind of death-in-life'. Its source, she assumes, when its power was vested in the hands of the chiefs and rulers, lay within the social power structure. But 'Over the years it had become dispersed throughout the whole society like a lingering and malignant ailment that was difficult to cure.' Mma-Mabele's struggle against the forces of witchcraft, treated here almost as a case study, is presented as being all the more commendable because of the chauvinistic nature of contemporary society. Nor was it, she insists, Mma-Mabele's belief in Christianity—the other main 'spiritual' force in the village—which led to her eventual triumph, but her own integrity and inner strength.

The final group of stories are of the oral tradition, variously rendered into English in recent times from different African languages of the region. With them, we reach back into a vast and rich stock of folklore—and into a kind of literature quite unlike anything else in this collection.[3] For among other things, the story-teller becomes a performer and the audience participators, reshaping the tales to suit the immediate conditions. Ideally, it is a shared artistic experience, with the matter itself springing from the very bowels of the society—recording its fears and problems, its acts of courage and its system of values and beliefs. Although often regarded as irrelevant to modern African life and dismissed because of their apparent simplicity, these tales are able to strike chords within us of a particularly basic kind. Their reality is of the archetypal sort universally found in myth, fable and proverb.

'About a Girl Who Met a Dimo', the most lyrical of the group, begins with a conventional phrase which makes it clear immediately that it happened in the distant past. Expressed mainly in dialogue and song, with scant background material or narrative embellishment, the central exchange is between the little girl Sediadie and a dimo. Using magic grass, given to her by her grandmother, Sediadie outwits and kills the giant, and is able to return safely to her home. With 'The Dishonest Chief' questions are raised about the rights of individual members and the responsibilities of chiefs. Is the farmer, in fact, to be condoned for his behaviour, not only in defending his property but in slaying the thief? And does it alter the situation when it is discovered that the thief is the chief? Moral contradictions abound in oral literature, and interpretations of characters and events can be too easily made. But the issue of group survival is fundamental, and anything that threatens social cohesion is readily perceived.

'Tselane and the Giant', unlike the tale of Sediadie and the dimo, is much more leisurely paced. It tells of how a ravaged valley is restored to prosperity by the death of a giant, of how human and natural forces redress themselves. The fairly explicit references to time and place, the ample descriptions and explanations, the later allusions and less impersonal approach—these and other features quite definitely indicate relatively recent adaptation, in all probability directed at a less homogeneous audience, of a more traditional work. Among other things, point out Schoffeleers and Roscoe, '... it is a sign that the tradition is still alive, reflecting contemporary surroundings and phenomena, updating itself to meet the demands of a changing society and scene.'[4] The last tale, of almost epic proportions, concerns itself with noble and heroic exploits. To this end, the style is generally elevated and the form ritualistic, making considerable use of symbolism and magic. But more specifically it returns again to the theme of the individual in society. The princess, who has been betrothed to a snake, the King of the Waters, by her brother, must extricate herself from this evil. Though the final confrontation must be made by her alone, direct assistance is given by her aunt and uncle. Moreover, as the entire society is also threatened, her victory over this destructive force is their victory as well. So the celebrations that follow are as natural as they are impressive. The individual within the oral tradition, despite acts of adventure and courage, functions within the body politic and must ultimately be subject to it.

Notes

1. This information is provided at the beginning of the stories concerned.
2. See for example, Minnie Postma, Translator's Introduction, *Tales from the Basotho*, trans. from Afrikaans by Susie McDermid, American Folklore Society, Memoir Series, 59 (Austin: University of Texas, 1974), p. xvi.
3. For further discussion see Ruth Finnegan, *Oral Literature in Africa* (Oxford: Clarendon Press, 1970).
4. The unpublished manuscript of J.M. Schoffeleers and A.A. Roscoe, *Land of Fire: Oral Literature from Central Africa*, Chap. VII, Notes on 'The Lazy Boys and the Witch'.

Notes on Contributors

Dan Jacobson has written a number of stories, articles and reviews for a wide range of newspapers and periodicals on both sides of the Atlantic. His novels include *A Dance in the Sun* and *The Price of Diamonds*. He now resides in London.

Can Themba was born in Marabastad, Northern Transvaal. After graduating from Fort Hare, he worked in Johannesburg first as a teacher then as a journalist, mainly on *Drum* and *The Golden City Post*. In 1963 he moved to Swaziland and died there several years later.

Susheela Curtis is the editor of a collection of twenty-eight stories of folklore called *Mainane. Tswana Tales*, published in Botswana in 1975.

Ahmed Essop was born in India, and completed his education at the University of South Africa. Various short stories, published in such periodicals as *Contrast* and *Purple Renoster*, were collected in *The Hajji and Other Stories* and won the Olive Schreiner Award in 1979. Not long afterwards his first novel, *The Visitation*, made its appearance.

Pauline Smith was born in Oudtshoorn, Cape Province, the daughter of an English doctor. Her collection of short stories, *The Little Karoo*, was published in 1925 and was shortly followed by *The Beadle*, then *Platkop's Children*.

B.L. Leshoai is a Mosotho with extensive teaching experience in various African universities. He is also a writer of plays and short stories, and has translated *Masilo's Adventures and Other Stories* from his own language.

Nathaniel (Nat) Nakasa was a journalist in Johannesburg, contributing regularly to *Drum* and *The Golden City Post*. Moreover, he was the first black journalist on the *Rand Daily Mail*, and established *The Classic* magazine. In 1965, at the age of twenty-eight, he committed suicide in New York City.

Charles Mungoshi has published two collections of stories, *Coming of the Dry Season* and *Waiting for the Rain* (AWS 170), and a novel in Shona. He lives in Zimbabwe.

Nadine Gordimer is one of the most exceptional writers of fiction in English today. Her publications include seven collections of short stories and seven novels. The short-story collection, *Friday's Footprint*, won the W.H. Smith Literary Award in 1961, *A Guest of Honour* won the James Tait Black Memorial Prize in 1972 and in 1974 she shared the Booker Prize for *The Conservationist*. A selection of her critical essays, *The Black Interpreters*, deals with different aspects of African writing. She lives in Johannesburg.

Bessie Head's publications include three novels—*When Rain Clouds Gather, Maru* (AWS 101) and *A Question of Power* (AWS 149)—as well as a collection of short stories, *The Collector of Treasures* (AWS 182). Her latest book *Serowe: Village of the Rain-Wind* (AWS 220) recalls everyday village life. She now lives in Serowe, Botswana.

Luis B. Honwana is Chief of Staff to the President of Mozambique. As a journalist and accomplished photographer he has been actively engaged in the literary and artistic life of Mozambique's capital city, Maputo. A number of his short stories have been translated into English and collected in *We Killed Mangy-Dog and Other Mozambique Stories* (AWS 60).

Herman C. Bosman's considerable reputation as a writer rests mainly on his short stories, especially those about the Marico district of the Transvaal. Among his publications are *Mafeking Road, Unto Dust, Jurie Steyn's Post-Office* and *A Bekkersdal Marathon*.

Ellis Singano and **A.A. Roscoe** live in Malaŵi, the former as a freelance writer, the latter as a Professor of English at the university and one of the leading critics on African literature.

Mbulelo Mzamane was educated in Swaziland and Botswana and has lectured on African literature at the university in Botswana. His short stories have appeared in local journals, including *New Classic, Izwe* and *Contrast*. Recently a collection of them, *Mzala*, has been published as part of the Staffrider Series.

Doris Lessing was born in Persia (Iran) of English parents and moved to a farm in Southern Rhodesia (Zimbabwe) as a child. In 1949 she left Salisbury to live in London. The following year her first novel was published, *The Grass is Singing* (AWS 131), which was followed by others and by an impressive number of short stories, essays and reviews. Among various literary honours, she has received the Society of Author's Somerset Maugham Award and the Prix Medici.

Paul Zeleza was educated in Malawi, graduating from the university there in 1976. He has written plays and poems, and a selection of his short stories has been collected in *Night of Darkness and Other Stories*.

Richard Rive's publications include a volume of short stories (*African Songs*), a novel (*Emergency*) and two plays. He has also edited several anthologies and contributed essays to various literary journals. He lives in Cape Town.

Alan Paton's first novel, *Cry the Beloved Country* (1948), won international acclaim. It was followed by a second novel, *Too Late the Phalarope*, and by a collection of short stories, *Debbie Go Home*. He has also written numerous articles on South African problems for national newspapers and periodicals, and continues to do so. Among his later publications are *Apartheid and the Archbishop* and *Knocking on the Door*.

Dambudzo Marechera's first novel *The House of Hunger* (AWS 207), won the prestigious *Guardian* fiction prize in 1979. A year later he published a collection of short stories, *Black Sunlight* (AWS 237). He has recently returned to Zimbabwe.

A.C. Jordan was raised in the Transkei and in Cape Town, and later became Professor of African Languages and Literature at the University of Wisconsin. He was an outstanding teacher, novelist and scholar, his studies centring on the Xhosa oral traditions.

Jack Cope's literary work includes biography, poetry, translation, short story writing and some eight novels. He also edited *Contrast* and, with Uys Krige, *The Penguin Book of South African Verse*. He lives in Onrust, Cape Province.

Es'kia (Zeke) Mphahlele has returned, after twenty years abroad, to South Africa. Besides his autobiography, *Down Second Avenue*, which is now regarded as a classic of African literature, he has written two novels, several books of short stories and numerous critical articles.

Beggar My Neighbour

Dan Jacobson

Michael saw them for the first time when he was coming home from school one day. One moment the street had been empty, glittering in the light from the sun behind Michael's back, with no traffic on the roadway and apparently no pedestrians on the broad sandy pavement; the next moment these two were before him, their faces raised to his. They seemed to emerge directly in front of him, as if the light and shade of the glaring street had suddenly condensed itself into two little piccanins with large eyes set in their round, black faces.

'*Stukkie brood?*' the elder, a boy, said in a plaintive voice. A piece of bread. At Michael's school the slang term for any African child was just that: *stukkie brood*. That was what African children were always begging for.

'*Stukkie brood?*' the little girl said. She was wearing a soiled white dress that was so short it barely covered her loins; there seemed to to be nothing at all beneath the dress. She wore no socks, no shoes, no cardigan, no cap or hat. She must have been about ten years old. The boy, who wore a torn khaki shirt and a pair of grey shorts much too large for him, was about Michael's age, about twelve, though he was a little smaller than the white boy. Like the girl, the African boy had no shoes or socks. Their limbs were painfully thin; their wrists and ankles stood out in knobs, and the skin over these protruding bones was rougher than elsewhere. The dirt on their skin showed up as a faint greyness against the black.

'I've got no bread,' the white boy said. He had halted in his surprise at the suddenness of their appearance before him. They must have been hiding behind one of the trees that were planted at intervals along the pavement. 'I don't bring bread from school.'

They did not move. Michael shifted his school case from one hand to the other and took a pace forward. Silently, the African children stood aside. As he passed them, Michael was conscious of the movement of their eyes; when he turned to look back he saw that they were standing still to watch him go. The boy was holding one of the girl's hands in his.

It was this that made the white child pause. He was touched by their dependence on one another, and disturbed by it too, as he had been by the way they had suddenly come before him, and by their watchfulness and silence after they had uttered their customary, begging request. Michael saw again how ragged and dirty they were, and thought of how hungry they must be. Surely he could give them a piece of bread. He was only three blocks from home.

He said, 'I haven't got any bread here. But if you come home with me, I'll see that you get some bread. Do you understand?'

They made no reply; but they obviously understood what he had said. The three children moved down the pavement, the two piccanins as silent as the shadows that slid over the rough sand ahead of them. The Africans walked a little behind Michael, and to one side of him. Once Michael asked them if they went to school, and the boy shook his head; when Michael asked them if they were brother and sister, the boy nodded.

When they reached Michael's house, he went inside and told Dora, the cook-girl, that there were two piccanins in the lane outside, and that he wanted her to cut some bread and jam for them. Dora grumbled that she was not supposed to look after every little beggar in town, and Michael answered her angrily, 'We've got lots of bread. Why shouldn't we give them some?' He was particularly indignant because he felt that Dora, being of the same race as the two outside, should have been even readier than he was to help them. When Dora was about to take the bread out to the back gate, where the piccanins waited, Michael stopped her. 'It's all right, Dora,' he said in a tone of reproof, 'I'll take it,' and he went out into the sunlight, carrying the plate in his hand.

'*Stukkie brood*,' he called out to them. 'Here's your *stukkie brood*.'

The two children stretched their hands out eagerly, and Michael let them take the inch-thick slices from the plate. He was pleased to see that Dora had put a scraping of apricot jam on the bread. Each of the piccanins held the bread in both hands, as if afraid of dropping it. The girl's mouth worked a little, but she kept her eyes fixed on the white boy.

'What do you say?' Michael asked.

They replied in high, clear voices, 'Thank you, baas.'

'That's better. Now you can eat.' He wanted to see them eat it; he wanted to share their pleasure in satisfying their strained appetites. But without saying a word to him, they began to back away, side by side. They took a few paces, and then they turned and ran along the lane towards the main road they had walked down earlier. The little girl's dress fluttered behind her, white against her black body. At the corner they halted, looked back once, and then ran on, out of sight.

A few days later, at the same time and in the same place, Michael saw them again, on his way home from school. They were standing in the middle of the pavement, and he saw them from a long way off. They were obviously waiting for him to come. Michael was the first to speak, as he approached them.

'What? Another piece of bread?' he called out from a few yards away.

'Yes, baas,' they answered together. They turned immediately to join him as he walked by. Yet they kept a respectful pace or two behind.

'How did you know I was coming?'

'We know the baas is coming from school.'

'And how do you know that I'm going to give you bread?'

There was no reply; not even a smile from the boy, in response to Michael's. They seemed to Michael, as he glanced casually at them, identical in appearance to a hundred, a thousand, other piccanins, from the peppercorns on top of their heads to their wide, calloused, sand-grey feet.

When they reached the house, Michael told Dora, 'Those *stukkie broods* are waiting outside again. Give them something, and then they can go.'

Dora grumbled once again, but did as she was told. Michael did not go out with the bread himself; he was in a hurry to get back to work on a model car he was making, and was satisfied to see, out of his bedroom window, Dora coming from the back gate a few minutes later with an empty plate in her hand. Soon he had forgotten all about the two children. He did not go out of the house until a couple of hours had passed; by then it was dusk, and he took a torch with him to help find a piece of wire for his model in the darkness of the lumber-shed. Handling the torch gave Michael a feeling of power and importance, and he stepped into the lane with it, intending to shine it about like a policeman on his beat. Immediately he opened the gate, he saw the two little piccanins standing in the half-light, just a few paces away from him.

'What are you doing here?' Michael exclaimed in surprise.

The boy answered, holding his head up, as if warning Michael to be silent. 'We were waiting to say thank you to the baas.'

'What!' Michael took a step towards them both, and they stood their ground, only shrinking together slightly.

For all the glare and glitter there was in the streets of Lyndhurst by day, it was winter, midwinter; and once the sun had set a bitter chill came into the air, as swiftly as the darkness. The cold at night wrung deep notes from the contracting iron roofs of the houses, and froze the fish-ponds in all the fine gardens of the white suburbs. Already Michael could feel its sharp touch on the tips of his ears and fingers. And the two African children stood there barefoot, in a flimsy dress and torn shirt, waiting to thank him for the bread he had had sent out to them.

'You mustn't wait,' Michael said. In the half-darkness he saw the white dress on the girl more clearly than the boy's clothing; and he remembered the nakedness and puniness of her black thighs. He stretched his hand out, with the torch in it. 'Take it,' he said. The torch was in his hand, and there was nothing else that he could give to them. 'It's nice,' he said. 'It's a torch. Look.' He switched it on and saw in its beam of light a pair of startled eyes, darting desperately from side to side. 'You see how nice it is,' Michael said, turning the beam upwards, where it lost itself against the light that lingered in the sky. 'If you don't want it, you can sell it. Go on, take it.'

A hand came up and took the torch from him. Then the two children ran off, in the same direction they had taken on the first afternoon. When they reached the corner all the street lights came on, as if at a single touch, and the children stopped and stared at them, before running on. Michael saw the torch glinting in the boy's hand, and only then did it occur to him that despite their zeal to thank him for the bread they hadn't thanked him for the torch. The size of the gift must have surprised them into silence, Michael decided; and the thought of his own generosity helped to console him for the regret he couldn't help feeling when he saw the torch being carried away from him.

Michael was a lonely child. He had neither brothers nor sisters; both his parents worked during the day, and he had made few friends at school. But he was not by any means unhappy in his loneliness. He was used to it, in the first place; and then, because he was lonely, he was all the better able to indulge himself in his own fantasies. He played for hours, by himself, games of his own inventions—games of war, of exploration, of seafaring, of scientific invention, of crime, of espionage, of living in a house beneath or above his real one. It was not long before the two African children, who were now accosting him regularly, appeared in some of his games, for their weakness, poverty and dependence gave Michael ample scope to display in fantasy his kindness, generosity, courage and decisiveness. Sometimes in his games Michael saved the boy's life, and was thanked for it in broken English. Sometimes he saved the girl's, and then she humbly begged his pardon for having caused him so much trouble. Sometimes he was just too late to save the life of either, though he tried his best, and then there were affecting scenes of farewell.

But in real life, Michael did not play with the children at all: they were too dirty, too ragged, too strange, too persistent. Their persistence eventually drove Dora to tell Michael's mother about them; and his mother did her duty by telling Michael that on no account should he play with the children, nor should he give them anything of value.

'Play with them!' Michael laughed at the idea. And apart from bread and the torch, he had given them nothing but a few old toys, a singlet or two, a pair of old canvas shoes. No one could begrudge them those gifts. And the truth was that Michael's mother begrudged the piccanins neither the old toys and clothes nor the bread. What she was anxious to do was simply to prevent her son playing with the piccanins, fearing that he would pick up germs, bad language, and 'kaffir ways' generally from them, if he did. Hearing both from Michael and Dora that he did not play with them at all, and that he had never even asked them into the backyard, let alone the house, Michael's mother was satisfied.

They came to Michael about once a week, meeting him as he walked back from school, or simply waiting for him outside the back gate. The spring winds had already blown the cold weather away, almost overnight, and still the children came. Their words of thanks varied neither in tone nor length, whatever Michael gave them; but they had revealed, in response to his questions, that the boy's name was Frans and the girl's name was Annie, that they lived in Green Point Location, and that their mother and father were both dead. During all this time Michael had not touched them, except for the fleeting contact of their hands when he passed a gift to them. Yet sometimes Michael wished that they were more demonstrative in their expressions of gratitude to him; he thought that they could, for instance, seize his hand and embrace it; or go down on their knees and weep, just once. As it was, he had to content himself with fantasies of how they spoke of him among their friends, when they returned to the tumbled squalor of Green Point Location; of how incredulous their friends must be to hear their stories about the kind white *kleinbaas* who gave them food and toys and clothing.

One day Michael came out to them carrying a possession he particularly prized—an elaborate pen and pencil set which had been given to him for a recent birthday. He had no intention of giving the outfit to the African children, and he did not think that he would be showing off with it in front of them. He merely wanted to share his pleasure in it with someone who had not already seen it. But as soon as he noticed the way the children were looking at the open box, Michael knew the mistake he had made. 'This isn't for you,' he said abruptly. The children blinked soundlessly, staring from the box to Michael and back to the box again. 'You can just look at it,' Michael said. He held the box tightly in his hand, stretching it forward, the pen and the propelling pencils shining inside the velvet-lined case. The two heads of the children came together over the box; they stared deeply into it.

At last the boy lifted his head. 'It's beautiful,' he breathed out. As he spoke, his hand slowly came up towards the box.

'No,' Michael said, and snatched the box away.

'Baas?'

'No.' Michael retreated a little, away from the beseeching eyes, and the uplifted hand.

'Please, baas, for me?'

And his sister said, 'For me also, baas.'

'No, you can't have this.' Michael attempted to laugh, as if at the absurdity of the idea. He was annoyed with himself for having shown them the box, and at the same time shocked at them for having asked for it. It was the first time they had asked for anything but bread.

'Please, baas. It's nice.' The boy's voice trailed away on the last word, in longing; and then his sister repeated the word, like an echo, her own voice trailing away too. 'Ni-ice.'

'No! I won't give it to you! I won't give you anything if you ask for this. Do you hear?'

Their eyes dropped, their hands came together, they lowered their heads. Being sure now that they would not again ask for the box, Michael relented. He said, 'I'm going in now, and I'll tell Dora to bring you some bread.'

But Dora came to him in his room a few minutes later. 'The little kaffirs are gone.' She was holding the plate of bread in her hand. Dora hated the two children, and Michael thought there was some kind of triumph in her voice and manner as she made the announcement.

He went outside to see if she was telling the truth. The lane was empty. He went to the street, and looked up and down its length, but there was no sign of them there either. They were gone. He had driven them away. Michael expected to feel guilty; but to his own intense surprise he felt nothing of the kind. He was relieved that they were gone, and that was all.

When they reappeared a few days later, Michael felt scorn towards them for coming back after what had happened on the last occasion. He felt they were in his power. 'So you've come back?' he greeted them. 'You like your *stukkies brood*, hey? You're hungry, so today you'll wait, you won't run away.'

'Yes, baas,' they said, in their low voices.

Michael brought the bread out to them; when they reached for it he jokingly pulled the plate back and laughed at their surprise. Then only did he give them the bread.

'Thank you, baas.'

'Thank you, baas.'

They ate the bread in Michael's presence; watching them, he felt a little more kindly disposed towards them. 'All right, you can come another day, and there'll be some more bread for you.'

'Thank you, baas.'

'Thank you, baas.'

They came back sooner than Michael had expected them to. He

gave them their bread and told them to go. They went off, but
again did not wait for the usual five or six days to pass, before
approaching him once more. Only two days had passed, yet here
they were with their eternal request—'*Stukkie brood*, baas?'

Michael said, 'Why do you get hungry so quickly now?' But he
gave them their bread.

When they appeared in his games and fantasies, Michael no
longer rescued them, healed them, casually presented them with
kingdoms and motor cars. Now he ordered them about, sent them
away on disastrous missions, picked them out to be shot for
cowardice in the face of the enemy. And because something similar
to these fantasies was easier to enact in the real world than his
earlier fantasies, Michael soon was ordering them about unrea-
sonably in fact. He deliberately left them waiting; he sent them
away and told them to come back on days when he knew he would
be in town; he told them there was no bread in the house. And
when he did give them anything, it was bread only now; never old
toys or articles of clothing.

So, as the weeks passed, Michael's scorn gave way to impatience
and irritation, irritation to anger. And what angered him most was
that the two piccanins seemed too stupid to realize what he now felt
about them, and instead of coming less frequently, continued to
appear more often than ever before. Soon they were coming almost
every day, though Michael shouted at them and teased them, left
them waiting for hours, and made them do tricks and sing songs for
their bread. They did everything he told them to do; but they
altogether ignored his instructions as to which days they should
come. Invariably, they would be waiting for him, in the shade of
one of the trees that grew alongside the main road from school, or
standing at the gate behind the house with sand scuffed up about
their bare toes. They were as silent as before; but more persistent,
inexorably persistent. Michael took to walking home by different
routes, but they were not to be so easily discouraged. They simply
waited at the back gate, and whether he went into the house by the
front or the back gate he could not avoid seeing their upright,
unmoving figures.

Finally, he told them to go and never come back at all. Often he
had been tempted to do this, but some shame or pride had always
prevented him from doing it; he had always weakened previously,
and named a date, a week or two weeks ahead, when they could

come again. But now he shouted at them, 'It's finished! No more bread—nothing! Come on, *voetsak*! If you come back I'll tell the garden boy to chase you away.'

From then on they came every day. They no longer waited right at the back gate, but squatted in the sand across the lane. Michael was aware of their eyes following him when he went by, but they did not approach him at all. They did not even get up from the ground when he passed. A few times he shouted at them to go, and stamped his foot, but he shrank from hitting them. He did not want to touch them. Once he sent out Jan, the garden boy, to drive them away; but Jan, who had hitherto always shared Dora's views on the piccanins, came back muttering angrily and incomprehensibly to himself; and when Michael peeped into the lane he saw that they were still there. Michael tried to ignore them, to pretend he did not see them. He hated them now; even more, he began to dread them.

But he did not know how much he hated and feared the two piccanins until he fell ill with a cold, and lay feverish in bed for a few days. During those days the two children were constantly in his dreams, or in his half-dreams, for even as he dreamed he knew he was turning on his bed; he was conscious of the sun shining outside by day, and at night of the passage-light that had been left on inside the house. In these dreams he struck and struck again at the children with weapons he found in his hands; he fled in fear from them down lanes so thick with sand his feet could barely move through it; he committed lewd, cruel acts upon the bare-thighed girl, and her brother shrieked to tell the empty street of what he was doing. Michael struck out at him with a piece of heavy cast-iron guttering. Its edge dug sharply into Michael's hands as the blow fell, and when he lifted the weapon he saw the horror he had made of the side of the boy's head, and how the one remaining eyeball still stared unwinkingly at him.

Michael thought he was awake, and suddenly calm. The fever seemed to have left him. It was as though he had slept deeply, for days, after the last dream of violence; yet his impression was that he had woken directly from it. The bedclothes felt heavy on him, and he threw them off. The house was quite silent. He got out of bed and went to look at the clock in the kitchen: it was early afternoon. Dora and Jan were resting in their rooms across the yard, as they always did after lunch. Outside, the light of the sun was unremitting, a single golden glare. He walked back to his bedroom; there, he put on his dressing-gown and slippers, feeling the coolness inside his slippers on his bare feet. He went through the kitchen again, quietly, and on to the back stoep, and then across the backyard. The sun seemed to seize the back of his neck as firmly as a hand grasping, and its light was so bright he was aware of it only as a darkness beyond the little stretch of ground he looked down upon. He opened the back gate. Inevitably, as he had known they would be, the two were waiting.

He did not want to go beyond the gate in his pyjamas and dressing-gown, so, shielding his eyes from the glare with one hand, he beckoned them to him with the other. Together, in silence, they rose and crossed the lane. It seemed to take them a long time to come to him, but at last they stood in front of him, with their hands interlinked. Michael stared into their dark faces, and they stared into his.

'What are you waiting for?' he asked.

'For you.' First the boy answered; then the girl repeated, 'For you.'

Michael looked from the one to the other; and he remembered what he had been doing to them in his dreams. Their eyes were black to look into, deep black. Staring forward, Michael understood what he should have understood long before: that they came to him not in hope or appeal or even in reproach, but in hatred. What he felt towards them, they felt towards him; what he had done to them in his dreams, they did to him in theirs.

The sun, their staring eyes, his own fear came together in a sound that seemed to hang in the air of the lane—a cry, the sound of someone weeping. Then Michael knew that it was he who was crying. He felt the heat of the tears in his eyes, he felt the moisture running down his cheeks. And with the same fixity of decision that had been his in his dreams of violence and torture, Michael knew what he must do. He beckoned them forward, closer. They came. He stretched out his hands, he felt under his fingers the springy hair he had looked at so often before from the distance between himself and them; he felt the smooth skin of their faces; their frail, rounded shoulders, their hands. Their hands were in his, and he led them inside the gate.

He led them into the house, through the kitchen, down the passage, into his room, where they had never been before. They looked about at the pictures on the walls, the toys on top of the low cupboard, the twisted white sheets and tumbled blankets on the bed. They stood on both sides of him, and for the first time since he had met them, their lips parted into slow, grave smiles. And Michael knew that what he had to give them was not toys or clothes or bread, but something more difficult. Yet it was not difficult at all, for there was nothing else he could give them. He took the girl's face in his hands and pressed his lips to hers. He was aware of the darkness of her skin, and of the smell of it, and of the faint movement of her lips, a single pulse that beat momentarily against his own. Then it was gone. He kissed the boy, too, and let them go. They came together, and grasped each other by the hand, staring at him.

'What do you want now?' he asked.

A last anxiety flickered in Michael and left him, as the boy slowly shook his head. He began to step back, pulling his sister with him; when he was through the door he turned his back on Michael and they walked away down the passage. Michael watched them go. At the door of the kitchen, on their way out of the house, they paused, turned once more, and lifted their hands, the girl copying the boy, in a silent, tentative gesture of farewell.

Michael did not follow them. He heard the back gate swing open and then bang when it closed. He went wearily back to his bed, and as he fell upon it, his relief and gratitude that the bed should be there to receive him, changed suddenly into grief at the knowledge that he was already lying upon it—that he had never left it.

His cold grew worse, turned into bronchitis, kept him in bed for several weeks. But his dreams were no longer of violence; they were calm, spacious, and empty of people. As empty as the lane was, when he was at last allowed out of the house, and made his way there immediately, to see if the children were waiting for him.

He never saw them again, though he looked for them in the streets and lanes of the town. He saw a hundred, a thousand, children like them; but not the two he hoped to find.

Kwashiorkor

Can Themba

'Here's another interesting case …'

My sister flicked over the pages of the file of one of her case studies, and I wondered what other shipwrecked human being had there been recorded, catalogued, statisticized and analysed. My sister is a social worker with the Social Welfare Department of the Non-European Section of the Municipality of Johannesburg. In other words, she probes into the derelict lives of the unfortunate poor in Johannesburg. She studies their living habits, their recreational habits, their sporting habits, their drinking habits, the incidence of crime, neglect, malnutrition, divorce, aberration, and she records all this in cyclostyled forms that ask the questions ready-made. She has got so good that she can tell without looking whether such-and-such a query falls under paragraph so-and-so. She has got so clinical that no particular case rattles her, for she has met its like before and knows how and where to classify it.

Her only trouble was ferocious Alexandra Township, that hell-hole in Johannesburg where it was never safe for a woman to walk the streets unchaperoned or to go from house to house asking testing questions. This is where I come in. Often I have to escort her on her rounds just so that no township roughneck molests her. We arranged it lovely so that she only went to Alexandra on Saturday afternoons when I was half-day-off and could tag along.

'Dave,' she said, 'here's another interesting case. I'm sure you would love to hear about it. It's Alex again. I'm interested in the psychological motivations and the statistical significance, but I think you'll get you a human-interest story. I know you can't be objective, but do, I beg you, do take it all quietly and don't mess me up with your sentimental reactions. We'll meet at two o'clock on Saturday, okay?'

That is how we went to that battered house on 3rd Avenue,

Alexandra. It was just a lot of wood and tin knocked together gawkily to make four rooms. The house stood precariously a few yards from the sour, cider-tasting gutter, and in the back there was a row of out-rooms constructed like a train and let to smaller families or bachelor men and women. This was the main source of income for the Mabiletsa family—mother, daughter and daughter's daughter.

But let me refer to my sister Eileen's records to get my facts straight.

Mother—Mrs Sarah Mabiletsa, age 62, widow, husband Abner Mabiletsa died 1953 in motor-car accident. Sarah does not work. Medical Report says chronic arthritis. Her sole sources of support are rent from out-rooms and working daughter, Maria. Sarah is dually illiterate.

Daughter—Maria Mabiletsa, age 17, Reference Book No. F/V 118/32N1682. Domestic servant. Educational standard: 5. Reads and writes English, Afrikaans, Sepedi. Convictions: 30 days for shoplifting. One illegitimate child unmaintained and of disputed paternity.

Child—Sekgametse Daphne Lorraine Mabiletsa, Maria's child, age 3 years. Father undetermined. Free clinic attendance. Medical report: Advanced Kwashiorkor.

Other relatives—Sarah's brother, Edgar Mokgomane, serving jail sentence, 15 years, murder and robbery.

Remarks (Eileen's verdict)—This family is desperate. Mother: ineffectual care for child. Child: showing malnutrition effects. Overall quantitative and qualitative nutritional deficiency. Maria: good-time girl, seldom at home, spends earnings mostly on self and parties. Recommend urgent welfare aid and/or intervention.

Although Eileen talks about these things clinically, *objectively*, she told me the story and I somehow got the feel of it.

Abner Mabiletsa was one of those people who was not content with life in the reserves in Pietersburg district where he was born and grew up. He did not see where the tribal set-up of chief and *kgotla*—the tribal council—and customs, taboos, superstitions, witchcraft and the lackadaisical dreariness of rotating with the sun from morn till eve would take the people and would take him. Moreover, the urge to rise and go out to do things, to conquer and become someone, the impatience of the blood, seized him. So he upped and went to Johannesburg, where else? Everybody went there.

First, there were the ordinary problems of adjustment: the tribal boy had to fit himself into the vast, fast-moving, frenetic life in the big city. So many habits, beliefs, customs had to be fractured overnight. So many reactions that were sincere and instinctive were laughed at in the city. A man was continually changing himself, leaping like a flea from contingency to contingency. But Abner made it, though most of the time he did not know who he was or whither he was going. He only knew that this feverish life had to be lived, identity becoming so large that a man sounded ridiculous for boasting he was a Mopedi or a Mosuto or a Xhosa or a Zulu—nobody seemed to care. You were just an African *here*, and somewhere *there* was a white man: two different types of humans that impinged now and then—indeed often—and painfully.

Abner made it. He was helped by his homeboys, those who had come before. They showed him the ropes. They found him a job. They accommodated him during those first few months until he found a room of his own in Alexandra. They took him to parties, to girls, to dice schools. Ultimately, they showed him where he could learn to drive a car. Soon, soon, he could negotiate all the by-ways and back-alleys of Johannesburg by himself. He had escapades, fun, riotous living ... until one day one of his escapades became pregnant and bore him a daughter. He paid the *lobola*—that hard-dying custom of paying the brideprice—getting some of his friends and homeboys to stand for him *in loco parentis;* he did not even apprise his folk back home in Pietersburg of his marriage; he did it all himself.

But life in Johannesburg was such that he did not find much time to look after his family. He was not exactly the delinquent father, but there was just not the time or the room for a man to become truly family-bound. Then suddenly, crash! He died in a motor-car accident, and his unprovided-for wife had to make do.

His daughter, Maria, grew up in the streets of Alexandra. The spectre of poverty was always looming over her life; and at the age of fourteen she left school to work in the white man's kitchens. It helped, at first, to alleviate the grim want, the ever-empty larder at home. But soon she got caught up in the froth of Johannesburg's titillating nether life. She had a boyfriend who came pretty regularly to sleep in her room at the back of her place of employment; she had other boyfriends in the city, in the townships, with whom she often slept. And of the billions of human seed so recklessly strewn, one was bound sometime to strike target.

When her condition became obvious, Maria nominated the boy she liked best, the swankiest, handsomest, most romantic and most moneyed swain in her repertoire. But he was a dangerous tsotsi, and when she told him of what he had wrought, he threatened to beat the living spit out of her. She fondly, foolishly persisted; and he assaulted her savagely. The real boyfriend—the one who slept in her room—felt bitter that she had indicated another. Had he not already boasted to his friends that he had 'bumped' her? Now the whole world judged that he had been cuckolded.

Poor Maria tried the somersault and turned to him, but by then he would have none of it. He effectively told the Native Commissioner, 'I am this girl's second opinion. She does not know who is responsible for her condition. There she stands, now too scared to nominate the man she first fancied, so she looks for a scapegoat, me.'

The commissioner had some biting things to say to Maria and concluded that he could not, in all conscience, find this man guilty of her seduction. As they say, he threw out the case.

So Sekgametse Daphne Lorraine was born without a father: an event in Alexandra, in Johannesburg, in all the urban areas of our times, that excites no surprise whatsoever.

First, Maria shed all her love—that is, the anguish and pain she suffered, the bitterness, the humiliation, the sense of desolation and collapse of her tinsel world—upon this infant. But people either perish or recover from wounds; even the worst afflictions do not gnaw at you forever. Maria recovered. She went back to her domestic work, leaving the baby with her mother. She would come home every Thursday—Sheila's Day—the day off for all the domestics in Johannesburg. She came to her baby, bringing clothing, blankets, pampering little goodies and smothering treacly love.

But she was young still, and the blood burst inside her once she recovered. Johannesburg was outside there calling, calling, first wooingly, alluringly, then more and more stridently, irresistibly. She came home less often, but remorsefully, and would crush the child to her in those brief moments. Even as she hugged the rose, the thorns tore at her feet. Then suddenly she came home no more ...

'It is quite a typical case of recidivism,' Eileen explained scholastically to me on our way to Alexandra. 'You see, there's a moment's panic as a result of the trauma. The reaction varies according to the victim. One way is that for most of our girls there's stubborn residue of moral upbringing from home or school or church, sometimes really only from mamma's personality, and mamma probably comes from an older, steadier, more inhibited and tribe-controlled environment ...' Eileen shrugged helplessly, '... and detribalization, modernization, adaptation, acculturation, call it what you like, has to tear its way into their psychological pattern, brute-like. At first, before the shock, these girls really just float loosely about in the new freedoms, not really willing evil, not consciously flouting the order. But they're nevertheless playing with fire, and no one knows how to tell them no. Their parents themselves are baffled by what the world's come to, and there's no invisible reality like tribe or comprehensible code like custom or taboo to keep some kind of balance. Meanwhile, the new dispensation—the superior culture, they call it; the diabolical shadow-life, I call it—pounds at them relentlessly. Suddenly some traumatic event, a jail sentence, a sudden encounter with brute, bloody death, or a first pregnancy, pulverizes them into what we credulous monitors consider repentance. It's really the startled whimper of a frightened child vaguely remembering that in some remote distance mamma or tribe or school or church has whispered, "Thou shalt not," and the horror that it's too late.

'But,' Eileen almost cursed out the words, 'the superior culture keeps pounding at them, and it's a matter of time before your repentant maiden sings again, "Jo'burg, here I come".'

I was shaken. 'Eileen, you know that much and yet you continue tinkering with statistics!'

She pulled herself together with an effort. But though she spoke confidently, it sounded unconvincing: 'Lad, I'm a social scientist, not a conjuress.'

So we went to that house on 3rd Avenue, off Selbourne Road. A deep gully ran in front of the house but the uneven street did not allow it to function effectively as a drain, and puddles of murky, noisome water and collected waste-matter stood pooled in it, still, thick, appalling, like foul soup that makes you nauseous—as if some malevolent devil bade you gulp it down. On the other side, the rotting carcass of a long-dead dog was sending malodorous miasmata from its surface to befoul the air. And on both sides of the street, moated by these stinking gullies, lived people.

Eileen jumped smartly over the trench and I followed. We walked into the fenceless yard, round to the back of the house, and she knocked. After a moment a wrinkled old lady opened the door. The ploughshares of the years had wobbled across her face; but then again, you thought it could not have been the years alone that had ravaged her so; something else ...

'Oh, come in, nurse.' They called everybody 'nurse' who came to their hovels to promise assuagement of their misery.

Although it was a bright day outside, you had to get used to the dark inside, and then when your eyes, by slow degrees, adjusted themselves, things seemed to come at you. A big sideboard tilted into view first. Then a huge stove whose one grey arm reached into the ceiling hole obscenely, and near it a double bed, perched on four large polish tins filled with sand. The bed was sunken in the middle like a crude canoe, and the blankets on it were yellow with age and threadbare with wear. In the middle of the top blanket was a great hole from some past misadventure, and through the hole glowered a crimson eye, the red disc of a piece-patched quilt-like thing.

I stumbled into a wooden table in the centre, and in my retreat hit a kitchen dresser. Dark-brown cockroaches scrambled for cover.

'Don't be so clumsy,' Eileen hissed, and in the same syntax, as it were, said to the old lady, 'Mother Mabiletsa, it's so dark in here. You really must open that window.'

I had not known there was a window there, but Eileen swept a piece of blanket aside and in flushed the light of day.

'How are you, Mother Mabiletsa? How are the legs today? Sit down please and tell me how is the baby.'

Mother Mabiletsa groaned into a chair, and I took a bench by the side of the table. Eileen stood a moment holding the old woman in scrutiny. When the old woman did not reply, Eileen lifted her bag and put it on the table.

'Look, I've brought little Sekgametse some skimmed milk. It's very good for babies, you know.'

I turned to look at the old lady and it seemed to me she was past caring about either Grace or Damnation. She was just enveloped in a dreadful murk of weariness.

She pressed down on arthritic knees, rose painfully and limped into another room. I could hear her moving about, heaving with effort though she sounded alone. Then she came in with a bundle in her arms which she put down on the great bed beside Eileen.

'Come and look,' Eileen whispered to me as she unfurled the bundle.

There sat a little monkey on the bed. It was a two to three years' old child. The child did not cry or fidget, but bore an unutterably miserable expression on its face, in its whole bearing. It was as if she was the grandmother writ small; pathetically, wretchedly, she looked out upon the world.

'Is it in pain?' I asked in an anxious whisper.

'No, just wasting away.'

'But she looks quite fat.'

To be sure, she did. But it was a ghastly kind of fatness, the fatness of the 'hidden hunger' I was to know. The belly was distended and sagged towards the bed. The legs looked bent convexly and there were light-brown patches on them, and on the chest and back. The complexion of the skin was unnaturally light here and there so that the creature looked piebald. The normally curly hair had a rusty tint and had lost much of its whorl. Much of it had fallen out, leaving islets of skull surfacing.

The child looked aside towards me, and the silent reproach, the quiet, listless, abject despair flowed from the large eyes wave upon wave. Not a peep, not a murmur. The child made no sound of complaint except the struggling breathing.

But those haunted eyes of despair. Despair? I brooded. To despair you should have had knowledge before. You should have gone through the tart sensations of experience, have felt the first flush of knowledge, the first stabs of hope, have encountered reality and toyed with the shifting, tantalizing promises that shadow-play across life's tapestries, have stretched out first tentative arms then wildly grasping hands, and have discovered the disappointment of the evanescence of all things that come from the voids to tickle men's fancies, sharpen men's appetites and rouse their futile aspirations, only to vanish back into the voids. Ultimately you should have looked into the face of death and known the paralysing power of fear.

What of all this could this little monkey know? And, yet, there it all was in those tragic eyes.

Then I thought, '*So this is kwashiorkor!*' Hitherto, to me, the name had just been another scare-word that had climbed from the dark caves of medical nomenclature to rear its head among decent folk; it had just been another disgusting digit, a clipped statistic that health officials hurled at us reporters, and which we laced our copy with to impress sensation-seeking editors who would fulminate under headlines like KWASHIORKOR AT YOUR DOOR. It had seemed right, then, almost sufficient that we should link it with the other horrors like 'Infant Mortality', 'Living Below the Bread-Line', 'The Apathy of the People' and 'The Cynical Indifference of the Affluent Society to the Problem'.

But here, in this groanless, gloomy room, it seemed indecent to shriek banner headlines when the child, itself, was quiet. It spoke no protest, it offered no resistance.

But while I was romanticizing, my sister was explaining to the old lady how to care for and feed the child, how to prepare and use the skim milk, how often to give it Cod-Liver Oil, how often to take it out into the air and the sunlight, how often to take it to the clinic.

Her mistressy voice, now urgent and straining, now clucking and scolding, now anxiously explaining, thinking in English, translating to itself first into Sepedi, begging, stressing, arguing, repeating, repeating, repeating—that restless voice tinkled into my consciousness, bringing me back.

The old lady muttered, 'I hear you, child, but how can I buy all these things with the R1.500 that's left over each month, and how can I carry this child to the clinic with my creaking bones?'

I was subdued.

'Well,' said Eileen later to me as we returned to the bus stop. 'Think you've seen bottomless tragedy? I could give you figures for kwashiorkor in Alexandra alone ...'

'Please, Eileen, please.'

My life, a reporter's life, is rather full and hectic, and I am so vortically cast about in the whirlpools of Johannesburg that no single thought, no single experience, however profound, can stay with me for long. A week, two weeks, or less, and the picture of the kwashiorkor baby was jarred out of me, or perhaps lost into the limbo where the psyche hides unpleasant dreams.

Every day during that spell I had to traffic with the ungodly, the wicked, the unfortunate, the adventurous, the desperate, the outcast and the screwy.

One day I was in E Court waiting for a rather spectacular theft case to come up. I had to sit through the normal run of petty cases. I was bored and fishing inside myself for a worthwhile reverie when suddenly I heard: 'Maria Mabiletsa! Maria Mabiletsa!' My presence of mind hurried back.

The prosecutor said, 'This one is charged with receiving stolen goods, Your Worship.'

A white man rose and told the court, 'Your Worship, I appear for the accused. I. M. Karotsky, of Mendelsohn and Jacobs, Sansouci House, 235 Bree Street.'

The prosecutor asked for an adjournment as 'other members of the gang are still at large'.

There was a wrangle about bail, but it was refused and the case was adjourned to August 25th.

It jolted me. After my case, I went down to the cells and there, after sundry buffetings despite the flashing of my Press Card, I managed to see her.

She was sweet, I mean, looked sweet. Of course now she was a mixture of fear and defiance, but I could see beyond these façades the real simplicity of her.

I do not know how long she had been in the cell, but she was clean and looked groomed. Her hair was stretched back and neatly tied in the ring behind the crown. She had an oval face, eyes intelligent and alive. Her nose stood out with tender nostrils. Her mouth was delicate but now twisted into a bitter scowl, and a slender neck held her head like the stem of a flower. Her skin colour was chestnut, but like ... like ... like the inside of my hand. She had a slight figure with pouts for breasts, slight hips, but buttocks rounded enough to insist she was African.

She wore atop a white blouse with frills, and amidships one of those skirts cut like a kilt, hugging her figure intimately and suddenly relenting to flare out.

But now she was importunate. For her all time was little, and lots had to be said quickly. Before I could talk to her she said, '*Au-boetie*, please, my brother, please, go and tell Lefty I'm arrested. Marshall Square, maybe No. 4. Tell him to bail me out. I'm Maria Mabiletsa, but Lefty calls me Marix. Please, *Au-boetie*, please.'

'Easy Maria,' I soothed, 'I know about you. I'm Dave from *The Courier*.'

'*Hô-man*, *Boeta* Dave, man. You we know, man. I read *The Courier*. But, please, *Boeta* Dave, tell Lefty my troubles, my mother's child.'

A cop was hurrying them away. 'Come'n, *phansi!*—down! *Phansi!*—down!'

'Please, *Au-boetie* Dave, don't forget to tell Lefty!'

'Maria,' I shouted as she was being rushed off, 'I've seen Sekgametse. She's well looked after.'

'Oh!—'

'*Phansi*—down!' Bang! The iron gates fell with a clangour.

That night I told Eileen. She stared at me with knitted brows for a long time. Then she said, 'The main thing is not to panic the old lady. Saturday, you and I will have to go there, but don't do or say anything to make her panic. Leave me to do all the talking.' But I could see Eileen was near panic herself.

Then I went to see Lefty. He was suave, unperturbed, taking all this philosophically.

'You reporter-boys take everything to head. Relax. You must have rhythm and timing. I've already got Karotsky to look after her and tomorrow Marix will be out. Relax, and have a drink.'

She was not out that tomorrow nor the day after. She had to wait for August 25th. Meantime, Saturday came and Eileen and I went to the house on 3rd Avenue, Alexandra. When we got there we found—as they say—'House To Let'. The old lady had heard about what had happened to Maria; she was faced with debts and the threat of starvation, so she packed her things, took the child, and returned to the reserve in Pietersburg.

The neighbours shrugged their shoulders and said, 'What could the old lady do?'

Eileen was livid.

'Dave, do you know what this means?' she erupted. 'It means that child is doomed. In the country they love children, they look after them, they bring them up according to a code and according to what they *know*, but what they know about the nutrition of children is homicidal and, s'true's God, they live under such conditions of poverty that they may turn cannibals any moment. That's where goes the child I tried to rehabilitate. And when adversity strikes them, when drought comes and the land yields less and less, and the cows' udders dry up, who are the first to go without? The children, those who need the milk most, those who need the proteins, the fats, the oils, the vegetables, the fruit; of the little there is, those who need it most will be the first to go without. There, indeed, they live on mieliepap and despair. A doctor once told me, Dave, "Kwashiorkor hits hardest between the ages of one and five when protein is needed most and when it's least available to African children". Least available! Why, Dave, why? Because the ignorant African does not realize that when milk is short, give the children first; when meat is little, give the children first. It's not as if …' she wailed, '… it's not as if my over-detribalized self wants to give grown-ups' food to children, but my Sekgametse's sick. I've been trying to coax her back from unnecessary and stupid child-death. Now this.'

Tactlessly, I said, 'Come now, Eileen, you've done your bit. Go and make your report, you're not a nurse, and in any case you can't solve the whole world's troubles one-out.'

'The whole world's troubles!' She spat at me as if I was a child-stealer. 'I only wanted to save that one child, damn you!'

Of course, she made her social worker's report, and other human problems seized her, and I often wondered later whether she had forgotten her kwashiorkor baby. Once, when I asked her if she had heard anything about the baby, she gave a barbed-wire reply, 'Outside our jurisdiction'. It sounded too official to be like Eileen, but I sensed that she felt too raw about it to be anything else than professional, and I held my war within me.

Then I met Maria. It was at a party in Dube, one of those class affairs where thugs and tarts appear in formal dress, and though none of the chicken flew, the liquor flowed.

'Remember me?' I asked her in the provocative style in vogue. She screwed her face and wrinkled her nose and said, 'Don't tell me, don't tell me, I know I know you.' But strain as hard as she tried, she could not identify me. So in mercy I told her I was the news reporter she once sent to Lefty when she was arrested. It half-registered. I told her my sister was the 'nurse' who looked after her Sekgametse. A cloud crossed her brow.

'*Hê*, man, *Au-boetie*, man, Africans are cruel,' she moaned. 'You know, I sent my child to the reserve in Pietersburg, and every month I used to send her nice things until she was the smartest kid in the countryside. Then they bewitched her. Kaffir-poison!' she said darkly. 'The child's stomach swelled and swelled with the beast they'd planted in it, until the child died. The Lord God will see those people, *mmcwi!*'

Viciously, I asked: 'And did you ever send the child soya beans?'

About a Girl Who Met a Dimo

translated from Setswana by
Susheela Curtis

It is said that long, long ago there was a girl called Sediadie who lived with her grandmother. When the corn began to ripen, she was sent to live at the fields by herself and scare birds away.

One day she said to herself, 'I shall go to see my grandmother now,' and set off for the village, which was some distance away.

When she arrived at her grandmother's house, the old woman was happy to see her and said, 'Sediadie, where have you come from?'

'I have come from the fields, grandmother,' replied the girl.

They talked for a while and then Sediadie said, 'I must now go back.'

Her grandmother gave her two small tins of magic grass and said, 'You may meet a dimo on the way. If you do, you must use this to kill him.'

Sediadie then went on her way.

As she walked through the bush, she met a dimo, who growled, 'Where are you coming from?'

Sediadie sang timidly,

I am coming from Borolong, teleng,
I have come with my magic grass, teleng,
If I point it at you, you will die, teleng.

The dimo asked mockingly, 'Die? Die forever?'
Sediadie sang, 'Yes, teleng.'
The dimo, unable to believe her, said, 'Never to walk this road?'
Sediadie sang, 'Never, teleng.'
The dimo said, 'To lie with my feet turned up!'
'Yes, yes, teleng,' sang Sediadie.
The dimo said, 'Take it out and let me see.'

So the girl pointed the magic grass at the dimo, and he died, and Sediadie reached the fields safely.

Hajji Musa
and the Hindu Fire-Walker

Ahmed Essop

'Allah has sent me to you, Bibi Fatima.'

'Allah, Hajji Musa?'

'I assure you, Allah, my good lady. Listen to me carefully. There is something wrong with you. Either you have a sickness or there is an evil spell cast over your home. Can you claim that there is nothing wrong in your home, that your family is perfectly healthy and happy?'

'Well, Hajji Musa, you know my little Amir has a nasty cough that even Dr Kamal cannot cure and Soraya seems to have lost her appetite.'

'My good woman, you believe me now when I say Allah has sent me to you?'

Bibi Fatima's husband, Jogee, entered the room. Hajji Musa took no notice of him and began to recite (in Arabic) an extract from the Koran. When he had done he shook hands with Jogee.

'Listen to me, Bibi Fatima and brother Jogee. Sickness is not part of our nature, neither is it the work of our good Allah. It is the work of that great evil-doer Iblis, some people call him Satan. Well, I, by the grace of Allah' (he recited another extract from the Koran), 'have been given the power to heal the sick and destroy evil. That is my work in life, even if I get no reward.'

'But Hajji Musa, you must live.'

'Bibi Fatima, Allah looks after me and my family. Now bring me two glasses of water and a candle.'

She hurried to the kitchen and brought the articles.

'Now bring me the children.'

'Jogee, please go and find Amir in the yard while I look for Soraya.'

Husband and wife went out. Meanwhile Hajji Musa drew the

curtains in the room, lit the candle and placed the two glasses of water on either side of the candle. He took incense out of his pocket, put it in an ash-tray and lit it.

When husband and wife returned with the children they were awed. There was an atmosphere of strangeness, of mystery, in the room. Hajji Musa looked solemn. He took the candle, held it about face level and said:

'Look, there is a halo around the flame.'

They looked and saw a faint halo.

He placed the candle on the table, took the glasses of water, held them above the flame and recited a verse from the Koran. When he had done he gave one glass to the boy and one to the girl.

'Drink, my children,' he said. They hesitated for a moment, but Bibi Fatima commanded them to drink the water.

'They will be well,' he said authoritatively. 'They can now go and play.'

He extinguished the candle, drew the curtains, and sat down on the settee. And he laughed, a full-throated, uproarious, felicitous laugh.

'Don't worry about the children. Allah has performed miracles and what are coughs and loss of appetites.' And he laughed again.

Bibi Fatima went to the kitchen to make tea and Jogee and I kept him company. She returned shortly with tea and cake.

'Jogee,' she said, 'I think Hajji Musa is greater than Dr Kamal. You remember last year Dr Kamal gave me medicines and ointments for my aching back and nothing came of it?'

'Hajji Musa is not an ordinary doctor.'

'What are doctors of today,' Hajji Musa said, biting into a large slice of cake, 'but chancers and frauds? What knowledge have they of religion and the spiritual mysteries?'

'Since when have you this power to heal, Hajji Musa?'

'Who can tell the ways of Allah, Bibi Fatima. Sometimes his gifts are given when we are born and sometimes when we are much older.'

'More tea?'

She filled the cup. He took another slice of cake.

'Last month I went to Durban and there was this woman, Jasuben, whom the doctors had declared insane. Even her own yogis and swamis had given her up. I took this woman in hand and today she is as sane as anyone else.'

'Hajji Musa, you know my back still gives me trouble. Dr Kamal's medicine gave me no relief. I have even stopped making roti and Jogee is very fond of roti.'

'You should let me examine your back some day,' the healer said, finishing his tea.

'Why not now?'

'Not today,' he answered protestingly. 'I have some business to attend to.'

'But Hajji Musa, it will only take a minute or two.'

'Well that's true, that's true.'

'Will you need the candle and water?'

'Yes.'

She hurriedly went to refill the glass with water.

'Please, Jogee and Ahmed, go into the kitchen for a while,' she said, returning.

We left the room, Jogee rather reluctantly. She shut the door. I sat down on a chair and looked at a magazine lying on the table. Jogee told me he was going to buy cigarettes and left. He was feeling nervous.

I was sitting close to the door and could hear Hajji Musa's voice and the rustle of clothing as he went on with the examination.

'I think it best if you lie down on the settee so that I can make a thorough examination. ... Yes, that is better. ... Is the pain here ...? Bibi Fatima, you know the pain often has its origin lower down, in the lumbar region. Could you ease your ijar a little ...? The seat of the pain is often here. ... Don't be afraid.'

'I can feel it getting better already, Hajji Musa.'

'That is good. You are responding very well.'

There was silence for some time. When Jogee returned Hajji Musa was reciting a prayer in Arabic. Jogee puffed at his cigarette.

When Bibi Fatima opened the door she was smiling and looked flushed.

'Your wife will be well in a few days,' Hajji Musa assured the anxious man. 'And you will have your daily roti again. Now I must go.'

'Hajji Musa, but we must give you something for your trouble.'

'No nothing, Bibi Fatima. I forbid you.'

She was insistent. She told Jogee in pantomime (she showed him five fingers) how much money he should give. Jogee produced the money from his pocket, though inwardly protesting at his wife's willingness to pay a man who asked no fees. Bibi Fatima put the money into Hajji Musa's pocket.

In appearance Hajji Musa was a fat, pot-bellied, short, dark man, with glossy black wavy hair combed backwards with fastidious care. His face was always clean shaven. For some reason he never shaved in the bathroom, and every morning one saw him in the yard, in vest and pyjama trousers, arranging (rather precariously) his mirror and shaving equipment on the window-sill outside the kitchen and going through the ritual of cleaning his face with the precision of a surgeon. His great passion was talking and while shaving he would be conducting conversations with various people in the yard: with the hawker packing his fruit and vegetables in the cart; with the two wives of the motor mechanic Soni; with the servants coming to work.

Hajji Musa was a well-known man. At various times he had been a commercial traveller, insurance salesman, taxi driver, companion to dignitaries from India and Pakistan, Islamic missionary, teacher at a seminary, shopkeeper, matchmaker and hawker of ladies' underwear.

His career as a go-between in marriage transactions was a brief inglorious one that almost ended his life. One night there was fierce knocking at his door. As soon as he opened it an angry voice exploded: 'You liar! You come and tell me of dat good-for-nutting Dendar boy, dat he good, dat he ejucated, dat he good prospect. My foot and boot he ejucated. He sleep most time wit bitches, he drink and beat my daughter. When you go Haj? You nutting but liar. You baster! You baster!' And suddenly two shots from a gun rang out in quick succession. The whole incident took place so quickly that no one had any time to look at the man as he ran through the yard and escaped. When people reached Hajji Musa's door they found him prostrate, breathing hard and wondering why he was still alive (the bullets had passed between his legs). His wife and eight children were in a state of shock. They were revived with sugared water.

Hajji Musa's life never followed an even course: on some days one saw him riding importantly in the chauffeur-driven Mercedes of some wealthy merchant in need of his services; on others, one saw him in the yard, pacing meditatively from one end to the other, reciting verses from the Koran. Sometimes he would visit a friend, tell an amusing anecdote, laugh, and suddenly ask: 'Can you give me a few rands till tomorrow?' The friend would give him the money without expecting anything of tomorrow, for it was well known that Hajji Musa, liberal with his own money, never bothered to return anyone else's.

Hajji Musa considered himself a specialist in the exorcism of evil jinn. He deprecated modern terms such as neurosis, schizophrenia, psychosis. 'What do doctors know about the power of satanic jinn? Only God can save people who are no longer themselves. I have proved this time and again. You don't believe me? Then come on Sunday night to my house and you will see.'

On Sunday night we were clustered around Hajji Musa in the yard. As his patient had not yet arrived, he regaled us with her history.

'She is sixteen. She is the daughter of Mia Mohammed the Market Street merchant. She married her cousin a few years ago. But things went wrong. Her mother-in-law disliked her. For months she has been carted from doctor to doctor, and from one psychiatrist to another, those fools. Tonight you will see me bring about a permanent cure.'

After a while a car drove into the yard, followed by two others. Several men—two of them tall, bearded brothers—emerged from the car, approached Hajji Musa and shook hands with him. They pointed to the second car.

'She is in that car, Hajji Musa.'

'Good, bring her into the house.' And he went inside.

There were several women in the second car. All alighted but one, who refused to come out. She shook her face and hands and cried, 'No! No! Don't take me in there, please! By Allah, I am a good girl.'

The two brothers and several women stood beside the opened doors of the car and coaxed the young lady to come out.

'Sister, come, we are only visiting.'

'No, no, they are going to hit me.'

'No one is going to hit you,' one of the women said, getting into the car and sitting beside her. 'They only want to see you.'

'They can see me in the car. I am so pretty.'

Everyone living in the yard was present to witness the spectacle, and several children had clambered onto the bonnet of the car and were shouting: 'There she is! There she is! She is mad! She is mad!'

'Come now, Jamilla, come. The people are laughing at you,' one of the brothers said sternly.

Hajji Musa now appeared wearing a black cloak emblazoned with sequin-studded crescent moons and stars, and inscribed with Cufic writing in white silk. His sandals were red and his trousers white. His turban was of green satin and it had a large round ruby (artificial) pinned to it above his forehead.

He proceeded towards the car, looked at Jamilla, and then said to the bearded brothers, 'I will take care of her.' He put his head into the interior of the car. Jamilla recoiled in terror. The lady next to her held her and said, 'Don't be frightened. Hajji Musa intends no harm.'

'Listen, sister, come into the house, I have been expecting you.'

'No! No! I want to go home.' Jamilla began to cry.

'I won't let anyone hurt you.'

Hajji Musa tried to grab her hand, but she pushed herself backwards against the woman next to her and screamed so loudly that for a moment the healer seemed to lose his nerve. He turned to the brothers.

'The evil jinn is in her. Whatever I do now, please forgive me.'

He put his foot into the interior of the car, gripped one arm of the terrified Jamilla and smacked her twice with vehemence.

'Come out jinn! Come out jinn!' he shouted and dragged her towards the door of the car. The woman beside Jamilla pushed her and punched her on her back.

'Please help,' Hajji Musa said, and the two brothers pulled the screaming Jamilla out of the car.

'Drive the jinn into the house!' And they punched and pushed Jamilla towards the house. She pleaded with several spectators for help and then in desperation clung to them. But they shook her off and one or two even took the liberty of punching her and pulling her hair.

Jamilla was pushed into the house and the door closed on her and several of the privileged who were permitted to witness the exorcism ceremony. As soon as she passed through a narrow passage and entered a room she quietened.

The room was brilliantly lit and a fire was burning in the grate. A red carpet stretched from wall to wall and on the window-sill incense was burning in brass bowls. In front of the gate were two brass plates containing sun-dried red chillies.

We removed our shoes and sat down on the carpet. Jamilla was made to sit in front of the grate. She was awed and looked about at the room and the people. Several women seated themselves near her. Hajji Musa then began to recite the chapter 'The Jinn' from the Koran. We sat with bowed heads. When he had done he moved towards the grate. His wife came into the room with a steel tray and a pair of tongs. Hajji Musa took some burning pieces of coal and heaped them on the tray. Then he scattered the red chillies over the coals. Smoke rose from the tray and filled the room with an acrid, suffocating smell. He seated himself beside Jamilla and asked the two brothers to sit near her as well. He pressed Jamilla's head over the tray and at the same time recited a verse from the Koran in a loud voice. Jamilla choked, seemed to scream mutely and tried to lift her head, but Hajji Musa held her.

As the smell of burning chillies was unbearable, some of us went outside for a breath of fresh air. Aziz Khan said to us:

'That primitive ape is prostituting our religion with his hocus-pocus. He should be arrested for assault.'

We heard Jamilla screaming and we returned quickly to the room. We saw Hajji Musa and the two brothers beating her with their sandals and holding her face over the coals.

'Out Iblis! Out Jinn!' Hajji Musa shouted and belaboured her.

At last Jamilla fell into a swoon.

'Hold her, Ismail and Hafiz.' Hajji Musa sprinkled her face with water and read a prayer. Then he asked the two brothers to pick her up and take her into an adjoining room. They laid her on a bed.

'When she wakes up the jinn will be gone,' Hajji Musa predicted confidently.

We went outside for a while. Aziz Khan asked a few of us to go with him in his car to the police station. But on the way he surprised us by changing his mind.

'It's not our business,' he said, and drove back to the yard.

When we returned Jamilla had opened her eyes and was sobbing quietly.

'Anyone can ask Jamilla if she remembers what happened to her.'

Someone asked her and she shook her head.

'See,' said the victorious man, 'it was the evil jinn that was thrashed out of her body. He is gone!'

☆　☆　☆　☆　☆

There had been the singing of hymns, chanting and the jingling of bells since the late afternoon, and as evening approached there was great excitement in the yard. Everyone knew of the great event that was to take place that evening: the Hindu fire-walker was going to give a demonstration.

'There is nothing wonderful about walking on fire,' Hajji Musa declared in a scornful tone. 'The Hindus think they are performing miracles. Bah! Miracles!' And he exploded in laughter. 'What miracles can their many gods perform, I ask you? Let them extract a jinn or heal the sick and then talk of miracles.'

'But can you walk on fire or only cook on fire?' Dolly asked sardonically. There was laughter and merriment.

'Both, my dear man, both. Anyone who cooks on fire can walk on fire.'

'If anyone can, let him try,' said the law student Soma. 'In law, words are not enough; evidence has to be produced.'

'Funny you lawyers never get done with words. After gossiping for days you ask for a postponement.'

Everyone laughed boisterously.

'Hajji Musa,' Dolly tried again, 'can you walk on fire?'

'Are you joking, Dolly? When I can remove a jinn, what is walking on fire? Have you seen a jinn?'

'No.'

'See one and then talk. Evil jinn live in hell. What is walking on fire to holding one of hell's masters in your hands?'

'I say let him walk on fire and then talk of jinn,' said Rama the dwarfish Hindu watchmaker, but he walked away fearing to confront Hajji Musa.

'That stupid Hindu thinks I waste my time in performing tricks. I am not a magician.'

A fire was now lit in the yard. Wood had been scattered over an area of about twenty feet by six feet. An attendant was shovelling coal and another using the rake to spread it evenly.

Meanwhile, in a room in the yard, the voices of the chanters were rising and the bells were beginning to jingle madly. Every now and then a deeper, more resonant chime would ring out, and a voice would lead the chanters to a higher pitch. In the midst of the chanters, facing a small altar on which were placed a tiny earthenware bowl containing a burning wick, a picture of the god Shiva surrounded by votive offerings of marigold flowers, rice and coconut, sat the fire-walker in a cross-legged posture.

The yard was crowded. Chairs were provided but these were soon occupied. The balconies were packed and several agile children climbed onto rooftops and seated themselves on the creaking zinc. A few dignitaries were also present.

The chanters emerged from the doorway. In their midst was the fire-walker, his eyes focused on the ground. He was like a man eroded of his own will, captured by the band of chanters. They walked towards the fire which was now a glowing flames leaping here and there.

The chanters grouped themselves near the fire and went on with their singing and bell-ringing, shouting refrains energetically. Then, as though life had suddenly flowed into him, the fire-walker detached himself from the group and went towards the fire. It was a tense moment. The chanters were gripped by frenzy. The coal-bed glowed. He placed his right foot on the fire gently, tentatively, as though measuring its intensity, and then walked swiftly over from end to end. He was applauded. Two boys now offered him coconuts in trays. He selected two, and then walked over the inferno again, rather slowly this time, and as he walked he banged the coconuts against his head several times until they cracked and one saw the snowy insides. His movement now became more like a dance than a walk, as though his feet gloried in their triumph over the fire. The boys offered him more coconuts and he went on breaking them against his head.

While the fire-walker was demonstrating his salamander-like powers, an argument developed between Aziz Khan and Hajji Musa.

'He is not walking over the fire,' Hajji Musa said. 'Our eyes are being deceived.'

'Maybe your eyes are being deceived, but not mine,' Aziz answered.

'If you know anything about yogis then you will know how they can pass off the unreal for the real.'

'What do you mean by saying if I know anything about yogis?'

'He thinks he knows about everything under the sun,' Hajji Musa said jeeringly to a friend. He turned to Aziz.

'Have you been to India to see the fakirs and yogis?'

'No, and I don't intend to.'

'Well, I have been to India and know more than you do.'

'I have not been to India, but what I do know is that you are a fraud.'

'Fraud! Huh!'

'Charlatan! Humbug!'

'I say, Aziz!' With a swift movement Hajji Musa clutched Aziz Khan's wrist.

'You are just a big-talker and one day I shall shut your mouth for you.'

'Fraud! Crook! You are a disgrace to Islam. You with your chillies and jinn!'

'Sister ...!' This remark Hajji Musa uttered in Gujarati.

'Why don't you walk over the fire? It's an unreal fire.' And Aziz laughed sardonically.

'Yes, let him walk,' said the watchmaker. 'Hajji Musa big-talker.'

'The fire is not as hot as any of your jinn, Hajji Musa,' Dolly said slyly, with an ironic chuckle.

'Dolly, anyone can walk on fire if he knows the trick.'

'I suppose you know,' Aziz said tauntingly.

'Of course I do.'

'Then why don't you walk over the fire?'

'Jinn are hotter!' Dolly exclaimed.

'Fraud! Hypocrite! Degraded infidel, you will never walk. I dare you!'

'I will show you, you fool. I will show you what I can do.'

'What can you show but your lying tongue, and beat up little girls!'

'You sister ...! I will walk.'

While the argument had been raging, many people had gathered around them and ceased to look at the Hindu fire-walker. Now, when Hajji Musa accepted the challenge, he was applauded.

Hajji Musa removed his shoes and socks and rolled up his trousers. All eyes in the yard were now focused on him. Some shouted words of encouragement and others clapped their hands. Mr Darsot, though, tried to dissuade him.

'Hajji Musa, I don't think you should attempt walking on fire.'

But Dolly shouted in his raucous voice:

'Hajji Musa, show them what you are made of!'

Hajji Musa, determined and intrepid, went towards the fire. The Hindu fire-walker was now resting for a while, his body and clothes wet with sweat and juice from broken coconuts, and the chanters' voices were low. When Hajji Musa reached the fire he faltered. His body tensed with fear. Cautiously he lifted his right foot over the glowing mass. But any thought he might have had of retreat, of giving up Aziz Khan's challenge and declaring himself defeated, was dispelled by the applause he received.

Crying out in a voice that was an invocation to God to save him, he stepped on the inferno:

'Allah is great!'

What happened to Hajji Musa was spoken of long afterwards. Badly burnt, he was dragged out of the fire, drenched with water and smothered with rags, and taken to hospital.

We went to visit him. We expected to find a man humiliated, broken. We found him sitting up in bed, swathed in bandages, but as ebullient and resilient as always, with a bevy of young nurses eagerly attending to him.

'Boys, I must say fire-walking is not for me. Showmanship ... that's for magicians and crowd-pleasers ... those seeking cheap publicity.'

And he laughed in his usual way until the hospital corridors resounded.

The Sisters

Pauline Smith

Marta was the eldest of my father's children, and she was sixteen years old when our mother died and our father lost the last of his water-cases to old Jan Redlinghuis of Bitterwater. It was the water-cases that killed my mother. Many, many times she had cried to my father to give in to old Jan Redlinghuis whose water-rights had been fixed by law long before my father built his water-furrow from the Ghamka river. But my father could not rest. If he could but get a fair share of the river-water for his furrow, he would say, his farm of Zeekoegatt would be as rich as the farm of Bitterwater and we should then have a town-house in Platkops dorp and my mother should wear a black cashmere dress all the days of her life. My father could not see that my mother did not care about the black cashmere dress or the town-house in Platkops dorp. My mother was a very gentle woman with a disease of the heart, and all she cared about was to have peace in the house and her children happy around her. And for so long as my father was at law about his water-rights there could be no peace on all the farm of Zeekoegatt. With each new water-case came more bitterness and sorrow to us all. Even between my parents at last came bitterness and sorrow. And in bitterness and sorrow my mother died.

In his last water-case my father lost more money than ever before, and to save the farm he bonded some of the lands to old Jan Redlinghuis himself. My father was surely mad when he did this, but he did it. And from that day Jan Redlinghuis pressed him, pressed him, pressed him, till my father did not know which way to turn. And then, when my father's back was up against the wall and he thought he must sell the last of his lands to pay his bond, Jan Redlinghuis came to him and said:

'I will take your daughter, Marta Magdalena, instead.'

Three days Jan Redlinghuis gave my father, and in three days, if

Marta did not promise to marry him, the lands of Zeekoegatt must be sold. Marta told me this late that same night. She said to me:

'Sukey, my father has asked me to marry old Jan Redlinghuis. I am going to do it.'

And she said again: 'Sukey my darling, listen now! If I marry old Jan Redlinghuis he will let the water into my father's furrow, and the lands of Zeekoegatt will be saved. I am going to do it, and God will help me.'

I cried to her: 'Marta! Old Jan Redlinghuis is a sinful man, going at times a little mad in his head. God must help you before you marry him. Afterwards it will be too late.'

And Marta said: 'Sukey, if I do right, right will come of it, and it is right for me to save the lands of my father. Think now, Sukey my darling! There is not one of us that is without sin in the world and old Jan Redlinghuis is not always mad. Who am I to judge Jan Redlinghuis? And can I then let my father be driven like a poor-white to Platkops dorp?' And she drew me down on to the pillow beside her, and took me into her arms, and I cried there until far into the night.

The next day I went alone across the river to old Jan Redlinghuis's farm. No one knew that I went, or what it was in my heart to do. When I came to the house Jan Redlinghuis was out on the stoep smoking his pipe.

I said to him: 'Jan Redlinghuis, I have come to offer myself.'

Jan Redlinghuis took his pipe out of his mouth and looked at me. I said again: 'I have come to ask you to marry me instead of my sister Marta.'

Old Jan Redlinghuis said to me: 'And why have you come to do this thing, Sukey de Jager?'

I told him: 'Because it is said that you are a sinful man, Jan Redlinghuis, going at times a little mad in your head, and my sister Marta is too good for you.'

For a little while old Jan Redlinghuis looked at me, sitting there with his pipe in his hand, thinking the Lord knows what. And presently he said:

'All the same, Sukey de Jager, it is your sister Marta that I will marry and no one else. If not, I will take the lands of Zeekoegatt as is my right, and I will make your father bankrupt. Do now as you like about it.'

And he put his pipe in his mouth, and not one other word would he say.

I went back to my father's house with my heart heavy like lead. And all that night I cried to God: 'Do now what you will with me, but save our Marta.' Yes, I tried to make a bargain with the Lord so that Marta might be saved. And I said also: 'If He does not save our Marta I will know that there is no God.'

In three weeks Marta married old Jan Redlinghuis and went to live with him across the river. On Marta's wedding-day I put my father's Bible before him and said:

'Pa, pray if you like, but I shall not pray with you. There is no God or surely He would have saved our Marta. But if there is a God as surely will He burn our souls in Hell for selling Marta to old Jan Redlinghuis.'

From that time I could do what I would with my father, and my heart was bitter to all the world but my sister Marta. When my father said to me:

'Is it not wonderful, Sukey, what we have done with the water that old Jan Redlinghuis lets pass to my furrow?'

I answered him: 'What is now wonderful? It is blood that we lead on our lands to water them. Did not my mother die for it? And was it not for this that we sold my sister Marta to old Jan Redlinghuis?'

Yes, I said that. It was as if my heart must break to see my father water his lands while old Jan Redlinghuis held my sister Marta up to shame before all Platkops.

I went across the river to my sister Marta as often as I could, but not once after he married her did old Jan Redlinghuis let Marta come back to my father's house.

'Look now, Sukey de Jager,' he would say to me, 'your father has sold me his daughter for his lands. Let him now look to his lands and leave me his daughter.' And that was all he would say about it.

Marta had said that old Jan Redlinghuis was not always mad, but from the day that he married her his madness was to cry to all the world to look at the wife that Burgert de Jager had sold to him.

'Look,' he would say, 'how she sits in her new tent-cart—the wife that Burgert de Jager sold to me.'

And he would point to the Zeekoegatt lands and say: 'See now, how green they are, the lands that Burgert de Jager sold me his daughter to save.'

Yes, even before strangers would he say these things, stopping his cart in the road to say to them, with Marta sitting by his side.

My father said to me: 'Is it not wonderful, Sukey, to see how Marta rides through the country in her new tent-cart?'

I said to him: 'What is now wonderful? It is to her grave that she rides in the new tent-cart, and presently you will see it.'

And I said to him also: 'It took you many years to kill my mother, but believe me it will not take as many months for old Jan Redlinghuis to kill my sister Marta.' Yes, God forgive me, but I said that to my father. All my pity was for my sister Marta, and I had none to give my father.

And all this time Marta spoke no word against old Jan Redlinghuis. She had no illness that one might name, but every day she grew a little weaker, and every day Jan Redlinghuis inspanned the new tent-cart and drove her round the country. This madness came at last so strong upon him that he must drive from sun-up to sun-down crying to all whom he met:

'Look now at the wife that Burgert de Jager sold to me!'

So it went, day after day, day after day, till at last there came a day when Marta was too weak to climb into the cart and they carried her from where she fell into the house. Jan Redlinghuis sent for me across the river.

When I came to the house old Jan Redlinghuis was standing on the stoep with his gun. He said to me: 'See here, Sukey de Jager! Which of us now had the greatest sin—your father who sold me his daughter Marta, or I who bought her? Marta who let herself be sold, or you who offered yourself to save her?'

And he took up his gun and left the stoep and would not wait for an answer.

Marta lay where they had put her on old Jan Redlinghuis's great wooden bed, and only twice did she speak. Once she said:

'He was not always mad, Sukey my darling, and who am I that I should judge him?'

And again she said: 'See how it is, my darling! In a little while I shall be with our mother. So it is that God has helped me.'

At sun-down Marta died, and when they ran to tell Jan Redlinghuis they could not find him. All that night they looked for him, and the next day also. We buried Marta in my mother's grave at Zeekoegatt. ... And still they could not find Jan Redlinghuis. Six days they looked for him, and at last they found his body in the mountains. God knows what madness had driven old Jan

Redlinghuis to the mountains when his wife lay dying, but there it was they found him, and at Bitterwater he was buried.

That night my father came to me and said: 'It is true what you said to me, Sukey. It is blood that I have led on my lands to water them, and this night will I close the furrow that I built from the Ghamka river. God forgive me, I will do it.'

It was in my heart to say to him: 'The blood is already so deep in the lands that nothing we can do will now wash it out.' But I did not say this. I do not know how it was, but there came before me the still, sad face of my sister Marta, and it was as if she herself answered for me.

'Do now as it seems right to you,' I said to my father. 'Who am I that I should judge you?'

Tselane and the Giant

translated from Sesotho by
B.L. Leshoai

During the days of King Chaka of the Amazulu a widow lived in Lesotho at a place called Lekhalong La 'Mantsopa. Mantsopa was a Mosotho prophetess who was said to have lived sometime after Noah's great flood. There is a large imprint of an ostrich's foot on a rock in this area. It is said that during Noah's flood even the hard rocks became soft from being covered in water for such a long time. When the floods went down the animals left the Ark in search of food; and this is the time when the ostrich, whose imprint was left on the rock, went in his search for food to Mantsopa's valley.

It was in this valley that our widow lived, many years after Mantsopa's death. The valley was very far from any other place — secret and quiet, and occupied by a huge giant called Limo, who made life very miserable for the people living there. He killed their cattle and sheep and even the people themselves with his great axe. At nightfall the people locked themselves and their children behind strong doors. They shut their animals up behind well-built kraals made from the wood of Mimosa trees. Even so, they did not manage to stop the evil giant from getting to the cattle and sheep when he wanted meat. Sometimes angry armed men and their vicious hunting dogs went out to fight the giant to put him to death. He waited for them to approach his cave before he rushed out to attack them with his huge axe. He always waited for them and their yelping dogs to get quite near before he appeared. Limo very much enjoyed the days when the people came to hunt him down.

Before he left the darkness of the cave he bellowed like an angry bull and the noise echoed up and down the valley. The yelping of the dogs stopped as soon as they heard this dreadful bellow. They hid their tails between their legs in great fear. The men stopped chanting their war songs as though they had already come face to face with the enemy. Limo had great fun watching what happened when he eventually appeared. The dogs were always the first to turn tail, yelping as though scalded with boiling water. As soon as the dogs ran away the men started to follow. Some dropped their heavy spears and round-headed sticks. The earth trembled under their feet. Some threw off their colourful blankets which flew in the wind and impeded their progress in the race for their lives. Their womenfolk and children, who were waiting in the hope of seeing the men return victorious with the giant's head, ran into their huts and bolted the doors behind them when they saw that they were defeated. This sight always made Limo laugh loudly. The cruel, mocking sound of his laugh upset the people even more. When they reached their homes, the dogs and the masters had to throw themselves against the strong doors. The men struck the doors with their sticks and fists. They yelled and screamed at their frightened womenfolk and children to let them in. When a door was opened or was broken down the dogs were always the first to find their way into the huts, through the men's legs. Once in, the men slammed the doors behind them and leaned against them with their backs, feet planted firmly on the floor, in an attempt to keep out the threatening giant.

Afterwards Limo would return to his cave, rocking with laughter at the foolish men and dogs. Sometimes to spite them he would follow to where their cattle and sheep were grazing and kill a few with his axe for his evening meal. Limo was a terrifying giant. His timid but kindly wife feared him like the plague. He was tall and strong, with a large round head covered with dirty, kinky hair. His face and chin were overgrown with a grizzly beard, and his huge eyes shone at night like two lights in the darkness. His large teeth always had bits of meat stuck between them. The meat rotted and so his breath had a very bad smell. His chest was big and strong, as were his thighs—larger and stronger than those of a bull! Beneath his muscular shoulders and arms was a big round and fat belly. His feet were flat and large. He ran like the wind, that one! His presence made the people of the valley feel very unsafe and one by one they began to leave. They took all their belongings and moved to a place far away. The giant began to starve because there were no longer any sheep and cattle to eat. So he began to eat human beings.

Now this widow had a beautiful daughter called Tselane. Tselane refused to leave the valley with her mother because she loved the beautiful hut where she lived and the valley with its sunken lake and trees and flowers. Her mother therefore left her in the hut and promised that she would bring her bread and meat every second day. She also told Tselane that she would sing a song at the door so that Tselane would know it was her mother outside. For many days she brought her daughter food in a basket and sang at the door in her sweet and tender motherly voice:

Tselane my child,
Tselane my child,
Open the door, my child,
Open the door, my child;
I've brought you bread to eat,
Tselane, my child.

Tselane listened with her ear against the door and when she was certain it was her mother's voice she sang in reply:

I hear you my mother,
I hear you my mother.

Then she opened the door and let her mother in. When she had finished her food, Tselane let her mother out and locked the door from the inside so that no one could come in.

Limo soon discovered that Tselane had stayed behind and began to make plans to catch her. He also found out the days on which her mother visited her and what she did to be allowed into the hut. So one day, when Limo knew that her mother wasn't coming, he went to the hut carrying his hunting sack. He tiptoed quietly to the door of the hut and began to sing in his gruff voice, which shook the tiny hut:

Tselane my child,
Tselane my child,
Open the door, my child,
Open the door, my child;
I've brought you bread to eat,
Tselane, my child.

Tselane didn't have to put her ear against the door for she knew it was not her mother's voice. Then she said, 'Go away, Limo; I know you, evil one. My mother's voice is sweet and gentle and not gruff like yours.'

Limo went home very angry and nagged his wife, making her very unhappy because Tselane had been too clever for him. At night he tossed sleeplessly on his mat until he had an idea: 'Aha, I've got it!' After that he slept soundly and snored loudly and his wife knew he was thinking up some mischief.

Next day Tselane's mother, after she heard her daughter's story of how Limo had tried to cheat her, attempted to persuade Tselane to go with her to her new home. But Tselane refused. On the following day Limo got up early and took his hunting sack with him. When his wife asked him where he was going he looked at her with bloodshot eyes and walked away without a word. When he was some distance from his cave he picked up a round smooth stone about the size of an ostrich's egg. He made a big fire and baked the stone. When it was red-hot he swallowed it quickly. The stone burnt his throat, though he did not feel much pain. After this he went to Tselane's hut and sang to her to open the door, but she was not deceived although his voice sounded much softer and pleasanter.

Limo went home in a very bad mood and made his wife run around doing unnecessary jobs. But this did not soothe his nerves. That night again he was unable to sleep and tossed restlessly on his mat. When his wife tried to sleep he scolded her and made her very unhappy. Towards morning, after he had been thinking and thinking, he exclaimed excitedly, 'Aha, I've got it!' and immediately fell into a deep sleep, filling the cave with his heavy snores.

That day Tselane recounted her experiences to her mother, who again tried to persuade her to leave the dangerous valley. Tselane refused once more, so her mother left her with a heavy heart and wept all the way home.

Limo woke up in the late afternoon and looked for a hoe among his old implements. He put it into his hunting sack and tried to be very pleasant to his wife. She knew that when he behaved like that and tried to be nice to her he usually had some hidden plan. Next morning he was up early, with the sack over his shoulder and the hoe inside. Some distance from Tselane's hut he lit a great big fire and threw the hoe into it until it was white-hot. Then he snatched it up and swallowed it quickly. The hoe burnt his throat and a great smoke issued from his mouth. His throat was so sore that he could not sing loudly. His voice was now soft and sweet like Tselane's mother's voice.

When he got to her hut he imitated her mother's voice perfectly:

Tselane my child,
Tselane my child,
Open the door, my child,
Open the door, my child;
I've brought you bread to eat,
Tselane, my child.

Tselane, who had pressed her ear against the door to listen, had two hearts. Her good heart told her that it wasn't her mother's voice and her bad heart told her that it was. After she had thought for a while she replied, 'If you are my mother, you will sing to me again.'

Limo replied in a soft voice, 'Yes, my child, I will sing.' Then he licked his ugly lips with his huge red tongue as though he already had his prey in the bag. He sang in an even sweeter and softer voice:

Tselane my child,
Tselane my child,
Open the door, my child,
Open the door, my child;
I've brought you bread to eat,
Tselane, my child.

She pressed her ear closer to the door. She was sure it was her mother's voice; and though she had two hearts and her good heart was beating fast, she replied tenderly:

I hear you my mother,
I hear you my mother.

Then Limo heard her turn the key in the door and prepared to grab hold of her as soon as the door opened. When he felt sure she had unlocked it, he gave it a violent push, knocking down the poor girl inside. When she saw who it was she fainted with fright. He picked her up and put her into his hunting sack, locked the door and went back to his cave.

His timid and kind-hearted wife could always tell when Limo had caught a human being because his face looked even more sour and cruel than usual. He hated to share human flesh with her. So when he got home in the evening he was humourless and moody and spoke harshly to his wife, his red eyes glowering at her like a lion. Cautiously she asked, 'What animal have you caught today?'

His reply was harsh and full of meaning: 'Nothing, just a lean buck!'

She pretended to be excited and asked him, 'And when do we eat it?'

'When I've rested,' was the cross reply. He put the wriggling sack into his special room and immediately went to sleep. He had instructed his wife to light the fire in the special room and to boil the water in the huge pot early next morning.

When Limo was sound asleep his wife crept to the sack to find out what was in it. When she put her ear to it she heard the faint sound of a girl's voice saying, 'Oh mother, dear mother, come to my rescue; save me from the cruel giant. Oh my mother dear, if my life is saved I shall always obey your wise advice.' Tselane then started to sob bitterly, her whole body trembling with sorrow and terror. Limo's wife was touched and moved by the child's bitter weeping, so she opened the sack and let her out. As there was no time to speak, she hurriedly hid the girl in one of the huge unused pots and told her to be very quiet. She then put a heavy lid over it. For the time being Tselane was safe, but Limo's wife did not know how to get her away from the cave, or what she would say if Limo discovered that Tselane had disappeared in the morning. She was very agitated and ran on tiptoe between the special room and Limo's bedroom, wringing her hands and racking her brain for a plan before he woke up. She just couldn't think of anything. Her motherly tears began to flow down her cheeks. She was not sorry for herself. She was worried about what would happen to Tselane when her husband woke up.

When morning was about to break, the wretched woman got up from where she had fallen asleep. Her head was aching and she was trembling with fear. The fire had to be lit and the water boiled for Limo to cook his 'lean buck'. As the cocks began to crow she went to the door of the cave to bring in the logs for the fire. Now near the entrance to the cave was a large tree on which were numerous bee hives and wasps' and hornets' nests. Suddenly an idea struck her when she saw the tree, and she exclaimed excitedly, 'I have it!'

She ran back with the pile of logs and lit the fire to boil the water.

Dawn was rapidly approaching and Limo was turning restlessly on his bed. This made his wife work feverishly to get her plan ready. When the fire had caught, she snatched up the empty sack and ran to the tree. With great skill she raked the sleepy bees and wasps and hornets into the sack with her hands. She then rolled away a big stone at the foot of the tree and also swept the many fat scorpions, with their poisonous stings, into the sack. She tied it as it was and put it back in the place where Limo had left it the night before. She had just put the sack down when she heard him yawn like a roaring lion and lick his lips with relish. While he rubbed his blood-red eyes he yelled at her to put the sack near the boiling pot. When he was ready he went into the special room and bolted the door, closing the holes in the walls with stones to prevent his quarry from escaping. The sun was up. The cattle and sheep were already grazing. Even the young herdboys were out, chanting their hunting songs, their tiny spears poised for action:

You're fat field mouse,
You're delicious field mouse.

Tselane's mother, meanwhile, had tossed restlessly the whole night. Her head was full of ugly dreams about snakes and lions. She was outside her daughter's hut at the first streaks of dawn. This was about the same time that Limo woke from his sleep. She began to sing her song with a trembling voice. There was no reply. She repeated the song again and again, each time singing louder and louder, with tears of anguish streaming down her cheeks. But still there was no reply. Then terror-stricken, she beat the door with her hands and with stones, shouting and screaming, 'Tselane my child, open the door! Tselane my child, wake up and eat your bread!' And still there was no answer except the hollow echo from the empty hut. In despair she sat on the door-step with her head in her hands and wept bitterly, for she had seen the big footprints and realized that Limo had taken her only daughter. She sat there for a great while and wept a long, long time.

When Limo was sure the door and the holes in the walls were secure, he lifted the sack onto his back. A scorpion stung him. Thinking that it was Tselane who had bitten him, he put the sack down and scratched his back while he smiled to himself, 'Well, the last kicks of a dying animal are always vicious. Kick as much as you like, die you shall die!' He swung the sack onto his back again. This time a bee and a wasp and a hornet stung him and he let the sack fall to the ground with a curse. And he could curse, that man! The stings itched like scabies, forcing him to scratch his back violently as he pranced about the room like a wild horse. His wife had her ear pressed to the door. She did not see his pranks, yet she smiled with satisfaction as she imagined what he was suffering. She thought with pleasure, 'Aha, the one who eats last also enjoys his food!' Had he not always been unkind to her? Well, now he would soon be face to face with his equals.

The last three stings had been particularly painful. Although Limo was a strong and cruel man he was not going to take chances with this girl with the stinging teeth. He approached the sack very carefully. He wanted to open it so that it would be ready for him to dump the contents into the boiling cauldron quickly.

The bees, wasps and hornets were buzzing angrily now. Limo thought this buzzing was that of a person weeping. It made him feel braver. He carefully loosened the opening of the sack, ready to tip his 'lean buck' into the pot. But alas, poor fellow, this was not to be! As soon as the sack was open, a buzzing swarm of bees and wasps and hornets flew out and immediately attacked him. He was completely stunned and stood there for a moment wondering what had happened.

Hundreds of scorpions had also crawled out of the fallen sack. Their piercing, poisonous stings roused him from his state of helplessness. The wild creatures had covered his entire body. He tried frantically to scrape them off. Suddenly he realized that his wife had tricked him. He forgot about Tselane and rushed off to find her. But who can think of killing when he is fighting against bees and wasps and hornets and scorpions? His only thought now was to save himself. Because his wife was not cruel she did not mock him. He screamed and hit the door with his fists and butted the walls with his head and kicked them with his large feet. His wife was busy all this time trying to think of how to save Tselane. Limo fought so furiously that the door soon flew open and he dashed out, howling with pain. The bees and wasps and hornets flew out after their victim.

The deadly scorpions had not been idle either. Near the cave there was a deep sunken lake. As he ran towards it, the distance

between him and the bees and wasps increased. But once you have
disturbed a hornets' nest you have to face the results. Although he
moved much faster than they did and his running feet stirred up a
cloud of dust behind him, still they followed. When he plunged
into the water the mad bees and wasps caught up with him again.
He was forced to put his head under the water to escape the
dreadful stings. His screams and howls filled the whole valley.
Tselane's mother heard his drowning cries from the hut where she
was still sitting weeping. That is how the cruel, bad giant died.

When Limo's wife was absolutely certain that he was dead, she
took the heavy lid off the pot and let Tselane out. Tselane fell on
her knees sobbing and thanked Limo's wife and asked her to go to
the hut with her. The poor woman, who had always wanted to lead
a good life, went with Tselane. They found Tselane's sad mother at
the hut. When she saw her daughter she wept again—this time
with joy. After Limo's wife had told the story of her husband's
death, they all went off to find their old friends to tell them the good
news.

There was much rejoicing and many people returned to live in
the valley. They invited Limo's wife to live with them. Ever since,
Lekhalong La 'Mantsopa has been a happy, safe and prosperous
place.

And that is the end of the story!

Johannesburg, Johannesburg

Nathaniel (Nat) Nakasa

People who have the best time in Johannesburg are the visitors. People who stay in town for a month or two and then fly out to their homes across the seas, with memories as their only link with Johannesburg. I've seen them sniff and stare at the city's narrow lanes where men smoke dagga. I've watched them enchanted by the opulence of the northern suburbs where whites live. These men, usually foreign correspondents from newspapers abroad, even find warmth in the squalor of the black slums. They look at Johannesburg from all angles, in much the same way as they would besiege a celebrated statesman at a press conference. They ask crucial questions without getting emotionally involved with the town's preoccupations.

I have often tried to put myself in this position, to approach Johannesburg with the attitude of a disengaged visitor. Unfortunately for me, I cannot succeed in doing this. I am a part of Johannesburg. The most I can do is regard myself as someone who has, unwittingly, volunteered to become the guinea pig in some incredible experiment by a quack scientist.

That's how I felt during my first few years in Johannesburg. I had travelled from Durban, over four hundred miles by train, to start working as a journalist. After work, I often slept on a desk at the office or stayed overnight when friends invited me to dinner in their homes.

This was not because of a Bohemian bent in me. Far from it. According to the law, 'native' bachelors are supposed to live in hostels in Johannesburg. I should have shared a dormitory with ten or more strange men. Some could have been office clerks, messengers, night-watchmen, road-diggers, school teachers or witch-doctors. We could each be at liberty to play our concertinas or strum guitars while others read books or brewed beer in the dormitory.

Instead of this, I chose to be a wanderer. It would have been too difficult to get a hostel bed anyway. I remember trying once, just for the hell of it. I picked up the telephone and spoke in a faked Oxford accent. 'My name is Brokenshaw,' I said. 'Is there a vacant bed in your hostel by any chance?'

'Yes, we have some beds,' the voice at the other end answered. It must have been the white superintendent. 'But I must explain to you that we are only taking special boys now,' he added.

'What sort of boys are those?' I asked.

'Special boys,' he repeated, 'boys employed in the essential services; milk-delivery boys, sanitation boys, and so on. Boys who have to be in town very early in the morning or till late at night.'

'Jolly good,' I said, 'my boy is actually quite special. He has to remain in town till quite late from time to time. He is a journalist.'

'Well, Mr Brokenshaw, I can't promise anything. You can send him along if you like. We'll have to deal with every case according to its merits.'

I didn't go to the superintendent. I didn't really want a hostel bed. Neither did I wish to switch from journalism to the essential services. Thus, for roughly eighteen months, on and off, I wandered about without a fixed home address. I determined to make the best of it. The idea was to regard complications of my relationship with Johannesburg as part of the incredible experiment. That way I could get on with the business of living without getting too depressed.

Fortunately, like most young men from the smaller towns in South Africa, I was thrilled by simply being in Johannesburg. While others made for their homes hurriedly at the end of the day, I took long leisurely walks from one end of the city to another. On some nights I spent long hours reading London papers in the *Rand Daily Mail* library. Friends who invited me to their flats soon got used to me turning up for a bath in addition to dinner and a drink.

At times I slept in the night-watchman's room on the top of our office block. The night-watchman was a tall, very dark man, always in blue overalls, and Zulu-speaking. He seemed to welcome my appearance and spoke a lot of politics with me. How long, he wanted to know once, did I think the white man would remain on top of us? Did I think the time would ever come when we would be on top? *Bathin' abelungu manje*? What are the whites saying now?

Answering these questions made me feel I was earning the watchman's hospitality. He saw me as an interpreter of the white man's ways because some of my friends were white. In the suburbs, over a drink, people plied me with questions about Africans. These conversations often developed into dull tales about the effects of apartheid on Africans, with me giving a rather false picture of the 'latest developments'. I knew very little about the African townships. Like many other people, I could have lived illegally in the townships, but I wanted to be in town, not five or fifteen miles outside.

I was especially fascinated with Johannesburg by night. Because of the curfew regulations, most Africans rushed out of town at the end of the day. Dozens of long brown trains whined out of town carrying thousands of Africans to their homes. By eleven o'clock, when the curfew regulations came into operation, almost all the faces in town would be white.

By day, the city became a depressing mess. There were too many Africans sweating away on company bicycles or lingering on pavements in search of work. More depressing would be the newly-recruited 'mine boys', scores of black men from all over Africa. They walked through town with blankets on their shoulders and loaves of bread under their armpits, to be housed in the hostels of the gold mines. They looked like prisoners to me. Some had blank, innocent faces and gazed openly, longingly, at women passing by. Most of them, if not all, were illiterate and doomed to stay that way for the rest of their lives. I resented them because I felt a responsibility towards them and I was doing nothing about it. They spoiled my image of Johannesburg as the throbbing giant which threw up sophisticated gangsters, brave politicians and intellectuals who challenged white authority.

This image of Johannesburg survived best at night. I shared a theory with a friend who also spent much of his time about town because of the housing problem. We believed that the best way to live with the colour bar in Johannesburg was to ignore it.

The theory worked remarkably well at times. I remember one night when we went to drink coffee at the Texan, a coffee bar reserved for whites in Commissioner Street. The place was run by an American from Texas. He had the American flag in the bar as well as a portrait of President Eisenhower, wearing his famous grin. My friend and I perched on two stools at the counter and placed our order for two coffees. The Texan's son went to fetch the coffee, obviously expecting us to drink it on the pavement, anywhere outside the bar. Meanwhile, my friend and I began to talk loudly about President Eisenhower's portrait. 'Look at the bum,' my friend started, looking at the President's portrait, 'there is something seriously wrong with America's choice of its heroes. Imagine the millions of American children whose ambition is to grow into the grinning emptiness which Ike symbolizes! To think that there are eggheads who could be built up instead of fellows like this.'

By the time the Texan's son brought our coffee, his father was embroiled in violent argument with us, all about Ike. The Texan confessed that he didn't know much about politics but he knew a man of God when he saw one. The argument was still raging when we finished drinking the coffee and left. Nobody seemed to remember the colour bar.

Apart from Cape Town, Johannesburg has what must be the largest number of whites who don't want the colour bar. Some people say this is because of the degree of industrial and commercial development which the city has achieved. Whatever the explanation may be, there can be no doubt that the University of Witwatersrand is leaving its own marks on the city's racial attitudes.

Wits has never been as 'open' as its Public Relations Office may suggest. It is predominantly white, taking a limited number of black students. Nevertheless, its non-racial character has facilitated a profound social intercourse between black and white men, people who might otherwise not have met except as master and servant or deadly enemies.

As a journalist, I was granted permission to borrow books from the university's library. To me, the opportunity to browse in that library, among students of all races, to go through any number of the books which line all the walls, transformed theories about the universality of education into a living reality.

Because of their common background of racial segregation, the students were intrigued with their discovery of an area of life relatively free from the colour bar. There was a general eagerness, often pretentious, to rush into each other's arms. But those who transcended the superficiality of this back-slapping brotherhood managed to establish warm, unaffected relationships.

It was students like these who descended on Uncle Joe's restaurant in Fordsburg, the predominantly Indian quarter at the west end of town. They came to eat Indian curry and listen to jazz in what was the only restaurant that allowed jam sessions before mixed audiences.

Although there was a police station nearby, nothing was done to stop the sessions at Uncle Joe's restaurant. We concluded that the police refrained from interfering because Uncle Joe gave them take-away food on credit.

People who speak of the decline of conversation in Europe and America ought to come to Johannesburg for their research on the subject. For what one finds here is worse than a decline—it is paralysis of conversation. The colour bar, which dominates the lives of all South Africans, haunts and plagues the dinner-tables monotonously all over town. I've often thought how irritating this must be to people who are sufficiently resourceful to make good conversation without dragging the business of segregation into it. I can survive because I am not one of them.

My conversations in Johannesburg have always centred around colour. Fortunately, some of this talk can be both meaningful and warm. I remember having dinner with a friend in one of the less prosperous white suburbs. One of the guests that night was a talented Afrikaner painter. He had a hungry, lean face which reminded me of a picture of Arthur Miller. He even wore glasses to complete the image. My host had hinted earlier that the painter was a Nationalist, a supporter of Dr Verwoerd's apartheid policy. The same man had spent much of his afternoon trying to keep alive a newborn African baby which had been abandoned on a pavement. He had taken the child in his arms, found warm clothes for it and phoned hospitals and the police.

Having talked about his paintings and jazz, we gravitated inevitably to the colour question. I wanted to know if he really was a Nationalist, and he said yes. We had, by now, warmed to each other, lighting cigarettes for one and all, sharing the same concern about the food which seemed to take a long time getting ready.

'But what kind of Nationalist are you?' I asked.

'But why?'

'How can you vote for apartheid and then come and drink brandy with me?'

'But there's nothing wrong in drinking with you. I would like to drink with you anywhere. At my place or yours, for that matter.'

'What if I told you that I have no place?'

'What do you mean?'

'Just that, I have no place and that's because of the laws you vote for.'

'What? Where are you going to sleep tonight, for instance?'
'I don't know. I may sleep here; wherever I can find a bed tonight.'

The painter was moved. I liked seeing his puzzled face.

'Well, if ... if you mean what you've said, you can come and live with me. We have a whole empty room in that house.'

Now I stopped being amused. Something was wrong somewhere.

'But the party you vote for has passed laws which say that's illegal, too,' I said.

Now the painter was blushing. He looked the other way and picked up his glass. I was becoming more and more irritated.

'Why are you a Nationalist if you are willing to stay with me? Don't you want the races to be separated?'

Suddenly, the painter took off his glasses and looked at me appealingly: 'You see,' he said, 'I am an Afrikaner. The National Party is my people's party. That's why I vote for it.'

Coming of the Dry Season

Charles Mungoshi

One Wednesday Moab Gwati received a letter from Rusape. His mother was seriously ill. He decided to wait till he got his pay on Friday: Saturday he would go home.

He had his pay on Friday afternoon, and, as always happened with his money when he had it, it seemed to fly in all directions.

That Friday night he got hopelessly drunk with a girl he had picked up in Mutanga's earlier in the evening. Her name was Chipo but he did not know it till Sunday. They slept together in his room till eight o'clock Saturday morning.

He was still drunk and, after a cold shower he took together with Chipo, he ordered two quarts of Castle lager to take with their breakfast of fried liver and eggs.

After breakfast, with five other friends, they drank till they dropped unconscious and their friends dumped them on the bed.

Early Sunday morning they had a beer and breakfast. They stayed in bed all morning. Moab felt his head beginning to ache. He had no more money and he did not want Chipo to know it.

At two o'clock he accompanied her to the bus station. He gave her a shilling for bus fare and a two-shilling piece for the fine weekend and patted her back in farewell. She said she had never been so happy in all her life. She stood in the queue to get on to the bus to Mufakose. Moab left before the ticket checker punched her ticket. As he was going away, the bus Chipo had taken passed him. He heard her yell and saw her wave to him. But he did not wave back. The black mood was on him.

When he felt this way Moab would walk for miles completely blind. It started always at the same emotional point, when, after a good time and he had no more money, he saw a gnarled old woman, thin as a starved cow, with a weak, saliva-flecked mouth and trembling limbs; very small dark eyes in carven sockets—a monkey face—and on her spare body threadbare rags wound as on a scarecrow stick. He would hear over and over the small mousy voice that was full of tears and self-pity, the voice that was a protest: '*Zindoga mwana'ngu*, remember where you come from.' A warning, a remonstrance, a curse and an epitaph. With it, he could never have a good time in peace. Guilt, frustration and fury ate at his nerves.

When he spent four years without employment she had almost died from despair. She had cooked beer to the ancestors and then he told her he was working. And her health had improved. He knew that she had stood on her thin little legs and danced the *mbavarira*, which is both a praise to the ancestors and a prayer for the dead. He knew she had burned good luck roots for him.

It seemed he could never do enough for her. He had sent her money and clothes and a hundred-pound bag of mealie meal with his first pay. After this he had promised himself he would send her some more money—which he had done—yet there seemed no end to the things she needed. Her voice asked for far more than he could give. She had said once, when he had let her come to the city, 'Couldn't you find work somewhere near me? You know it won't be long and as you are my first-born you must know all that you must do for me—for your own good—before I am gone. When I am gone you won't ever set anything right by yourself.' There were many things wrong with the family, she had told him. And she had been glad that he was working now because he would be able to set them right and release her from bondage.

It had so depressed him that, wishing her gone, he had told her that one day he would take a leave and she would say all she wanted done and he would do it. He had told her to console herself and remember that she would be always in his thoughts. She had cried, whether for joy or sorrow he had not known. But her tears had stayed with him and a guilt—about what he could not say—had dogged him like his shadow.

He smelled a sudden familiar smell. Dry, harvest-time smoke of burning maize-leaves. A shiver. Across the vlei the sun danced on the late red rapoko heads which nodded in the slight wind. In a pond of rust-coloured water rice was turning yellow and grass, rotting in the pond, stank. There had been unusually heavy rains this year. It was still raining, even now, in April. Another shiver. Why it should remind him of his mother, now very ill—at death's door as the letter had said—he did not know. He walked along the vlei, at the edge of Highfield Village. When he thought he should turn back, he entered Highfield from the west, having left it from the east.

He walked round and round Highfield. Night caught him still on the streets. Soon people left for bed and the dogs began their restless barking that would end with the coming of day.

In the northern sky he saw the bright arc of light that was the city. It reminded him of a veld fire at home. Only there was not the familiar smell of burning grass. If there had been, he knew he would have cried.

He watched the dogs trotting, mating, overturning bins in search of left-overs and relieving themselves on the streets. When he felt tired he went home.

The severe yellow light of his room, mixed with the strong smell of onions in dripping and rotting sofa sackcloth, brought before him a prison cell and his mother. She was there now, imprisoned by life, trapped by her conscience, holding on tight till he was there to leave whatever it was she wanted to leave him. Her little cell, probably.

But she would have to let go without him. He had no money now. It was all finished. He switched off the light and lay on the bed unable to sleep till the milkman's bell. Lying in bed he heard rain falling. Thinking of his mother and a childhood belief, he thought:

Soft earth
Wide spade
Are good friends.

He was listless the whole of the next day, a sunny Monday. His boss told him to take aspirin and go to bed, but he said he was all right. The boss, an understanding jovial man, had advised him not to take these weekends so severely.

Afraid of his yellow room, he slept at a friend's that night. On Tuesday, while walking to work, a bushy-tailed squirrel crossed and then recrossed his path. His heart sank. He asked for a sick leave that day and went home.

He found a telegram waiting for him next door where the postman had left it with his neighbours.

His mother had died on Saturday night.

Moab walked dazedly into his room. He sat in a chair and looked into a mean backyard of motor-car scraps and hen manure. He was thinking of nothing.

'Hello.'

It came weak and faraway as if it were his own mother's voice greeting him from the grave. He turned towards the bed.

Chipo lay naked under a pink sheet. She smiled at him. For a long time he looked at her, dumb.

'I came yesterday evening. Your door was unlocked. I waited for you all night. Where have you been?' She sounded exactly like his mother. He hated her.

'Why have you come here? What do you want with me?'

Chipo looked confused, as if she had found herself, by mistake, in the Gents.

'But ... but ... you slept with me.'

'So what's that? Haven't you slept with many others? Why do you come to me?'

'But you are different, Moab, I wish you would marry me. I ask for nothing else.'

She looked at him sadly and her mouth twisted as if she had a pain somewhere. 'I have been alone too long.'

Suddenly he felt helpless, trapped. He said weakly, 'I did not ask you to come back.'

'I know. I just came back. You were so kind to me.'

He wondered what he had done for her. She was talking like his mother, suffering and saying things he did not understand. Why must they receive something else from what he intended to give— and then come back later to ask him for more of what he did not know how to give? He despised her. She had come back only to complicate his world.

'I don't have any more money,' he said harshly. 'That's what you want, isn't it? I don't have even a penny.'

'I know that, Moab. I didn't come for your money. I have too much of that.'

'Then why did you come back? Your type always comes back for money!' He glared at her.

She looked at him and did not answer. Her mouth twisted again, and there was a whiff of dry season air in the room. Moab's eyes filled.

'Go back where you come from! I didn't call you here!'

He stood up and yanked the sheet off her. She gasped but did not scream. She covered her private parts and hastily put on her dress. Moab noticed that her body was pitifully thin and starved.

He slumped back into his chair.

When she had finished putting on her clothes she took her handbag from a peg above the bed. From it she took a purse. Tilting the purse towards the light, so that Moab saw the thick wad of pound notes in it, Chipo extracted a shilling and a two-shilling piece and slapped them on the table beside Moab's right elbow. Then quietly she went out of the room.

Alone, Moab stared at the three shillings on the table. The ragged figure of his mother moved into focus. He felt damned.

His hand reached down for the money. He looked at it, wondering whether he should throw it out of the window on to the scrap heap. His head tightened and untightened with indecision: unclean money. But he had not even a penny in his pocket.

And his cheeks burning with shame, he furtively put the money into his pocket. He stood up and flung himself on the bed. He cried for something that was not the death of his mother.

A Soldier's Embrace

Nadine Gordimer

The day the cease-fire was signed she was caught in a crowd. Peasant boys from Europe who had made up the colonial army and freedom fighters whose column had marched into town were staggering about together outside the barracks, not three blocks from her house in whose rooms, for ten years, she had heard the blurred parade-ground bellow of colonial troops being trained to kill and be killed.

The men weren't drunk. They linked and swayed across the street; because all that had come to a stop, everything *had* to come to a stop: they surrounded cars, bicycles, vans, nannies with children, women with loaves of bread or basins of mangoes on their heads, a road gang with picks and shovels, a Coca-Cola truck, an old man with a barrow who bought bottles and bones. They were grinning and laughing in amazement. That it could be: there they were, bumping into each other's bodies in joy, looking into each other's rough faces, all eyes crescent-shaped, brimming greeting. The words were in languages not mutually comprehensible, but the cries were new, a whooping and crowing all understood. She was bumped and jostled and she let go, stopped trying to move in any self-determined direction. There were two soldiers in front of her, blocking her off by their clumsy embrace (how do you do it, how do you do what you've never done before) and the embrace opened like a door and took her in—a pink hand with bitten nails grasping her right arm, a black hand with a big-dialled watch and thong bracelet pulling at her left elbow. Their three heads collided gaily, musk of sweat and tang of strong sweet soap clapped a mask to her nose and mouth. They all gasped with delicious shock. They were saying things to each other. She put up an arm round each neck, the rough pile of an army haircut on one side, the soft negro hair on the other, and kissed them both on the cheek. The embrace broke. The crowd wove her away behind backs, arms, jogging heads; she was returned to and took up the will of her direction again—she was walking home from the post office, where she had just sent a telegram to relatives abroad: ALL CALM DON'T WORRY.

The lawyer came back early from his offices because the courts were not sitting although the official celebration holiday was not until next day. He described to his wife the rally before the Town Hall, which he had watched from the office-building balcony. One of the guerilla leaders (not the most important; he on whose head the biggest price had been laid would not venture so soon and deep into the territory so newly won) had spoken for two hours from the balcony of the Town Hall. 'Brilliant. Their jaws dropped. Brilliant. They've never heard anything on that level: precise, reasoned—none of them would ever have believed it possible, out of the bush. You should have seen De Poorteer's face. He'd like to be able to get up and open his mouth like that. And be listened to like that ...' The Governor's handicap did not even bring the sympathy accorded to a stammer; he paused and gulped between words. The blacks had always used a portmanteau name for him that meant the-crane-who-is-trying-to-swallow-the-bullfrog.

One of the members of the black underground organization that could now come out in brass-band support of the freedom fighters had recognized the lawyer across from the official balcony and given him the freedom fighters' salute. The lawyer joked about it, miming, full of pride. 'You should have been there—should have seen him, up there in the official party. I told you—really— you ought to have come to town with me this morning.'

'And what did you do?' She wanted to assemble all details.

'Oh I gave the salute in return, chaps in the street saluted *me* ... everybody was doing it. *It was marvellous*. And the police standing by; just to think, last month—only last week—you'd have been arrested.'

'Like thumbing your nose at them,' she said, smiling.

'Did anything go on around here?'

'Muchanga was afraid to go out all day. He wouldn't even run up to the post office for me!' Their servant had come to them many years ago, from service in the house of her father, a colonial official in the Treasury.

'But there was no excitement?'

She told him: 'The soldiers and some freedom fighters mingled outside the barracks. I got caught for a minute or two. They were dancing about; you couldn't get through. All very good-natured. —Oh, I sent the cable.'

An accolade, one side a white cheek, the other a black. The white one she kissed on the left cheek, the black one on the right cheek, as if these were two sides of one face.

That vision, version, was like a poster; the sort of thing that was soon peeling off dirty shopfronts and bus shelters while the months of wrangling talks preliminary to the take-over by the black government went by.

To begin with, the cheek was not white but pale or rather sallow, the poor boy's pallor of winter in Europe (that draft must have only just arrived and not yet seen service) with homesick pimples sliced off by the discipline of an army razor. And the cheek was not black but opaque peat-dark, waxed with sweat round the plump contours of the nostril. As if she could return to the moment again, she saw what she had not consciously noted: there had been a narrow pink strip in the darkness near the ear, the sort of tender stripe of healed flesh revealed when a scab is nicked off a little before it is ripe. The scab must have come away that morning: the young man picked at it in the the troop carrier or truck (whatever it was the freedom fighters had; the colony had been told for years that they were supplied by the Chinese and Russians indiscriminately) on the way to enter the capital in triumph.

According to newspaper reports, the day would have ended for the two young soldiers in drunkenness and whoring. She was, apparently, not yet too old to belong to the soldier's embrace of all that a land-mine in the bush might have exploded forever. That was one version of the incident. Another: the opportunity taken by a woman not young enough to be clasped in the arms of the one who (same newspaper, while the war was on, expressing the fears of the colonists for their women) would be expected to rape her.

She considered this version.

She had not kissed on the mouth, she had not sought anonymous lips and tongues in the licence of festival. Yet she had kissed. Watching herself again, she knew that. She had—god knows why

—kissed them on either cheek, his left, his right. It was deliberate, if a swift impulse: she had distinctly made the move.

She did not tell what happened not because her husband would suspect licence in her, but because he would see her—born and brought up in the country as the daughter of an enlightened white colonial official, married to a white liberal lawyer well known for his defence of blacks in political trials—as giving free expression to liberal principles.

She had not told, she did not know what had happened.

She thought of a time long ago when a school camp had gone to the sea and immediately on arrival everyone had run down to the beach from the train, tripping and tearing over sand dunes of wild fig, aghast with ecstatic shock at the meeting with the water.

De Poorteer was recalled and the lawyer remarked to one of their black friends, 'The crane has choked on the bullfrog. I hear that's what they're saying in the Quarter.'

The priest who came from the black slum that had always been known simply by that anonymous term did not respond with any sort of glee. His reserve implied it was easy to celebrate; there were people who 'shouted freedom too loud all of a sudden'.

The lawyer and his wife understood: Father Mulumbua was one who had shouted freedom when it was dangerous to do so, and gone to prison several times for it, while certain people, now on the Interim Council set up to run the country until the new government took over, had kept silent. He named a few, but reluctantly. Enough to confirm their own suspicions—men who perhaps had made some deal with the colonial power to place its interests first, no matter what sort of government might emerge from the new constitution? Yet when the couple plunged into discussion their friend left them talking to each other while he drank his beer and gazed, frowning as if at a headache or because the sunset light hurt his eyes behind his spectacles, round her huge-leaved tropical plants that bowered the terrace in cool humidity.

They had always been rather proud of their friendship with him, this man in a cassock who wore a clenched fist carved of local ebony as well as a silver cross round his neck. His black face was habitually stern—a high seriousness balanced by sudden splurting laughter when they used to tease him over the fist—but never inattentively ill-at-ease.

'What was the matter?' She answered herself; 'I had the feeling he didn't want to come here.' She was using a paper handkerchief dipped in gin to wipe greenfly off the back of a pale new leaf that had shaken itself from its folds like a cut-out paper lantern.

'Good lord, he's been here hundreds of times.'

'—Before, yes.'

What things were they saying?

With the shouting in the street and the swaying of the crowd, the sweet powerful presence that confused the senses so that sound, sight, stink (sweat, cheap soap) ran into one tremendous sensation, she could not make out words that came so easily.

Not even what she herself must have said.

A few wealthy white men who had been boastful in their support of the colonial war and knew they would be marked down by the blacks as arch exploiters, left at once. Good riddance, as the lawyer and his wife remarked. Many ordinary white people who had lived contentedly, without questioning its actions, under the colonial government, now expressed an enthusiastic intention to help build a nation, as the newspapers put it. The lawyer's wife's neighbourhood butcher was one. 'I don't mind blacks.' He was expansive with her, in his shop that he had occupied for twelve years on a licence available only to white people. 'Makes no difference to me who you are so long as you're honest.' Next to a chart showing a beast mapped according to the cuts of meat it provided, he had hung a picture of the most important leader of the freedom fighters, expected to be first President. People like the butcher turned out with their babies clutching pennants when the leader drove through the town from the airport.

There were incidents (newspaper euphemism again) in the Quarter. It was to be expected. Political factions, tribally based, who had not fought the war, wanted to share power with the freedom fighters' Party. Muchanga no longer went down to the Quarter on his day off. His friends came to see him and sat privately on their hunkers near the garden compost heap. The ugly mansions of the rich who had fled stood empty on the bluff above the sea, but it was said they would make money out of them yet—they would be bought as ambassadorial residences when independence came, and with it many black and yellow diplomats. Zealots who claimed they belonged to the Party burned shops and houses of the poorer whites who lived, as the lawyer said, 'in the inevitable echelon of colonial society', closest to the Quarter. A house in the lawyer's street was noticed by his wife to be accommodating what was certainly one of those families, in the outhouses; green nylon curtains had appeared at the garage window, she reported. The suburb was pleasantly overgrown and well-to-do; no one rich, just white professional people and professors from the university. The barracks was empty now, except for an old man with a stump and a police uniform stripped of insignia, a friend of Muchanga, it turned out, who sat on a beer-crate at the gates. He had lost his job as night-watchman when one of the rich people went away, and was glad to have work,

The street had been perfectly quiet; except for that first day.

The fingernails she sometimes still saw clearly were bitten down until embedded in a thin line of dirt all round, in the pink blunt fingers. The thumb and thick fingertips were turned back coarsely even while grasping her. Such hands had never been allowed to take possession. They were permanently raw, so young, from unloading coal, digging potatoes from the frozen Northern Hemisphere, washing hotel dishes. He had not been killed, and now that day of the cease-fire was over he would be delivered back across the sea to the docks, the stony farm, the scullery of the grand hotel. He would have to do anything he could get. There was unemployment in Europe where he had returned, the army didn't need all the young men any more.

A great friend of the lawyer and his wife, Chipande, was coming home from exile. They heard over the radio he was expected, accompanying the future President as confidential secretary, and they waited to hear from him.

The lawyer put up his feet on the empty chair where the priest had sat, shifting it to a comfortable position by hooking his toes, free in sandals, through the slats. 'Imagine, Chipande!' Chipande had been almost a protégé—but they didn't like the term, it smacked of patronage. Tall, cocky, casual Chipande, a boy from the slummiest part of the Quarter, was recommended by the White Fathers' Mission (was it by Father Mulumbua himself?—the lawyer thought so, his wife was not sure they remembered correctly). A bright kid who wanted to be articled to a lawyer. That was asking a lot, in those days—nine years ago. He never finished his apprenticeship because while he and his employer were soon close friends, and the kid picked up political theories from the books in the house he made free of, he became so involved in politics that he had to skip the country one jump ahead of a detention order signed by the crane-who-was-trying-to-swallow-the-bullfrog.

After two weeks the lawyer phoned the offices the guerilla-movement-become-Party had set up openly in the town, but apparently Chipande had an office in the former colonial secretariat. There he had a secretary of his own; he wasn't easy to reach. The lawyer left a message. The lawyer and his wife saw from the newspaper pictures he hadn't changed much: he had a beard and had adopted the Muslim cap favoured by political circles in exile on the East Coast.

He did come to the house eventually. He had the distracted, insistent friendliness of one who has no time to re-establish intimacy; it must be taken as read. And it must not be displayed. When he remarked on a shortage of accommodation for exiles now become officials, and the lawyer said the house was far too big for two people, he was welcome to move in and regard a self-contained part of it as his private living quarters, he did not answer but went on talking generalities. The lawyer's wife mentioned Father Mulumbua, whom they had not seen since just after the cease-fire. The lawyer added, 'There's obviously some sort of big struggle going on, he's fighting for his political life there in the Quarter.' 'Again,' she said, drawing them into a reminder of what had only just become their past.

But Chipande was restlessly following with his gaze the movements of old Muchanga, dragging the hose from plant to plant, careless of the spray; 'You remember who this is, Muchanga?' she had said when the visitor arrived, yet although the old man had given, in their own language, the sort of respectful greeting even an elder gives a young man whose clothes and bearing denote rank and authority, he was not in any way overwhelmed nor enthusiastic—perhaps he secretly supported one of the rival factions?

The lawyer spoke of the latest whites to leave the country—people who had got themselves quickly involved in the sort of currency swindle that draws more outrage than any other kind of crime, in a new state fearing the flight of capital: 'Let them go, let them go. Good riddance.' And he turned to talk of other things—there were so many more important questions to occupy the attention of the three old friends.

But Chipande couldn't stay. Chipande could not stay for supper; his beautiful long velvety black hands with their pale lining (as she thought of the palms) hung impatiently between his knees while he sat forward in the chair, explaining, adamant against persuasion. He should not have been there, even now; he had official business waiting, sometimes he drafted correspondence until one or two in the morning. The lawyer remarked how there hadn't been a proper chance to talk; he wanted to discuss those fellows in the Interim Council Mulumbua was so warily distrustful of—what did Chipande know?

Chipande, already on his feet, said something dismissing and very slightly disparaging, not about the Council members but of Mulumbua—a reference to his connection with the Jesuit missionaries as an influence that 'comes through'. 'But I must make a note to see him sometime.'

It seemed that even black men who presented a threat to the Party could be discussed only among black men themselves, now. Chipande put an arm round each of his friends as for the brief official moment of a photograph, left them; he who used to sprawl on the couch arguing half the night before dossing down in the lawyer's pyjamas. 'As soon as I'm settled I'll contact you. You'll be around, ay?'

'Oh we'll be around.' The lawyer laughed, referring, for his part, to those who were no longer. 'Glad to see you're not driving a Mercedes!' he called with reassured affection at the sight of Chipande getting into a modest car. How many times, in the old days, had they agreed on the necessity for African leaders to live simply when they came to power!

On the terrace to which he turned back, Muchanga was doing something extraordinary—wetting a dirty rag with Gilbey's. It was supposed to be his day off, anyway; why was he messing about with the plants when one wanted peace to talk undisturbed?

'Is those thing again, those thing is killing the leaves.'

'For heaven's sake, he could use methylated for that! Any kind of alcohol will do! Why don't you get him some?'

There were shortages of one kind and another in the country, and gin happened to be something in short supply.

Whatever the hand had done in the bush had not coarsened it. It, too, was suede-black, and elegant. The pale lining was hidden against her own skin where the hand grasped her left elbow. Strangely, black does not show toil—she remarked this as one remarks the quality of a fabric. The hand was not as long but as distinguished by beauty as Chipande's. The watch a fine piece of equipment for a fighter. There was something next to it, in fact looped over the strap by the angle of the wrist as the hand grasped. A bit of thong with a few beads knotted where it was joined as a bracelet. Or amulet. Their babies wore such things; often their first and only garment. Grandmothers or mothers attached it as protection. It had worked; he was alive at cease-fire. Some had been too deep in the bush to know, and had been killed after the fighting was over. He had pumped his head wildly and laughingly at whatever it was she—they— had been babbling.

The lawyer had more free time than he'd ever remembered. So many of his clients had left; he was deputed to collect their rents and pay their taxes for them, in the hope that their property wasn't going to be confiscated—there had been alarmist rumours among such people since the day of the cease-fire. But without the rich whites there was little litigation over possessions, whether in the form of the children of dissolved marriages or the houses and cars claimed by divorced wives. The Africans had their own ways of resolving such redistribution of goods. And a gathering of elders under a tree was sufficient to settle a dispute over boundaries or argue for and against the guilt of a woman accused of adultery. He had had a message, in a roundabout way, that he might be asked to be consultant on constitutional law to the Party, but nothing seemed to come of it. He took home with him the proposals for the draft constitution he had managed to get hold of. He spent whole afternoons in his study making notes for counter or improved proposals he thought he would send to Chipande or one of the other people he knew in high positions: every time he glanced up, there through his open windows was Muchanga's little company at the bottom of the garden. Once, when he saw they had straggled off, he wandered down himself to clear his head (he got drowsy, as he never did when he used to work twelve hours a day at the office). They ate dried shrimps, from the market: that's what they were doing! The ground was full of bitten-off heads and black eyes on stalks. His wife smiled. 'They bring them. Muchanga won't go near the market since the riot.' 'It's ridiculous. Who's going to harm him?'

There was even a suggestion that the lawyer might apply for a professorship at the university. The chair of the Faculty of Law was vacant, since the students had demanded the expulsion of certain professors engaged during the colonial regime—in particular of the fuddy-duddy (good riddance) who had gathered dust in the Law chair, and the quite decent young man (pity about him) who had had Political Science. But what professor of Political Science could expect to survive both a colonial regime and the revolutionary regime that defeated it? The lawyer and his wife decided that since he might still be appointed in some consultative capacity to the new government it would be better to keep out of the university context, where the students were shouting for Africanization, and even an appointee with his credentials as a fighter of legal battles for blacks against the colonial regime in the past might not escape their ire.

Newspapers sent by friends from over the border gave statistics for the number of what they termed 'refugees' who were entering the neighbouring country. The papers from outside also featured sensationally the inevitable mistakes and misunderstandings, in a new administration, that led to several foreign businessmen being held for investigation by the new regime. For the last fifteen years of colonial rule, Gulf had been drilling for oil in the territory, and just as inevitably it was certain that all sorts of questionable people, from the point of view of the regime's determination not to be exploited preferentially, below the open market for the highest bidder in ideological as well as economic terms, would try to gain concessions.

His wife said, 'The butcher's gone.'

He was home, reading at his desk; he could spend the day more usefully there than at the office, most of the time. She had left after breakfast with her fisherman's basket that she liked to use for shopping, she wasn't away twenty minutes. 'You mean the shop's closed?' There was nothing in the basket. She must have turned and come straight home.

'Gone. It's empty. He's cleared out over the weekend.'

She sat down suddenly on the edge of the desk; and after a moment of silence, both laughed shortly, a strange, secret, complicit laugh. 'Why, do you think?' 'Can't say. He certainly charged, if you wanted a decent cut. But meat's so hard to get, now; I thought it was worth it—justified.'

The lawyer raised his eyebrows and pulled down his mouth: 'Exactly.' They understood; the man probably knew he was marked to run into trouble for profiteering—he must have been paying through the nose for his supplies on the black market, anyway, didn't have much choice.

Shops were being looted by the unemployed and loafers (there had always been a lot of unemployed hanging around for the pickings of the town) who felt the new regime should entitle them to take what they dared not before. Radio and television shops were the most favoured objective for gangs who adopted the freedom fighters' slogans. Transistor radios were the portable luxuries of street life; the new regime issued solemn warnings, over those same radios, that looting and violence would be firmly dealt with but it was difficult for the police to be everywhere at once. Sometimes their actions became street battles, since the struggle with the looters changed character as supporters of the Party's rival political factions joined in with the thieves against the police. It was necessary to be ready to reverse direction, quickly turning down a side street in detour if one encountered such disturbances while driving around town. There were bodies sometimes; both husband and wife had been fortunate enough not to see any close up, so far. A company of the freedom fighters' army was brought down from the north and installed in the barracks to supplement the police force; they patrolled the Quarter, mainly. Muchanga's friend kept his job as gate-keeper although there were armed sentries on guard: the lawyer's wife found that a light touch to mention in letters to relatives in Europe.

'Where'll you go now?'

She slid off the desk and picked up her basket. 'Supermarket, I suppose. Or turn vegetarian.' He knew that she left the room quickly, smiling, because she didn't want him to suggest Muchanga ought to be sent to look for fish in the markets along the wharf in the Quarter. Muchanga was being allowed to indulge in all manner of eccentric refusals; for no reason, unless out of some curious sentiment about her father?

She avoided walking past the barracks because of the machine guns the young sentries had in place of rifles. Rifles pointed into the air but machine guns pointed to the street at the level of different parts of people's bodies, short and tall, the backsides of babies slung on mothers' backs, the round heads of children, her fisherman's basket—she knew she was getting like the others: what she felt was afraid. She wondered what the butcher and his wife had said to each other. Because he was at least one whom she had known. He had sold the meat she had bought that these women and their babies passing her in the street didn't have the money to buy.

It was something quite unexpected and outside their own efforts that decided it. A friend over the border telephoned and offered a place in a lawyers' firm of highest repute there, and some prestige in the world at large, since the team had defended individuals fighting for freedom of the press and militant churchmen upholding freedom of conscience on political issues. A telephone call; as simple as that. The friend said (and the lawyer did not repeat this even to his wife) they would be proud to have a man of his courage and convictions in the firm. He could be satisfied he would be able to uphold the liberal principles everyone knew he had always stood for; there were many whites, in the country still ruled by a white minority, who deplored the injustices under which their black population suffered etc. and believed you couldn't ignore the need for peaceful change etc.

His offices presented no problem; something called Africa Sea-beds (Formosan Chinese who had gained a concession to ship seaweed and dried shrimps in exchange for rice) took over the lease and the typists. The senior clerks and the current articled clerk (the lawyer had always given a chance to young blacks, long before other people had come round to it—it wasn't only the secretary to the President wession to ship seaweed and dried shrimps in exchange for rice) took over the lease and the typists. The senior clerks and the current articled clerk (the tes with the colonial government. The house would just have to stand empty, for the time being. It wasn't imposing enough to attract an embassy but maybe it would do for a Chargé d'Affaires—it was left in the hands of a half-caste letting agent who was likely to stay put: only whites were allowed in, at the country over the border. Getting money out was going to be much more difficult than disposing of the house. The lawyer would have to keep coming back, so long as this remained practicable, hoping to find a loophole in exchange control regulations.

She was deputed to engage the movers. In their innocence, they had thought it as easy as that! Every large vehicle, let alone a pantechnicon, was commandeered for months ahead. She had no choice but to grease a palm, although it went against her principles, it was condoning a practice they believed a young black state must stamp out before corruption took hold. He would take his entire legal library, for a start; that was the most important possession, to him. Neither was particularly attached to furniture. She did not know what there was she felt she really could not do without. Except the plants. And that was out of the question. She could not even mention it. She did not want to leave her towering plants, mostly natives of South America and not Africa, she supposed, whose aerial tubes pushed along the terrace brick, erect tips extending hourly in the growth of the rainy season, whose great leaves turned shields to the spatter of Muchanga's hose glancing off in a shower of harmless arrows, whose two-hand-span trunks were smooth and grooved in one sculptural sweep down their length, or carved by the drop of each dead leaf-stem with concave medallions marking the place and building a pattern at once bold and exquisite. Such things would not travel; they were too big to give away.

The evening she was beginning to pack the books, the telephone rang in the study. Chipande—and he called her by her name, urgently, commandingly—'What is this all about? Is it true, what I hear? Let me just talk to him—'

'Our friend,' she said, making a long arm, receiver at the end of it, towards her husband.

'But you can't leave!' Chipande shouted down the phone. '*You* can't go! I'm coming round. *Now*.'

She went on packing the legal books while Chipande and her husband were shut up together in the living-room.

'He cried. You know, he actually cried.' Her husband stood in the doorway, alone.

'I know—that's what I've always liked so much about them, whatever they do. They feel.'

The lawyer made a face: there it is, it happened; hard to believe.

'Rushing in here, after nearly a year! I said, but we haven't seen you, all this time … he took no notice. Suddenly he starts pressing me to take the university job, raising all sorts of objections, why not this … that. And then he really wept, for a moment.'

They got on with packing books like builder and mate deftly handling and catching bricks.

And the morning they were to leave it was all done; twenty-one years of life in that house gone quite easily into one pantechnicon. They were quiet with each other, perhaps out of apprehension of the tedious search of their possessions that would take place at the border; it was said that if you struck over-conscientious or officious freedom-fighter patrols they would even make you unload a piano, a refrigerator or washing machine. She had bought Muchanga a hawker's licence, a hand-cart, and stocks of small commodities. Now that many small shops owned by white shopkeepers had disappeared, there was an opportunity for humble itinerant black traders. Muchanga had lost his fear of the town. He was proud of what she had done for him and she knew he saw himself as a rich merchant; this was the only sort of freedom he understood, after so many years as a servant. But she also knew, and the lawyer sitting beside her in the car knew she knew, that the shortages of the goods Muchanga could sell from his cart, the sugar and soap and matches and pomade and sunglasses, would soon put him out of business. He promised to come back to the house and look after the plants every week; and he stood waving, as he had done every year when they set off on holiday. She did not know what to call out to him as they drove away. The right words would not come again; whatever they were, she left them behind.

Witchcraft

Bessie Head

It was one of the most potent evils in the society and people afflicted by it often suffered from a kind of death-in-life. Everything in the society was a mixture of centuries of acquired wisdom and experience, so witchcraft belonged there too; something people had carried along with them from ancestral times. Every single villager believed that at some stage in his life 'something' got hold of him; all his animals died and his life was completely smashed up. They could give long and vivid accounts of what happened to them at this time. The accounts were as solid as the reasons people give for believing in God or Jesus Christ, so that one cannot help but conclude that if a whole society creates a belief in something, that something is likely to become real. But unlike Christianity, which proposed the belief in a tender and merciful God eager to comfort and care for man, there was nothing pleasant in this 'dark thing' in village life. It was entirely a force of destruction which people experienced at many levels. Since in olden times the supreme power of sorcery or witchcraft was vested in the chiefs or rulers, it can be assumed that this force had its source in a power structure that needed an absolute control over the people. Over the years it had become dispersed throughout the whole society like a lingering and malignant ailment that was difficult to cure. Political independence seemed to have aggravated the disease more than anything else because people now said: 'Our old people used to say that you can't kill someone who is not your relative. You know what you are going to take from your relative. But these days they are killing everyone from jealousy ...'

This anxiety, that people were vulnerable to attack or to assault from an evil source, was always present; so that when an ordinary villager started a new yard and before he put up his fence, he would call the Tswana doctor to place protective charms and medicines all around the yard. He would call the Tswana doctor for almost every event in his life: for herbs to protect him in his employment, when he married, when his children were born, or when he was taking a long journey from home. Since supposedly the society was both Christian and rational, people laughingly explained their behaviour thus: 'The baloi are troubling us. The baloi are those people with a bad heart. No one openly walks around with the mark of the baloi, so we don't know who they are. Very often I can be your friend and laugh and joke with you. Then I see that your life is picking up and your goods are increasing, so I go to the Tswana doctor for medicine to kill you just because I am jealous. White people are better. They might suffer from jealously but they don't know how to kill people in this way. Batswana people know how to kill. This is how they kill: some day, some one might approach me for four teaspoons of tea leaves, which I lend to him because I think he is in need. But he takes these tea leaves straight to a Tswana doctor who makes a medicine out of them. Suddenly, my whole life falls apart; a sickness enters my body and I am ill from one day to the next. Before I can pass away, I go and consult a Tswana doctor. He throws the bones and straightaway sees the cause of my sickness. He says to me: "You remember you gave so-and-so four teaspoons of tea leaves? Well, he is injuring your life." If life is like this, then all the people are afraid of each other. There is a tendency these days for people to dislike consulting the Tswana doctor because they often find that he has not the power to drive out the baloi and they often waste money consulting him. But the baloi are troubling people ...'

To complicate matters further, people often used their own resources and wisdom to explain ailments like malnutrition and malaria fever or any other kind of ordinary sickness that could be treated in a hospital, so that everything in the end was reduced to witchcraft. And yet, tentatively, one could concede that there was a terrible horror present in the society. Was it only human evil, that in some inexplicable way could so direct its energies that it had the power to inflict intense suffering or even death on others?

Mma-Mabele belonged to that section of the village who rationalized quite clearly: 'I know I can be poisoned and so meet my end, but I cannot be bewitched. I don't believe in it.' They were the offspring of families who had deeply embraced Christianity and who were regular church-goers; when the hospital opened in the village, they had all their ailments attended to there and did not need to consult the Tswana doctor. All this provided some mental leverage to sort out the true from the false in the everyday round of village life, but not immunity to strange forms of assault.

Of all the people in her village ward, Mma-Mabele lived one of the most unspectacular lives. She had been born in a year when people had reaped a particularly rich harvest of corn and she was named Mma-Mabele, the corn mother, after this event. Also, the contentment and peace people feel when assured of a year's supply of food seemed deeply woven into her personality. She moved around the village quietly, never seeming flustered or anxious about anything. When her parents and grandparents were alive, she had shared with them the rhythmic life of people who live off what they can reap from the earth; but on their death she seemed to find herself incapable of moving out to the lands for the ploughing season, so that their land lay fallow now with no one to plough it. Her family was reduced to her sister Maggie and her illegitimate son, Banophi, herself and her own illegitimate child, Virginiah. For a year after the death of all the elderly relatives, her sister Maggie had held down a job as a housekeeper; Mma-Mabele, meanwhile had moved out into the village and offered to do any chores village women might need done for the day, in return for which she might either be given a plate of food or a dish of corn meal for her own house. They managed badly, and on some days only had water to drink.

Over a number of years, after the birth of her child, Mma-Mabele had acquired an unpleasant nickname in her surroundings. She was called 'he-man' and it was meant to imply that something was not quite right with her genitals, they were mixed up, a combination of male and female. The rumour had been spread by a number of men who had made approaches to her and whom she had turned down with quiet finality: 'I don't want to show myself any more,' she'd said.

The men never looked up as far as a quiet, sensitive face that might have suffered insult or injury. The only value women were given in the society was their ability to have sex; there was nothing beyond that. Mma-Mabele had been engaged to be married to the man by whom she had had her child; at least he had mentioned it before she conceived. Then he said nothing more and as soon as it could be seen that a baby was on the way, he simply disappeared from the village. There was nothing else to learn from men who boasted: 'We pick them off on our fingers, one-two-three-four-five!' There was nothing else to replace the knowledge that a man and a woman belonged together, in a family circle. What the men resented, because it was rare, was to come face to face with a woman not necessarily in a frenzy about satisfying her genitals, as they did. So they spread the nickname 'he-man' for Mma-Mabele. But her ability to observe that life was all wrong and a deep sensitivity to feel pain and desist from repeating errors, was all that stood between her and the misery that was soon to engulf her life.

Towards the end of the year when they had struggled so much, Mma-Mabele also found a job as a housekeeper with a particularly good employer, who was impressed with her quiet, respectful personality and her ability to work hard in a neat, orderly way. At the end of the month Mma-Mabele came home heaped with treasures, a salary which was twice that of her sister Maggie, a number of old cotton dresses and a pair of shoes. The two sisters made tea, then as darkness fell they sat outdoors, their backs leaning against the mud wall of a hut, and happily pooled their salaries together on Mma-Mabele's lap. Between them they had a fortune, in terms of village economics: R5.00 of Maggie's salary and R10.00 of Mma-Mabele's salary. Mma-Mabele's salary alone could feed the whole family for a month. So she sat with her head to one side and, with a thoughtful, serious face, worked out their budget for the month.

'I think we should start off by buying half a bag of corn,' she said. 'It will last us two months and give us time to pick up a little ...'

Maggie nodded her consent. Corn or mabele always lasted longer than half a bag of mealie meal because when the corn was stamped it was separated into two heaps: one of rough grains and one of smoother, stamped grains. The heap of rough grains was cooked first for about ten minutes, to which was then added the heap of smoothly-pounded grain. This technique swelled the pot of porridge to an enormous size.

'After I've spent R6.00 on the bag of corn,' Mma-Mabele continued, 'I'd like to buy one bag of bread flour and cooking oil for fat cakes so that we can have a change of food. That leaves us

R1.60 for meat for sixteen days and so my money is finished now.'

With a smile she handed the R5.00 back to Maggie.

'I think you would like to spend this money on clothes,' she said. 'Banophi's school shirts are in tatters and a dress for Virginiah only costs sixty cents; there will still be something left over for a dress for yourself if you like. For myself, I have need of nothing now.'

As Maggie put the R5.00 note in her pocket, Mma-Mabele added wistfully: 'If I can keep this job, we'll soon see what we are making of our lives. Perhaps some of the money can be saved.'

They all ate well that night, heaped plates of porridge and tripe, with the greasy intestinal fat of the ox richly spread over the porridge, and deeply contented the whole family went to sleep. But the following morning, the strange story began.

They were all seated outdoors, eating a breakfast of soft porridge when the small boy, Banophi, began to stare intently at Mma-Mabele's head. At last he remarked: 'Why have you cut your hair, my aunt?'

Mma-Mabele paused, surprised in the act of putting a spoonful of porridge into her mouth.

'But I haven't cut my hair, Banophi,' she said.

'But you have cut it, aunt,' he said. 'There's a smooth patch cut out on the side of your head.'

Apprehensively, Mma-Mabele raised her hand to the right side of her head and with suddenly trembling fingers felt the smooth, bald patch. Her fingers recoiled in alarm. But in a quick, practical, decisive way, she stood up and went to examine the nearly bare interior of her hut. The sleeping mats were neatly folded in a corner; a tin trunk with her clothes stood in another corner and she bent over and searched the bare earth floor for traces of her cut hair. There was nothing. No flesh-and-blood human being could have entered her hut at night; she had herself unlatched the door from the inside in the early morning. For a moment, she leaned one hand against the earth wall of the hut, faint with fear. In village lore, it was only one thing that could have touched her life—the baloi. On an impulse, to rid herself of the hideous, unknown presence that had invaded her life during the night, she walked back to her sister who was still seated near the fire eating her porridge and said: 'Maggie, you must cut off all my hair before I go to work. I cannot walk around like this.'

'What can the matter be?' Maggie asked, frightened.

'I think it is the baloi who have come to me,' Mma-Mabele said, almost in the same matter-of-fact voice with which she had discussed their budget the night before.

'You should go and see the prophet of the church or I can tell Lekena. Lekena knows about these things. They might help us,' Maggie said.

'Both the prophet and Lekena will want money from me,' Mma-Mabele replied aggressively. 'And where am I to get it? We are poor. But I don't believe in them, so we must keep this trouble to ourselves.'

Maggie, as the younger sister, kept silent. Mma-Mabele was the strength of the household and all her judgements on life and people were sane and kind. Obediently Maggie cut off all her hair, then they both left home for work. It was a Saturday morning, and the children, who were not at school that day, spread around the story of the patch of hair that had been cut out on Mma-Mabele's head in a mysterious way during the night. The news soon reached Lekena, the Tswana doctor of their village ward, who lived barely ten yards away from Mma-Mabele.

'I have a customer,' he said to himself.

When Mma-Mabele returned from work late that afternoon, she found Lekena patiently seated in her yard. He greeted her with unconcealed proprietory interest.

'I say, Mma-Mabele,' he said, astonished. 'You have cut your hair! What have you done with the cut hair?'

'I burnt it,' she said, seating herself politely near him.

'It's a good thing you have destroyed the very thing with which your enemy wishes to injure you. I must say I was very surprised when the story reached me this morning. I thought: "Who could want to injure a kind woman like Mma-Mabele? She has harmed no one. I must rush to help her".' With these words, he reached under his low stool and dramatically produced a bottle of dark medicine.

Mma-Mabele had been looking at him with an appeal-for-help expression on her face. It was the first time in her life that the baloi had visited her and she was deeply afraid of the event. But when he produced the bottle of medicine, she compressed her lips firmly. He would ask for R5.00 and she had no intention of parting with her money.

'I cannot take the medicine, Lekena,' she said, quickly inventing a defence. 'You know very well I am a church-goer and it is forbidden for us to use Tswana medicine.'

'The church doesn't know everything, Mma-Mabele,' he said earnestly. 'The trouble comes from Tswana custom and it is only Tswana medicine that can help you.'

Like all his clan, the Tswana doctors, Lekena had considerable dash and courage. They were like gymnastic performers of a very imaginative kind and for centuries, in their tradition, they had explained the world of phenomena to themselves and the people. They were the most clever men in the society and their hold on the people was very strong. It took a cold and logical mind to analyse all their activities because, in spite of repeated failures in their medical treatment of people, they were still consulted avidly. Coldness and logic were Mma-Mabele's special mental gifts. She had stood apart and watched all Lekena's failures, some of which were of a fatal nature. Lekena claimed to remove the poison of a scorpion bite through his medicine which gave power to his person. For years he appeared successful until the small boy, Molefe, of their village ward had been stung by a big, black scorpion and died while under Lekena's treatment. The same thing happened with snakebite which Lekena also claimed to cure. Mma-Mabele sorted it out for herself—there were poisonous snakes and scorpions and non-poisonous ones. Lekena's treatment only succeeded when the snakes and scorpions were non-poisonous. But what to make out of that cut-out patch of her hair?

'It is true I am puzzled, Lekena,' she said. 'I have never seen this thing before on myself. My hair was truly cut out like a smooth part of my skin.'

'There are no secrets here, Mma-Mabele. Everyone knows you now have a good job. Someone is jealous of you and wants you to lose that job,' he said.

At this, she compressed her lips again. No one else had experienced that year of near starvation behind her; at times she had stumbled around faint and dizzy with hunger. Whatever else happened, she wasn't going to lose her job.

'I'll throw the bones for you,' Lekena said persuasively. 'The bones will help me to see the one who is injuring your life. Throwing the bones is cheaper than the medicine. It only costs R1.00.'

Mma-Mabele shook her head slowly. To show that he only had good intentions towards her, Lekena touched his hands over his heart.

'Everyone can see my heart,' he said. 'There is no evil thing in it,' and with this assurance, he departed.

From then onwards Mma-Mabele was to find that it was a deep unhappiness to be afflicted by the things that dwelt in the dark side of human life. Formerly, the stories had come to her by hearsay, but their end was all the same—the people so afflicted sat down and began to rot; they would not work or do anything because they believed that the very attempt to prosper in life had brought the affliction on them; they sat like that until they died. Whereas formerly her life had been a vaguely pleasant round of work, sleep and idle chatter and gossip, it turned from this sunlit world to an inner world of gloomy brooding and pain.

There was something horribly disturbing about the nights. They always began the same way. She would see a small, pointed yellow light, which was followed by indistinct black shapes that bubbled in front of her with the liquid flow of water. Then she seemed caught up in a high wind-storm and was dashed about this way and that. But more persistent was a sensation that she was being strangled by an unseen hand. Then, one night, the source of her affliction took on embodied form. It was a misshapen thing walking towards her, with a huge, misshapen face. She lay on her side that night and the thing, it looked like a grotesque man, bent and placed its mouth on her chest and pressed a forefinger and thumb into her forehead. She was quite powerless to protest or move; she just lay there, her heart wildly pounding with fear. It was some time before she regained her senses and realized that she was quite alone in the dark hut. Thinking she had seen the Devil or worse, she arose trembling and, kneeling upright in bed, she prayed, piteously: 'Oh Lord Jesu, help me.'

As she said these words, a soft laugh sounded just behind her ear. She groped around in the dark for matches and lit the small oil lamp beside her bed. Except for herself, the hut was quite empty. She sat up for the rest of the night, too afraid to sleep. At one stage she cried out: 'Oh, poor me, what will become of me now!'

The following morning she felt the pain. Just as she was in the midst of her work at mid-morning, a blow struck her on the head. She slowly rocked from end to end with the violence of it and she held on to the household broom for support. She blinked her eyes rapidly in the intensity of her pain. It was some moments she stood like that, completely immobile, and the pain hanging there like a dull, heavy weight in her head as though an unseen ghoul had fastened its mouth there and was slowly sucking out her brains. This happened repeatedly at the same time each morning, until on the third morning her employer found her like that, clinging to the broom in her pain.

'Why, Mma-Mabele, what's wrong with you?' she asked.

'I think I am sick,' Mma-Mabele replied, fearfully. She had to say it, but she did not want to lose her job. But then neither did her employer want to lose her. Good housekeepers were hard to come by. So she made a sympathetic arrangement for Mma-Mabele to take two days off as sick-leave and go to the hospital for a check-up.

Lekena, who now kept a sharp eye on Mma-Mabele's yard, nodded his head in satisfaction as he saw Mma-Mabele come home long before her work hour was up. She walked with her head bent, broody and mournful and she had a small bag of oranges slung over her left shoulder. She had hardly entered her yard before he followed close on her heels and exclaimed: 'How is it you are so early from work, Mma-Mabele! I am much surprised at this!'

'I am sick, Lekena,' she said. 'I have just come from hospital.'

'What is your sickness, Mma-Mabele?'

'I have a terrible pain in my head.' Then she paused and with a note of surprise in her voice said: 'I was examined by the doctor and he said I am quite a healthy person. Then he asked what food I was eating and he said that crushed corn and meat is not enough; that is poor diet. I should try to eat some oranges too. The pain in my head might be caused by poor food.'

Lekena bent his head in deep thought, then he said: 'They don't know everything Mma-Mabele. I told you your trouble comes from Tswana custom and I can help you too.' He looked at her speculatively: 'I think I know who is injuring you. You do not care about Tswana medicine, but I took pity on you and threw the bones, for free. I saw that it is Molema who is injuring your life. He has spread such a bad word about you in the village that I am ashamed to repeat it.'

She looked at Lekena with her steady, honest eyes: 'Molema cannot injure me,' she said. 'He only cares about drink and the bed. Most times he has fallen somewhere, dead drunk. He was angry at one time because I refused to show myself to him, that is why he said that bad word about me. My special parts are quite normal, but a woman can be too much hurt by these men, which is why I refuse to show them.'

Not to be outdone by Mma-Mabele's reasoning powers, Lekena said: 'I can throw the bones again, Mma-Mabele. I don't mean you to pay me. Your sickness has worked up my mind. In Tswana custom ...'

Mma-Mabele jerked her head to one side, impatiently: 'I know we have Tswana custom as well as Christian custom, Lekena. But all the people respect Christian custom. There is no one who would laugh when a person mentions the name of the Lord. This thing which I see now laughs when I pray to the Lord.'

This so knocked Lekena off his medical feet that he drew in his breath with a gasp of surprise: 'You mean you have seen a new thing, Mma-Mabele? I must say I didn't know it. We can never tell what will happen these day, now that we have independence.'

After he had left, she sat in the shadow of the hut and slowly ate some of the oranges, but they didn't help her. She lived with the affliction. Once she realized this, she never asked for sick-leave again. The pain took precedence over everything else she experienced: sometimes it was like a blow in the head; sometimes it was like a blow in the heart—it moved from place to place. Soon her whole village ward noticed the struggle she was waging with death. She became thinner and thinner. She took to leaving very early for work, would walk a little way and then sit down in the pathway to rest. And she did the same on returning home in the evening.

Towards the end of that year her employer and family went away on a month's holiday. The strain to keep her job had reduced Mma-Mabele to a thin skeleton. She seemed about to die. She lay down in her hut for many days, like one stunned and dead. Just when everyone expected news of her death, she suddenly recovered and began to eat voraciously and recover her health. She was soon seen about the village at the daily task of drawing water and her friends would stop her and query: 'How is it you aren't sick any more, Mma-Mabele? Did you find a special Tswana doctor to help you, like the rich people?'

And she would reply angrily: 'You all make me sick! There is no one to help the people, not even God. I could not sit down because I am too poor and there is no one else to feed my children.'

The Old Woman

Luis B. Honwana

translated from Portuguese by Dorothy Guedes

I swear I never really lost consciousness, although just before falling down I experienced the slowing-down of sensations which, when it seizes us, restricts our capacity for self-defence to those purely instinctive and stupidly slow gestures we all recognize in a groggy boxer. I think no one could estimate the tremendous effort I made in those long or perhaps brief moments to control my fists—brutally heavy before they regained movement, and floundering unbelievably after I raised them. Meanwhile, the blows I was receiving produced no corresponding physical sensation, because I was aware of them only through a fading echo slowly reverberating through my head. This cursed echo, and it alone, was responsible for my fall—for it confused me terribly, making me force myself to think of lifting my arm before I could lift it. I fell slowly, fully conscious that I was falling.

At first I felt a certain relief to be lying down, although the echo continued to fill my head. When I opened my eyes the buzzing started, and I was furious with myself for having fallen. The echo was affecting my sight so much that I wasn't at all sure what I saw, but afterwards when my eyes stopped trembling I became aware of the two darkly clad legs, stiff and tense, straddling my body, stretching way up, and converging onto the shining metal plaque of the belt. Above them, far above, close to the lamp on the ceiling, the face stared at me attentively, smiling with satisfaction. I closed my eyes again. I felt myself trembling, but the echo was easier to bear because it had ceased its disordered jumbling and resolved itself into a sort of regular throbbing. I only opened my eyes when I was sure he had gone away, fully satisfied with proving to everybody that he had hit me.

☆ ☆ ☆ ☆ ☆

I needed to go home. I think I already felt like going there even before I went into the bar, so really what had happened there wasn't the reason for my wanting so much to go home. I hadn't seen the old woman and the children for I don't know how long, because lately I'd been going home very late and leaving very early, but I still wasn't quite sure if I wanted to see them again. The old woman was so dull, and the children were such a nuisance with their constant squabbling and clamouring for attention. Of course this was nothing compared with what happened in the bar just now, and in all the other bars, restaurants, cinema foyers and those places where everybody eyed me strangely, as if they repudiated something in me—something queer, ridiculous, exotic: Heaven knows what else. They make me sick! And I having to restrain myself from exploding precisely for the sake of the wretched old woman and the snivelling kids!

That in the bar just now was really what had been happening all along. I didn't manage to hit the fellow because he was all the others, and it was exactly as such that he hit me. Let's face it—they're all the same. Even those who try to pretend that they are not like the others are only different on neutral ground, or only when they need me, because they too surround themselves with walls of taboos, and defend themselves with the same nauseous, nauseating stares against anyone who goes beyond those walls. And I should know!

I needed to go home. I would eat rice and peanut curry as they wanted me to, but not to fill my stomach. I needed to go home to fill my ears with screams, my eyes with misery and my conscience with rice and peanut curry.

Sitting on the straw mat, the old woman was quietly watching the children eat. Now and then one of them would get up and bring the aluminium plate for her to serve another helping. It was at one of those intervals that the old woman noticed me. She had the wooden spoon stretched out, filled with rice, and she was going to empty it onto the plate, when she seemed to remember something and turned towards the door. As soon as she saw me she glanced down to the bottom of the pot, and asked me if I wanted something to eat.

'I don't know yet whether I want to eat or not,' I replied.

She turned towards the fire, and waited some time with the ladle in the air, looking at the flames.

'Are you angry? Are you so angry that you can't eat, and don't even know whether you want to eat or not?'

'No, I'm not angry.'

The old woman thought for quite a long time, then muttered, 'Well, then that's all right, if you're not angry.'

While she was saying this she turned towards the child, so she asked him, as if this was more important to her than anything else: 'Quito! What's that you're chewing and chewing all the time, Quito?'

Before he could empty his mouth to reply, Khatidya yelled from the other end of the room: 'That Quito's chewing the meat he stole from my plate while I wasn't looking. It's mine, Mama! Chi! Quito, you're a thief!'

And she turned to me, 'It's mine, I'm telling you, brother!'

Quito held out his hand to show what he had taken out of his mouth, and said indignantly, 'This meat, Kati, this here? It's the meat Mama gave me, I'm telling you.' And to me, 'Didn't she, brother?'

By this time they had already started a disgusting row, and the old woman took control.

'Shhh.'

They all stopped at once, except for Khatidya, who still whined, 'It's mine. It's mine, he stole it. Chi! Quito, you should be ashamed of yourself, I saw you.'

But the other children helped the old woman.

'Shhh.'

Khatidya turned to them, 'Shhh.' And they all started to hiss as loud as they could.

With the wooden spoon still raised, the old woman watched them all. Then the children got tired of their nonsense and began eating, and Quito put back the food he had spat out into his hand. Only then did the old woman put a spoonful of food onto Quito's plate. Before giving him curry she thought a while and served him spoonful after spoonful of rice. When the children went away, she asked me, distractedly, 'But is it true you don't know whether you want to eat or not?'

'Well, and supposing I did want to?' Heavens! This insistence was irritating me!

The old woman seemed to be upset. She gazed at the bottom of the pot and smiled at me apologetically.

'All that's left is *ucoco*!'

From the other end the children started to comment, 'Chi! *Ucoco*!' Quito said, 'Shhh!' and they all hissed again. The old woman shouted at them and they went on eating.

'So why do you keep on asking me if I want to eat—anyway, what are you going to eat?'

'I'm not hungry,' the old woman replied.

'But there's no more food, isn't that it?'

'I'm not hungry, I'm not, really I'm not. But if you like I'll make some tea in a second. Would you like some?'

'I'm not hungry either.'

'Well, then I'll make some tea for the children in case they're still hungry after they've eaten.'

Then I could no longer resist the impulse to embrace the old woman. She remained quite still while I buried my head between her breasts. Laughing nervously, she protested, 'But you don't usually do this ...' And she continued to laugh until she had the courage to embrace me.

'My son ...'

I felt her rough fingers timidly caressing my face. Then she kissed me and laughed a lot.

I heard the children laughing too.

'You're not usually like this! What's happened to you? My son ... my son ... Are you hungry? Shall I make you some tea?'

I hadn't heard that tone of voice for I don't know how long, and perhaps I didn't remember ever having heard it.

'Did they hit you? Tell me, my son, did they hit you? Who was it?'

'No, they didn't hit me.'

'But they did something to you, didn't they, my son? You're angry with them, aren't you? ...'

I tried not to speak, but I had no time to think. 'They've destroyed everything ... they've stolen ... they don't want ...'

I felt her catch her breath and stiffen slightly. 'Don't you want to tell me? Don't you? Don't you?'

'It's no use.'

The children drew nearer, 'Tell us, tell us.'

'No, I won't, you'll have to grow up first. ... Don't be a nuisance now.'

'Yes, my son, there's time, there's time. ... Everything will change, everything will be better, and when they're grown up ...'

'They'll grow up all right. ... They'll have to grow up in all this ...'

'Do you really not want to tell?'

'Tell us, tell us!' The children gathered around us on the straw mat.

No, I wouldn't tell them. It wasn't for this that I had come home. Anyway, I wouldn't be the one to destroy anything for them, whatever it was. All in good time someone would be charged with telling them the truth about the lie, about all those lies. They themselves would feel the bitterness of having to destroy the monument to Youth and Faith, built on the lie of a hope. No, I would not tell.

'My son ...'

I was startled to hear the old woman speak. 'My son, I don't quite understand what you're trying to say, really I don't understand. But you are trembling; either you're frightened or very angry or something like that, and what you're saying can't be good, because you're trembling, you're actually trembling! ...'

Perhaps the old woman was right, because it is very rare for her to be mistaken. But anyway this made no difference. I wouldn't tell, and that was that ... and even if I did, what would be the good? Yes, what good would it do, seeing that the filth, the damned filth of it all would come to these children in other circumstances, with other details and with other names.

'Eh, all of you, go to sleep, go on! Yes, sleep. What are you looking at? Go to sleep!'

But, who knows? and also, why not believe? Why not believe in something really nice? Like, perhaps, that the upbringing of the children would be different from mine, and would endow them with a tolerance of things, a tolerance that my emotional make-up could not endure. And for them, perhaps, how should I know? Perhaps time would create more understanding, more tenderness, yes, more humanity. ... Because, perhaps, the old woman was right, there is time, time.

'My son, the children have gone.'

'Yes, I'll tell you, they did hit me.'

'Who was it? But is that all? You're trembling ...'

'Yes, this isn't everything, and it's not even anything. They made me small, and they succeeded in making me feel small. Yes, that's it. That is everything. And why? They don't even say it out loud. And everything falls on me, not as a slow soft erosion, for this no one feels, but it falls suddenly, with agonizing noises inside me, and falls, and falls. ...'

'Well, I think it's better if I don't know about this at all, because I don't understand anything you say.'

We both became silent, in so close an embrace that I didn't even know if she was the one who was trembling. It was only at this moment that I saw the flames, although I had been looking at them a long time. The heat enveloped us pleasantly, and the flames twisted and turned in a strange ruby dance. I only stopped looking when the old woman talked in a way that made me realize that she had long been meditating on how to say something she eventually did not say. She only said, 'My son.'

Her fingers were rough, but her dark velvet embrace was soft and warm, and exuded the strong, pure fragrance of the good years of my faith.

Dopper and Papist

Herman C. Bosman

It was a cold night (Oom Schalk Lourens said) on which we drove with Gert Bekker in his Cape cart to Zeerust. I sat in front, next to Gert, who was driving. In the back seat were the predikant, Rev Vermooten, and his ouderling, Isak Erasmus, who were on their way to Pretoria for the meeting of the synod of the Dutch Reformed Church. The predikant was lean and hawk-faced; the ouderling was fat and had broad shoulders.

Gert Bekker and I did not speak. We had been transport-drivers together in our time, and we had learnt that when it is two men alone, travelling over a long distance, it is best to use few words, and those well-chosen. Two men, alone in each other's company, understand each other better the less they speak.

The horses kept up a good, steady trot. The lantern, swinging from side to side with the jogging of the cart, lit up stray patches of the uneven road and made bulky shadows rise up among the thorn trees. In the back seat the predikant and ouderling were discussing theology.

'You never saw such a lot of brand-siek sheep in your life,' the predikant was saying, 'as what Chris Haasbroek brought along as tithe.'

We then came to a stony part of the road, and so I did not hear the ouderling's reply; but afterwards, above the rattling of the cart-wheels, I caught other snatches of God-fearing conversation, to do with raising of pew-rents.

From there the predikant started discussing the proselytizing activities being carried on among the local Bapedi kafirs by the Catholic mission at Vleisfontein. The predikant dwelt particularly on the ignorance of the Bapedi tribes and on the idolatrous form of the Papist Communion service, which was quite different from the Protestant Nagmaal, the predikant said, although to a Bapedi, walking with his buttocks sticking out, the two services might, perhaps, seem somewhat alike.

Rev Vermooten was very eloquent when he came to denouncing the heresies of Catholicism. And he spoke loudly, so that we could hear him on the front seat. And I know that both Gert Bekker and I felt very good, then, deep inside us, to think that we were Protestants. The coldness of the night and the pale flickering of the lantern-light among the thorn trees gave an added solemnity to the predikant's words.

I felt that it might perhaps be all right to be a Catholic if you were walking on a Zeerust side-walk in broad daylight, say. But it was a different matter to be driving through the middle of the bush on a dark night, with just a swinging lantern fastened to the side of a Cape cart with baling-wire. If the lantern went out suddenly, and you were left in the loneliest part of the bush, striking matches, then it must be a very frightening thing to be a Catholic, I thought.

This led me to thinking of Piet Reilly and his family, who were Afrikaners, like you and me, except that they were Catholics. Piet Reilly even brought out his vote for General Lemmer at the last Volksraad election, which we thought would make it unlucky for our candidate. But General Lemmer said no, he didn't mind how many Catholics voted for him. A Catholic's vote was, naturally, not as good as a Dopper's, he said, but the little cross that had to be made behind a candidate's name cast out the evil that was of course otherwise lurking in a Catholic's ballot paper. And General Lemmer must have been right, because he got elected, that time.

While I was thinking on those lines, it suddenly struck me that Piet Reilly was now living on a farm about six miles on the bushveld side of Sephton's Nek, and that we would be passing his farmhouse, which was near the road, just before daybreak. It was comforting to think that we would have the predikant and the ouderling in the Cape cart with us, when we passed the homestead of Piet Reilly, a Catholic, in the dark.

I tried to hear what the predikant was saying, in the back seat, to the ouderling. But the predikant was once more dealing with an abstruse point of religion, and had lowered his voice accordingly. I could catch only fragments of the ouderling's replies.

'Yes, dominie,' I heard the ouderling affirm, 'you are quite right. If he again tries to overlook your son for the job of anthrax inspector, then you must make it clear to the Chairman of the

Board that you have all that information about his private life. ...'

I realized then that you could find much useful guidance for your everyday problems in the conversation of holy men.

The night got colder and darker.

The palm of my hand, pressed tight around the bowl of my pipe, was the only part of me that felt warm. My teeth began to chatter. I wished that, next time we stopped to let the horses blow, we could light a fire and boil coffee. But I knew that there was no coffee left in the chest under the back seat.

While I sat silent next to Gert Bekker, I continued to think of Piet Reilly and his wife and children. With Piet, of course, I could understand it. He himself had merely kept up the religion—if you could call what the Catholics believe in a religion—that he had inherited from his father and his grandfather. But there was Piet Reilly's wife, Gertruida, now. She had been brought up a respectable Dopper girl. She was one of the Drogedal Bekkers, and was, in fact, distantly related to Gert Bekker, who was sitting on the Cape cart next to me. There was something for you to ponder about, I thought to myself, with the cold all the time looking for new places in my skin through which to strike into my bones.

The moment Gertruida met Piet Reilly she forgot all about the sacred truths she had learnt at her mother's knee. And on the day she got married she was saying prayers to the Virgin Mary on a string of beads, and was wearing a silver cross at her throat that was as soft and white as the roses she held pressed against her. Here was now a sweet Dopper girl turned Papist.

As I have said, I knew that there was no coffee left in the box under the back seat; but I did know that under the front seat there was a full bottle of raw peach brandy. In fact, I could see the neck of the bottle protruding from between Gert Bekker's ankles.

I also knew, through all the years of transport-driving that we had done together, that Gert Bekker had already, over many miles of road, been thinking how we could get the cork off the bottle without the predikant and the ouderling shaking their heads reprovingly. And the way he managed it in the end was, I thought, highly intelligent.

For, when he stopped the cart again to rest the horses, he alighted beside the road and held out the bottle to our full view.

'There is brandy in this bottle, dominie,' Gerk Bekker said to the predikant, 'that I keep for the sake of the horses on cold nights, like now. It is an old Marico remedy for when horses are in danger of getting the *floute*, I take a few mouthfuls of the brandy, which I then blow into the nostrils of the horses, who don't feel the cold so much, after that. The brandy revives them.'

Gert commenced blowing brandy into the face of the horse on the near side, to show us.

Then he beckoned to me, and I also alighted and went and stood next to him, taking turns with him in blowing brandy into the eyes and nostrils of the offside horse. We did this several times.

The predikant asked various questions, to show how interested he was in this old-fashioned method of overcoming fatigue in draught animals. But what the predikant said at the next stop made me perceive that he was more than a match for a dozen men like Gert Bekker in point of astuteness.

When we stopped the cart, the predikant held up his hand.

'Don't you and your friend trouble to get off this time,' the predikant called out when Gert Bekker was once more reaching for the bottle, 'the ouderling and I have decided to take turns with you in blowing brandy into the horses' faces. We don't want to put all the hard work on to your shoulders.'

We made several more halts after that, with the result that daybreak found us still a long way from Sephton's Nek. In the early dawn we saw the thatched roof of Piet Reilly's house through the thorn trees some distance from the road. When the predikant suggested that we call at the homestead for coffee, we explained to him that the Reillys were Catholics.

'But isn't Piet Reilly's wife a relative of yours?' the predikant asked of Gert Bekker. 'Isn't she your second-cousin, or something?'

'They are Catholics,' Gert answered.

'Coffee,' the predikant insisted.

'Catholics,' Gert Bekker repeated stolidly.

The upshot of it was, naturally enough, that we outspanned shortly afterwards in front of the Reilly homestead. That was the kind of man that the predikant was in an argument.

'The coffee will be ready soon,' the predikant said as we walked up to the front door. 'There is smoke coming out of the chimney.'

Almost before we had stopped knocking, Gertruida Reilly had

opened both the top and bottom doors. She started slightly when she saw, standing in front of her, a minister of the Dutch Reformed Church. In spite of her look of agitation, Gertruida was still pretty, I thought, after ten years of being married to Piet Reilly.

When she stepped forward to kiss her cousin, Gert Bekker, I saw him turn away, sadly; and I realized something of the shame that she had brought on her whole family through her marriage to a Catholic.

'You looked startled when you saw me, Gertruida,' the predikant said, calling her by her first name, as though she was still a member of his congregation.

'Yes,' Gertruida answered. 'Yes—I was—surprised.'

'I suppose it was a Catholic priest that you wanted to come to your front door,' Gert Bekker said, sarcastically. Yet there was a tone in his voice that was not altogether unfriendly.

'Indeed, I was expecting a Catholic priest,' Gertruida said, leading us into the voorkamer. 'But if the Lord has sent the dominie and his ouderling, instead, I am sure it will be well, also.'

It was only then, after she had explained to us what had happened, that we understood why Gertruida was looking so troubled. Her eight-year-old daughter had been bitten by a snake; they couldn't tell from the fang-marks if it was a ringhals or a bakkop. Piet Reilly had driven off in the mule-cart to Vleisfontein, the Catholic Mission Station, for a priest.

They had cut open and cauterized the wound and had applied red permanganate. The rest was a matter for God. And that was why, when she saw the predikant and the ouderling at her front door, Gertruida believed that the Lord had sent them.

I was glad that Gert Bekker did not at the moment think of mentioning that we had really come for coffee.

'Certainly, I shall pray for your little girl's recovery,' the predikant said to Gertruida. 'Take me to her.'

Gertruida hesitated.

'Will you—will you pray for her the Catholic way, dominie?' Gertruida asked.

Now it was the predikant's turn to draw back.

'But, Gertruida,' he said, 'you, you whom I myself confirmed in the Enkel-Gereformeerde Kerk in Zeerust—how can you now ask me such a thing? Did you not learn in the catechism that the Romish ritual is a mockery of the Holy Ghost?'

'I married Piet Reilly,' Gertruida answered simply, 'and his faith is my faith. Piet has been very good to me, Father. And I love him.'

We noticed that Gertruida called the predikant 'Father', now, and not 'Dominie'. During the silence that followed, I glanced at the candle burning before an image of the Mother Mary in a corner of the voorkamer. I looked away quickly from that unrighteousness.

The predikant's next words took us by complete surprise.

'Have you got some kind of a prayer-book,' the predikant asked, 'that sets out the—the Catholic form for a ...'

'I'll fetch it from the other room,' Gertruida answered.

When she had left, the predikant tried to put our minds at ease.

'I am only doing this to help a mother in distress,' he explained to the ouderling. 'It is something that the Lord will understand. Gertruida was brought up a Dopper girl. In some ways she is still one of us. She does not understand that I have no authority to conduct the Catholic service for the sick.'

The ouderling was going to say something.

But at that moment Gertruida returned with a little black book that you could almost have taken for a Dutch Reformed Church psalm-book. Only, I knew that what was printed inside it was as iniquitous as the candle burning in the corner.

Yet I also began to wonder if, in not knowing the difference, a Bapedi really was so very ignorant, even though he walked with his buttocks sticking out.

'My daughter is in this other room,' Gertruida said, and started in the direction of the door. The predikant followed her. Just before entering the bedroom he turned round and faced the ouderling.

'Will you enter with me, Brother Erasmus?' the predikant asked.

The ouderling did not answer. The veins stood out on his forehead. On his face you could read the conflict that went on inside him. For what seemed a very long time he stood quite motionless. Then he stooped down to the rusbank for his hat—which he did not need—and walked after the predikant into the bedroom.

The Dishonest Chief

translated from Chichewa by
Ellis Singano and A.A. Roscoe

Once upon a time there lived a certain chief who was a crook. The people in the village did not know this for he seemed to rule wisely. But whenever this man saw groundnuts or other crops in someone else's garden he would go in at once and steal them.

One day, the chief wanted some millet to eat. He had not got any in his own store so he went round the village peeping into gardens which might contain some. Luckily enough, he found one and soon began cutting the millet before sneaking back to his own house with a large bundle under his arm. When the millet was finished, he went again to steal some more.

The owner of the millet was angry when he realized that someone was stealing his crop, so he thought up a plan to catch the thief red-handed.

'Ah! I have an idea,' he said to his wife, who was beside him looking at the patch where the millet had been cut. 'Tomorrow, I will hide behind the bushes in our garden and then leap out and cut the fellow's head off when he comes.'

'That's a good plan,' his wife replied. 'We must catch this rascal at once before he steals any more.'

The following day, as the sun was setting, the man went to his millet garden and hid himself behind a clump of bushes. He had in his belt a big knife and lay quite still waiting for the thief to arrive. Not long after the sun had fallen away behind the mountains, the chief crept into the garden and began cutting the millet. As he was busy at his evil task, the garden owner suddenly hurled his large knife at him, striking him in the neck and cutting off his head completely. The chief now lay on the ground, his blood spattering the millet he had tried to steal. The man came out of hiding and approached the body. He could not believe his eyes when he saw it was the chief who was the culprit. He took a large basket which he always kept in the garden, picked up the chief's head, and placed it inside, covering the grisly thing with freshly-cut millet. Then taking his knife, he put the basket on his head and made his way to the chief's house. As he was approaching, he heard the chief's wife singing a song which went like this:

Alendo mwadzatiyendera?
    Limande
Mwandioneranji?
    Limande.
Pano amfumu kulibe.
    Limande, Mwationera? Limande.
Adapita ku Milimo.
    Limande, Mwandionera?
Kukatema Milimo
    Limande Mwandionera?
(Have you come to visit us?
Hush!
What makes you think that?
Hush!
The chief is not here.
Hush!
What makes you think that?
Do you want me to tell the secret)*

The man put the basket down beside the chief's wife and sang a song answering the questions he had heard in her song:

Inde tadzayenda.
Limande Mwandionera?
Pano amfumu kulibe
Mwandionera?
Adapita kukaba
Mwandionera?
Limande
Kukaba Mapira.
Mwandionera?
Limande.

*Song translated by Chris Kamlongera

Mutu uli M'dengumo.
Mwandionera?
Limande.

When the chief's wife had heard what the man sang, she started taking the millet out of the basket. Then she saw the head of her husband, and she fell to the ground shrieking and sobbing. The man later explained to the village people how and why their chief had died, and there the story ends.

The Soweto Bride

Mbulelo V. Mzamane

To most people in Soweto, Solomzi's marriage to a black American woman brought back memories of Dr Zuma's prestigious marriage to another black American more than a quarter of a century ago. Solomzi's reputation rose precipitously when the *World* carried the news on its front page. Both his family and friends awaited his return anxiously. I often went to his home to ask when they were expected back. Each time, his father told me they hadn't written yet. His friends spoke of nothing else. There was Samoosa shaking his head and smiling each time the bride's name was mentioned. Yster often said he wished to ask Solomzi what they tasted like. Tefo, who'd also studied in America, told us we were impressed by small things. He'd had the pick of American women, he said, though one could detect a hint of envy in his tone.

When Solomzi finally wrote to me to tell me when they were coming, I started arranging for a convoy of cars to fetch them from Jan Smuts Airport. I also planned to hold a rousing welcome party on the day of his arrival. His parents were also going to slaughter a sheep, though his father sounded hurt that his son had not written to him.

What struck me about Norma when I met her at Jan Smuts was her ordinary plainness. She wore her hair in the boyish Afro-style which was also common among our girls in Soweto. Her face looked all the way an African's, nothing to compel a second glance in her direction. She was dressed in a plain black skirt, a black skipper and manly windbreaker with navy socks and black canvas shoes of the type we call moosemocks. I had seen prettier and better dressed girls in the townships. Solomzi appeared by far the more impressive of the two in his white Arrow shirt, black pleatless Mayfair slacks, black cardigan and a pair of Florscheim shoes. He also sported an Afro and looked more American then Percy Sledge, Andrew Gardner or any of the other top American visitors who had graced the dusty streets of Soweto in recent years.

We shook hands all round in the airport's V.I.P. lounge. Solomzi introduced us to his wife. Her rich American drawl was impressive and surpassed anything you heard from Tefo, for instance. Tefo claimed to have studied Linguistics in America. He never tired of telling us how his accent had been improved by hours of hard work in a language laboratory, with complicated machinery, tape recorders and sophisticated gadgets. But we all thought his drawl rather artificial. Norma sounded like Cleopatra Jones in the movies.

The round of greetings over, we headed for our contingent of cars. I jumped into the front seat of the leading car — a new black Cadillac convertible specially hired for the occasion and blazoned in bold letters on the side, MBONANI WEDDING UNDERTAKERS. Norma and Solomzi climbed in the back. I ordered the driver to lock the doors amidst complaints of 'Why can't he ride in the cheap scrap he came in?' from Yster, who had been timidly trying to work his way back to the guest car. Nobody had invited him, but as we left the location I'd seen him in the front seat of the Cadillac and made up my mind to fix him later.

The driver pulled out.

'Man, how does it feel like to be back home a married man when you left a bachelor?' I began with my carefully rehearsed questions. I tried to sound cheerful and spontaneous.

'So, so, so,' Solomzi replied.

I shifted the conversation to Norma — a tip obtained from my booklet *Art of Conversation, How to Master it*. 'And don't you miss your native America?'

'I've been away from home before.'

'I mean, do you find a world of difference between us and the people back home?'

'I hardly know you.'

I shifted my gaze to Solomzi who was trying not to notice. I was beginning to wonder how he managed with her.

I needed a fresh start. 'Sol, there'll be a small do in your honour at my digs tonight.'

'Shucks, Phambili, not today, man. All we need is a good night's sleep.'

I chose another line. 'We have fixed for you to rest the whole afternoon. The party's for the evening.' I decided to pull out my trump card. 'Mr Sixishe is coming. He's the new Mayor. I also hope Mr Nelson who is the American Consul-General can make it. You two take a rest between two and five ...'

'Do you usually treat adults like kindergarten kids, hay? Telling us when we should or shouldn't take a nap?' Norma cut in.

What a strange woman, I thought, one who would in all likelihood pull out back to America as soon as it suited her. She didn't seem the assimilable type.

'*Kyk hier, Fana,*' I said, imagining that if I spoke in a language she didn't know she'd have less cause to interrupt, '*julle kan ons nie nou disorganize nie. Ons het die programme grand gestul.*'

'What's he saying?' she asked.

Solomzi laughed out. I only grinned for appearances.

'He says we can't disorganize them now, they already have the programme worked out. And that's true, you know, Norm. We can't let them down now.'

'I guess in planning their programme they might have asked our opinion. I certainly ain't in no mood for no cocktail.'

She seemed bent on cutting me down to size. I only hoped Solomzi would make her see sense. I wondered if you could safely deal this one a blue eye if she got in your way. She seemed the type who would lay a charge with the police against her husband. Give me my township type any time, I thought, as my mind automatically shifted to Kedibone — a staff nurse, double qualified, general and midwifery, yet she never said 'No' twice to a suggestion from me.

Norma eventually yielded to Solomzi's persuasion, although on her own terms. She was willing to spend an hour, and not more, at this 'cocktail'. Against my better judgement, I barged in to explain that it wasn't a 'cocktail' but a party. The look on her face wasn't to my liking so I froze the rest of my explanation.

☆   ☆   ☆   ☆   ☆

We stopped at Solomzi's. As they heard the cars pull in, Solomzi's relations who had gathered to welcome the bride burst out of the house, the women ululating at the top of their throats. I heard Norma mumble something like: 'But you said the cocktail wasn't due to start until this evening ...' before Solomzi gently pushed her out of the car. She clung to his side at first like a frightened child.

From all sides improvised confetti made of torn pieces of paper from discarded fahfee exercise books were showered on the couple and some of it landed on my Hector Powe suit. Norma, who seemed to have realized the futility of trying to beat them, put up her best efforts to join them. She dished out a patronizing smile all round. My attention was then drawn to the *World* reporter whom I had personally invited. He was preparing to shoot some photos so I drew as near the couple as I could. I murmured some reassuring words to Norma, though my real intention was to display my unique relationship with the couple. I fancied myself something of a best man, if you care to look at the show as a wedding. Small wonder I was allowed, or rather bulldozed my way, into the bridal suite while the others with whom we had been to Jan Smuts were provided with seats under the hired tent on the lawn. Outside, the women had begun singing wedding songs.

We were led by one of Solomzi's relatives, Aunt Bessie, into the dining-cum-sitting-room where we were left to ourselves for some time. I chatted away to an uninterested couple about a group of Soweto businessmen who had recently left on a study tour of business trends in the United States. My various anecdotes about the States which I was about to narrate were interrupted by a group of women from all over the township who came to shake hands with us and to ask after the bride's health. I ventured to hint that the *makoti* did not speak IsiXhosa whereupon MaMthethwa, the shebeen queen, promptly switched to Sesotho, an example followed by others. I shook my head sadly and looked at Solomzi to see how he took it. He did not seem to be with us. He went through the motions of greeting mechanically. At length he said, 'Aunt Bessie, I haven't seen Mama and Tata. Where are they?'

'Your father is with your mother. She is still weeping tears of gratitude. You see, when you wrote to say you'd married an American we all thought it was a white woman. How were we to know, my child? But when we saw you arrive just now and I explained to her that the *makoti* was as human as you and me, she broke down with tears of relief so we had to call your father to comfort her.'

Aunt Bessie ended her explanation as Solomzi's mother, led by his father, came into the room. The old couple stood transfixed at the door for a while. Steadily, Solomzi rose to meet them. In another moment he was covered in his mother's arms. Tears ran down her lined cheeks. I averted my eyes at this moving scene and checked back a stupid, involuntary tear. What would the American girl think? I could not help wondering.

Solomzi shifted his attention to his father, who greeted him with dignified composure. They shook hands simply and asked after each other's health. Solomzi introduced them to Norma, who smiled most agreeably and shook hands.

Predictably, a woman I had recognized from the outset by her uniform — she was dressed in the red blouse, black skirt and white hat of the Methodist Mothers' *Manyano* — burst into an impromptu rendition of *Umphefumlo Wam' Uyayibonga Inkos*. The house joined in. Torn between self-respect and my instinctive response, I hummed the baritone part as distinctly and audibly as I could but with my mouth firmly shut to create the illusion I was silent.

The same woman of the *Manyano* began a prayer of considerable length. She composed most of it as she went along. In her prayer she introduced herself as Solomzi's father's cousin, on his mother's side. She followed this by a brief singing of the family praises. She proceeded to trace Solomzi's biography, laying stress on his brilliant scholastic career (which, I can swear, had been very mediocre) and his parents' struggles preceding his departure for America. Comparing herself to some biblical character, she expressed a wish to die now that she had seen one of her own blood in a position where he could support all his relations and their friends and their friends' friends. She rounded off her prayer by condemning contraception and wishing the couple a houseful of children.

What would the American think of us? I kept on asking myself.

There were more speeches of welcome, first in IsiXhosa then, as MaMthethwa drew the speaker's attention to the bride's linguistic limitations, in Sesotho.

Solomzi appeared too emotionally involved to take in the situation. In muffled tones and as discreetly as I could, I reminded the couple of that evening's party and excused myself. I really thought any more of this speechifying could have no effect on an outsider than to shame our heritage.

The evening's party was proclaimed by our many guests, both the invited as well as the uninvited, as highly successful, by which the uninvited at least meant that they had neither been turned back nor discriminated against. The impressions of our guests were neatly summed up by Yster, an irrepressible gatecrasher with a radar for liquor, who intoned endlessly, '*Ons het ge-groove*, Jack. It was really groovy.'

I moved among our guests, urging them to rejoice at Solomzi's safe return and to drink to his bride's health. What also delighted everybody was that there were really no speeches to talk of. Mr Sixishe, the Mayor of Soweto by virtue of being Chairman of the Urban Bantu Council, spoke as briefly as he could in welcoming our long-lost sister back to Africa, where her ancestors, as she undoubtedly must have been told, had originated.

'You are probably related to me, here, or to your husband, there,' he added, at which we all laughed.

Then he said a few proud things about Solomzi, who had not only brought back a soul-sister but a certificate as well. Whereupon we shouted 'Soul Sister', 'Black Power', 'Black is Beautiful' and other American slogans we knew.

Yster wanted to know what a certificate was. I ignored the question and gave him a silencing stare.

Next on the programme was the toast, which I asked Tefo to propose to the people of Africa and America in general. In my mind the whole affair had acquired a distinctly international flavour. In fact, only the meeting of the Black Sash had prevented the Americam Consul-General from attending. What a pity he wasn't able to accept my invitation! I had met him at Jan Smuts that morning. Samoosa, who worked at the United States Information Service, pointed him out to me. I wasted no time in giving him a verbal invitation to his compatriot's party whom he had undoubtedly come to meet too. But it turned out he had come to meet some other distinguished guest and had been invited elsewhere that evening to address a meeting of the Black Sash. But for that we would have been rubbing shoulders with the big man himself. Perhaps he'd have brought his wife and daughters too.

Solomzi rose after the toast and simply thanked us for the singular honour bestowed on him and his wife.

As Master of Ceremonies I took over. I formally welcomed our guests and invited them all to 'partake of the waters of immortality and the other delicacies set before them'. That was the cue for Tefo to play the first record, James Brown's *I'm Black and I'm Proud*, which was calculated to get everybody, including the naturally inhibited, into the right spirit.

I dragged my Kedibone, who needed no second prompting, to the floor and we danced the Mayfair, adding the latest variations. Everybody simultaneously jumped onto the dance floor.

Later I noticed that Yster, who had the physique of a champion wrestler and the fiery temperament of a long-term prisoner, was yapping incessantly at Norma. I determined to rescue her and worked my way to where they stood.

'And who is this one, this other one, man?' Yster put one finger in his mouth. 'Agh! He died not so long ago. Used to play piano for the M.J.Q. . . . Ah! John Lewis, that's his name. Do you know him?'

A long-drawn yawn preceded Norma's 'No.'

'And what about our South African boys, Hugh Masekela, for instance? He's appeared in *Down Beat*.'

An inattentive Norma answered 'Yes.'

'*Hoor daar*, Jack,' Yster (who habitually called everybody Jack) nudged hard at my ribs with his elbows. 'She's probably sat at the same table with Hugh Masekela and has listened to live performances of *Grazing in the Grass* at night clubs in the U.S. Shake my hand, Soul Sister.'

After the handshaking I barged in and introduced Norma to the nearest friend who happened to be at hand, Samoosa. She told me with great annoyance that she'd already met him. Samoosa happily clung to her hand while he mumbled something about vacancies at the U.S.I.S.

I could see Yster wasn't too pleased at my interruption. But I wanted him to know I had more important things in mind.

'Norma,' I began, 'Mr Sixishe wants to have a few words with you before he leaves. Couldn't we join him while he's talking to Sol?'

'Tell Sol the hour I agreed to spend here is now over.'

'*Sy is moeg*, Jack,' Yster added.

I could tell as I shuffled away that Yster thought I had been fixed, good and square. I heard him shout the fashionable all-night party slogan *Akulalwa egiggin* before he promptly fell asleep.

I was wearing a broad smile as I approached my Kedibone to show anybody who cared that my acquaintances were class. I felt proud of her as she stood there chatting to some friends, colleagues

of hers from the hospital. She looked pretty in her hot pants and
halter-neck blouse. At least, prettier than Norma who hadn't
changed her crumpled skirt and skipper. Kedibone turned away
from her companions to face me.

'You look enchanted by our American friend,' she said.

'That kill-joy! You couldn't be more wrong, darling.'

'Haven't you been watching her the whole evening?'

'The evening's hardly begun.'

'Except for one dance with me,' she went on, 'you've been
paying attention to no one else but Norma. What's she got that's so
special?'

'Who's being jealous?' I tried to make a joke of it.

'I'm not being jealous, Phambili. But you are tied to me just as
I'm tied to you. You're my man until either of us declares the silver
cup broken.'

'Kedibone, you and I are the chief host and hostess, added to
which I'm the M.C. At any rate, would you seriously say there was
anything captivating about that woman?'

'That's where you men are fools. If mixed marriages were to be
permitted in our country, a good proportion of you would marry
the ugliest of whites, simply because they were whites. If you must
import a girl, at least bring home a rare catch.'

'I suppose *you* would marry into the cream of white society!'

After an uneasy silence I decided to steer the conversation into
safer channels.

'She wants me to tell Sol that they must now leave.'

'But the party's hardly started! Look,' I followed the direction of
her eyes, 'Sol and Mr Sixishe want you to join them. You're in very
great demand, aren't you? I hope old Sixishe is on his way home.
He's held up things a bit. Let's get on with the party without stiff
crocks like him.'

I edged my way in the direction of Solomzi and Mr Sixishe.

'I must congratulate you on your fine efforts, son.' Mr Sixishe
looked at Solomzi who nodded his approval. 'It calls for such small
gestures — not that I think your party a small affair — to make one
feel socially acceptable in an alien environment. Your gesture, I am
sure, will not be lost on our daughter. But for other arrangements,
I would love to have remained longer. I hope you enjoy yourselves.'

I led Mr Sixishe to Norma and they said goodnight. As we
walked back from the car I gave Solomzi Norma's message. Before

answering he helped himself to the bottle of Scotch we had bought specially for him and Mr Sixishe, who didn't drink anyway.

'I don't see how she hopes to get initiated to this part of the world if she shuns company. I think she's better left with people like Yster.'

He gulped his drink, poured himself another, disposed of it and continued addressing me as he poured himself yet another.

'You know, Phambi, I sometimes feel you and I with our "excuse me" fashions are far from being typical. Yster and his lot are more representative of the ordinary bloke in Soweto. That's what made Bobby Kennedy's tour of Soweto the success it was. Because he met the ordinary dustman's family. Americans still say it was the most successful visit by one of their politicians to a black township in South Africa. Right? So why not let Norma adjust the way I did in the States? There were no conducted tours for me.'

I really admired his firmness. That's how I would have handled Kedibone. But I tried to persuade him to be a bit sympathetic to Norma.

'At least for a coupla seconds, Sol,' I added, as he moved in her direction, dangling the whisky bottle like a drunkard's banner.

She still sat yawning where I had left her. Companionless because even Yster had found his feet and was shouting above the noise of the record player, '*Akulalwa egiggin,* never, no sleeping at a party.'

Norma's face lit up as Solomzi joined her. But it lost its lustre just as soon. I guessed from her expression that Solomzi was showing her just where women got off in Africa. She sulked for the next two hours, now looking like dough, now like fatcakes. The urge to pause and enjoy a hearty laugh at her expense was great. But I had a few announcements to make.

Some former schoolmates of ours from Swaziland, where Solomzi and I had been educated, had just arrived and found us at the party. In introducing Dudu and Neo I didn't let on that it was sheer coincidence they happened to be there on the same day as Solomzi. I let it look as though they had come on purpose to add to the international flavour. Amidst cries of 'Soul Brother' I rounded off the introduction and we began dancing to Herbie Mann's *Battle Hymn of the Underground*.

Two hours later I announced the departure of Solomzi and Norma. He was dragging her off to bed to give her, I hoped, a taste of African manhood. I remained wondering how he could have walked into this burning flame with both eyes open. Interesting, I thought, to see what happens to her high-and-mighty airs in another few weeks.

The party swung on even after our guests of honour had left. When the house ran dry, we invaded nearby shebeens for more — which is what I had meant to explain to Norma when she mistook our party for a 'cocktail'. Beer and spirits flowed like *ndambula* at the Municipal Beer Hall until black-outs had claimed a considerable proportion of our company, including myself.

When we came to at daybreak my home looked like a wrecked bar. Empty bottles littered the kitchen and overflowed into the yard. Clearly, something had to be done. Yster, dusting himself as he emerged from behind the stove, was for removing his hangover.

'Jack,' he said to no one in particular, '*ons moet gazaat.*'

This seemed a brilliant idea. We chipped in to raise the price of a case and two straights which we bought from MaMthethwa's.

To forestall arguments about the change I suggested we buy meat. 'We need something salty, gents.' The idea met with general approval. Despite Yster's obvious genius, I hadn't forgotten that we never invited him in the first place, so I took the initiative and suggested we continue the party at Solomzi's to whom we owed our togetherness.

Besides Yster and myself there was Dudu and Neo, whose car we used, and Kedibone who was still sulking after her idle claim that I had beaten her up for sweet nothing the previous evening. She hardly had a swollen eye to back her story. She had skipped work that morning at my suggestion. I promised to buy her a doctor's certificate from one of the township medicos.

We might as well have left the meat and augmented the liquor with another half-jack, for at Solomzi's a sheep had been slaughtered to thank the ancestors. We were welcomed with a communal dish of *mala le moholu*, the insides of the sheep, as we explained to Solomzi the purpose of our early invasion. He too complained that churchbells were ringing monotonously in his head and that since we were responsible for his state he would welcome whatever cure we adopted. Yster and I hopped out and soon returned with the stuff from the car.

We bumped into Norma as we came in carrying the liquor like hard-earned but well-deserved trophies. I gave her a hearty greeting which she returned with her accustomed terseness. She preceded us into the dining-cum-sitting-room where the guests greeted her. She placed herself beside Solomzi and returned the greetings in that high-nosed manner I had come to associate with her. Throughout our visit she sat like that, occasionally croaking in monosyllables when anyone directed a question at her. At least my Kedibone parked herself comfortably in a corner of the settee and snored away peacefully.

We reviewed the previous night's happening as we drank to clear our heads. Once a nosey aunt of Solomzi's came in clapping her hands together in supplication. I poured her two stiff fingers of brandy which she gulped down. She launched into a roundabout speech whose theme was pour-me-some-again, until Aunt Bessie came in to drag her out with the words — 'You certainly won't involve us in the unnecessary expense of buying *umqombothi* for you and your tribe and afterwards running away from it.'

We saw no more of her as she went to join the drinkers of the native brew who were seated under the shade of the hired tent.

As Solomzi brightened we switched to our blend of Afrikaans-*tsotsi taal* whenever what was said was not meant for Norma's ears. He told us he was no longer on speaking terms with her because of the previous evening's events. It was a measure of his wife's selfishness, he said, that she failed to appreciate his position.

Americans were known to be less conservative and more adaptable than the British, we tried to console him. It was probably just the novelty of it all. It wouldn't take her long to discard her own values and culture and adapt herself.

Generalizations are all very fine, I thought to myself, but inapplicable to individual human reality. I didn't believe Norma or any other U.S. citizen could exchange their American adult life and culture for our own. What happened to Andrew Gardener, the American boxing trainer? He married a local beauty queen. We even re-Christened him 'Sbali' to signify he had become one of us. He played the mouth-organ and was seen on several Soweto stages with some of our leading jazzmen. 'Destined to become the first Yank to acquire Soweto citizenship,' Mr Sixishe used to say. Always in top company. But he eventually left with his treasured wife. He must have realized how his sense of importance and

American charm, which he used to put on like an executive committee member's suit, had worn off with constant rubbing of shoulders. Whoever heard of an American localizing? Didn't Mrs Zuma go back to America after her husband's death? To me the 'back-to-Africa call' would always remain a black American myth, at best a rallying slogan and an emotional focus. A political weapon and little besides. As for Norma? 'Only time will tell, gents,' I said aloud. I was entering my first stage of intoxication, the intro-spective phase.

Solomzi further explained that he was arranging for Norma to obtain her residential papers. Her embassy would help her acquire a residence permit.

Would she also apply for a reference book? I wanted to know.

'It would be silly of her to drop her American citizenship,' Solomzi replied.

'Sy is American, Jack,' Yster added. 'You don't expect her to acquire Transkeian citizenship.'

'The point is, at a certain stage she qualifies for citizenship.'

'Not if she doesn't want to,' Solomzi said. 'She can apply for a temporary residence permit which is easier to get, and keep on renewing it ...'

'Till death do us part,' I said.

'That can be done through her embassy,' he continued. 'The Americans are very influential in this part of the world.'

'There would be no sense of security in all that,' I said. 'It would be merely exposing yourselves to the wild whims of the govern-ment. "What can be avoided whose end is purposed by the mighty government?" Can you remember who wrote that?'

'*Hier in Soweto is net Oswald Mtshali want so skry.*' It was Yster again.

'Nonsense! Such a fatalistic view of life is only found in the Old Testament.'

An argument ensued, with Dudu and Neo siding with me because they considered me more educated than Yster. Solomzi refused to be drawn into the argument which he had so skilfully started to divert attention from the more personal issues we had been discussing. I had passed on to my second stage of intoxica-tion, the argumentative phase. Solomzi who knew me better than any of the others had realized that any argument would do for me now.

'The essential quality of speech is talking,' he said and went into raucous fits of laughter joined by Dudu and Neo. That had been a favourite saying of mine at high school.

'*Kyk hier*, my sister, wasn't it Oswald Mtshali who wrote that?' Yster asked.

'What?' Norma asked.

'*Sê dit weer*, Jack,' he requested Solomzi.

Solomzi repeated the first quotation.

'Isn't that by Mtshali?'

'No.'

'Who said it then?' Yster demanded from Norma.

'Shakespeare.'

'We were both wrong, Jack,' Yster summed up.

How can I ever forget Norma's impressionistic entry into our lives and Solomzi's tragic exit from this world? Norma's eventual departure for America simply became the final unfolding of a pattern, dramatic only because of its unanticipated suddenness and less so because I had foreseen it.

Norma did obtain her temporary residence permit, valid for an initial period of two years but renewable for a further two years. She was also granted a special permit to be resident in Soweto. She got a job at the U.S.I.S. in Jo'burg as a secretary-typist. She had no use for our overcrowded Soweto trains either, because Samoosa drove her to work and back.

In another six months Solomzi bought his own car. He had struck a well-paying job with the Institute of Race Relations. We began to see less and less of them.

Once we invited them to a party, a weekend marathon in honour of the Malombo Jazzmen who had been booked for a visit to the United States. They turned down our invitation because of 'unforeseen commitments'. Solomzi told me later what this meant — they always spent their weekends in town with one or the other of Norma's several white co-workers.

'Jack, *daardie cherrie druk Sol met hom billy* — she's really dragging him by his sex,' Yster remarked. He had become a regular visitor at my place. I found myself warming towards him till I had embraced him as the only friend I had who could organize a drink in the driest of seasons, for which reason I now called him

The Four Seasons.

It happened in the second year of their marriage. She was expecting their first child and was on paid maternity leave.

'She finds life very dull in the township, so I have to drive her to her friends in town as often as I can, which is every day after knocking off from work. Every effing day,' Solomzi said.

'Boy! I guess marriage is for the birds, to judge by your experience. Thank God you got hooked before me,' I commented.

'It isn't so much the fact of marriage,' he said. 'All depends on who tricks you into it. Take your Kedi, for instance. ... May she bear you ten-times-ten kids!'

'Hell! Not that many!'

'She drives me like a slave, Phambi. Sometimes I'm so tired I'm almost asleep behind the wheel. But I must go on driving her to see her friends. What about *my* friends? I tell you it's hopeless. And when we return from these outings I'm mostly pissed. I wonder how I escape being ticketed for driving under the influence!'

They were on their way home from one of their visits when it happened. Solomzi missed a corner and the car ended in a ditch near Uncle Charley's garage.

He died a few hours later at the Baragwanath Hospital.

Norma was treated for shock and discharged.

The funeral was one of the largest Soweto has seen. Most people compared it to Dr Zuma's. A generous sprinkling of whites from the U.S.I.S. and the embassy were present.

Not so long after the funeral Norma arranged with her embassy to be flown back home. She left a few days later.

I have seldom seen Samoosa as excited as he was that afternoon. Yster and I were trying to clear a gargantuan hangover at MaMthethwa's when he joined us.

'I've been looking for you all over the township. Have you heard the news?'

'What news?' we both asked.

'*Shoot ons,* Jack, *wat gebeer?*'

'I heard my whites talking about it at the office. Norma's got a baby boy.'

'This will be very welcome news to Solomzi's parents. Let's go and tell them if they haven't heard already. Here, take a glass and let's celebrate ...'

We finished the half-jack of Oudemeester and ordered another.

The moon was just coming up when we left MaMthethwa's. We were singing Christmas carols.

We got into Samoosa's car and drove to Solomzi's, where we found his parents and Aunt Bessie clustered around a table. Before them was an album. We were offered seats round the table and shown the snaps. They were photos of Solomzi and Norma taken in America.

'Have you heard anything from her recently,' I asked, pointing at a snap of Norma.

'She did send us a postcard shortly after she arrived to tell us she was safe home. We haven't heard from her since,' Solomzi's father replied.

'And to imagine we once thought she was as human as you and me,' Aunt Bessie said.

'It would have been better if she had left after the official period of mourning,' his father continued. 'Is there much consideration and civilization in such irreverence for the dead? Is that the way of educated people?'

'*Shoot hulle,* Jack?' Yster said nudging at Samoosa.

'Have you heard the good news?' Samoosa asked.

'She could at least have left me my grandchild to be my comfort in my old age,' Solomzi's mother said.

'But the good news!'

'What news?' the father enquired.

I cleared my throat, but Samoosa spoke on.

'God on my forefathers!' Solomzi's mother exclaimed at the end, 'we must write to the child.'

'He can't read yet, Mama,' Yster said.

'Yes,' the father said, 'we must ask her to send us the baby's photos.'

'*Yebo*, she must be sent an invitation to come and visit us with the baby,' Aunt Bessie added.

'What shall we call him?' Solomzi's mother asked.

'We'll call him Vusumzi, for in him my son lives again.'

'Would you boys like to join us for a cup of tea?' Aunt Bessie asked.

'No thanks, Auntie,' I said. 'We must be on our way home. It's never safe to move about at night.'

We rose and said goodnight. They thanked us and saw us out.

At Yster's suggestion we clubbed together for the price of a half-jack and six beers and went back to MaMthethwa's where we carried on reminiscing until the early hours of the morning.

A Sunrise on the Veld

Doris Lessing

Every night that winter he said aloud into the dark of the pillow: Half past four! Half past four! till he felt his brain had gripped the words and held them fast. Then he fell asleep at once, as if a shutter had fallen; and lay with his face turned to the clock so that he could see it first thing when he woke.

It was half past four to the minute, every morning. Triumphantly pressing down the alarm-knob of the clock, which the dark half of his mind had outwitted, remaining vigilant all night and counting the hours as he lay relaxed in sleep, he huddled down for a last warm moment under the clothes, playing with the idea of lying abed for this once only. But he played with it for the fun of knowing that it was a weakness he could defeat without effort; just as he set the alarm each night for the delight of the moment when he woke and stretched his limbs, feeling the muscles tighten, and thought: Even my brain — even that! I can control every part of myself.

Luxury of warm rested body, with the arms and legs and fingers waiting like soldiers for a word of command! Joy of knowing that the precious hours were given to sleep voluntarily! — for he had once stayed awake three nights running, to prove that he could, and then worked all day, refusing even to admit that he was tired; and now sleep seemed to him a servant to be commanded and refused.

The boy stretched his frame full-length, touching the wall at his head with his hands, and the bedfoot with his toes; then he sprang out, like a fish leaping from water. And it was cold, cold.

He always dressed rapidly, so as to try and conserve his night-warmth till the sun rose two hours later; but by the time he had on his clothes his hands were numbed and he could scarcely hold his shoes. These he could not put on for fear of waking his parents, who never came to know how early he rose.

As soon as he stepped over the lintel, the flesh of his soles contracted on the chilled earth, and his legs began to ache with cold. It was night: the stars were glittering, the trees standing black and still. He looked for signs of day, for the greying of the edge of a stone, or a lightening in the sky where the sun would rise, but there was nothing yet. Alert as an animal he crept past the dangerous window, standing poised with his hand on the sill for one proudly fastidious moment, looking in at the stuffy blackness of the room where his parents lay.

Feeling for the grass-edge of the path with his toes, he reached inside another window farther along the wall, where his gun had been set in readiness the night before. The steel was icy, and numbed fingers slipped along it, so that he had to hold it in the crook of his arm for safety. Then he tiptoed to the room where the dogs slept, and was fearful that they might have been tempted to go before him; but they were waiting, their haunches crouched in reluctance at the cold, but ears and swinging tails greeting the gun ecstatically. His warning undertone kept them secret and silent till the house was a hundred yards back: then they bolted off into the bush, yelping excitedly. The boy imagined his parents turning in their beds and muttering: Those dogs again! before they were dragged back in sleep; and he smiled scornfully. He always looked back over his shoulder at the house before he passed a wall of trees that shut it from sight. It looked so low and small, crouching there under a tall and brilliant sky. Then he turned his back on it, and on the frowsting sleepers, and forgot them.

He would have to hurry. Before the light grew strong he must be four miles away; and already a tint of green stood in the hollow of a leaf, and the air smelled of morning and the stars were dimming.

He slung the shoes over his shoulder, veld skoen that were crinkled and hard with the dews of a hundred mornings. They would be necessary when the ground became too hot to bear. Now he felt the chilled dust push up between his toes, and he let the muscles of his feet spread and settle into the shapes of the earth; and he thought: I could walk a hundred miles on feet like these! I could walk all day, and never tire!

He was walking swiftly through the dark tunnel of foliage that in daytime was a road. The dogs were invisibly ranging the lower travelways of the bush, and he heard them panting. Sometimes he felt a cold muzzle on his leg before they were off again, scouting for a trail to follow. They were not trained, but free-running companions of the hunt, who often tired of the long stalk before the final shots, and went off on their own pleasure. Soon he could see them, small and wild-looking in a wild strange light, now that the bush stood trembling on the verge of colour, waiting for the sun to paint earth and grass afresh.

The grass stood to his shoulders; and the trees were showering a faint silvery rain. He was soaked; his whole body was clenched in a steady shiver.

Once he bent to the road that was newly scored with animal trails, and regretfully straightened, reminding himself that the pleasure of tracking must wait till another day.

He began to run along the edge of a field, noting jerkily how it was filmed over with fresh spiderweb, so that the long reaches of great black clods seemed netted in glistening grey. He was using the steady lope he had learned by watching the natives, the run that is a dropping of the weight of the body from one feet to the next in a slow balancing movement that never tires, nor shortens the breath; and he felt the blood pulsing down his legs and along his arms, and the exultation and pride of body mounted in him till he was shutting his teeth hard against a violent desire to shout his triumph.

Soon he had left the cultivated part of the farm. Behind him the bush was low and black. In front was a long vlei, acres of long pale grass that sent back a hollowing gleam of light to a satiny sky. Near him thick swathes of grass were bent with the weight of water, and diamond drops sparkled on each frond.

The first bird woke at his feet and at once a flock of them sprang into the air calling shrilly that day had come; and suddenly behind him, the bush woke into song, and he could hear the guinea-fowl calling far ahead of him. That meant they would not be sailing down from their trees into thick grass, and it was for them he had come: he was too late. But he did not mind. He forgot he had come to shoot. He set his legs wide, and balanced from foot to foot, and swung his gun up and down in both hands horizontally, in a kind of improvised exercise, and let his head sink back till it was pillowed in his neck muscles, and watched how above him small rosy clouds floated in a lake of gold.

Suddenly it all rose in him: it was unbearable. He leapt up into

the air, shouting and yelling wild, unrecognizable noises. Then he
began to run, not carefully, as he had before, but madly, like a wild
thing. He was clean crazy, yelling mad with the joy of living and a
superfluity of youth. He rushed down the vlei under a tumult of
crimson and gold, while all the birds of the world sang about him.
He ran in great leaping strides, and shouted as he ran, feeling his
body rise into the crisp rushing air and fall back surely on to sure
feet; and thought briefly, not believing that such a thing could
happen to him, that he could break his ankle any moment, in this
thick tangled grass. He cleared bushes like a duiker, leaped over
rocks; and finally came to a dead stop at a place where the ground
fell abruptly away below him to the river. It had been a two-mile-
long dash through waist-high growth, and he was breathing
hoarsely and could no longer sing. But he poised on a rock and
looked down at stretches of water that gleamed through stooping
trees, and thought suddenly, I am fifteen! Fifteen! The words came
new to him; so that he kept repeating them wonderingly, with
swelling excitement; and he felt the years of his life with his hands,
as if he were counting marbles, each one hard and separate and
compact, each one a wonderful shining thing. That was what he
was: fifteen years of this rich soil, and this slow-moving water, and
air that smelt like a challenge whether it was warm and sultry at
noon, or as brisk as cold water, like it was now.

There was nothing he couldn't do, nothing! A vision came to
him, as he stood there, like when a child hears the word 'eternity'
and tries to understand it, and time takes possession of the mind.
He felt his life ahead of him as a great and wonderful thing,
something that was his; and he said aloud, with the blood rising to
his head: All the great men of the world have been as I am now, and
there is nothing I can't become, nothing I can't do; there is no
country in the world I cannot make part of myself, if I choose. I
contain the world. I can make of it what I want. If I choose, I can
change everything that is going to happen: it depends on me, and
what I decide now.

The urgency, and the truth and the courage of what his voice was
saying exulted him so that he began to sing again, at the top of his
voice, and the sound went echoing down the river gorge. He
stopped for the echo, and sang again: stopped and shouted. That
was what he was! — he sang, if he chose; and the world had to
answer him.

And for minutes he stood there, shouting and singing and waiting for the lovely eddying sound of the echo; so that his own new strong thoughts came back and washed round his head, as if someone were answering him and encouraging him: till the gorge was full of soft voices clashing back and forth from rock to rock over the river. And then it seemed as if there was a new voice. He listened, puzzled, for it was not his own. Soon he was leaning forward, all his nerves alert, quite still: somewhere close to him there was a noise that was no joyful bird, nor tinkle of falling water, nor ponderous movement of cattle.

There it was again. In the deep morning hush that held his future and his past, was a sound of pain, and repeated over and over: it was a kind of shortened scream, as if someone, something, had no breath to scream. He came to himself, looked about him, and called for the dogs. They did not appear: they had gone off on their own business, and he was alone. Now he was clean sober, all the madness gone. His heart beating fast, because of that frightened screaming, he stepped carefully off the rock and went towards a belt of trees. He was moving cautiously, for not so long ago he had seen a leopard in just this spot.

At the end of the trees he stopped and peered, holding his gun ready; he advanced, looking steadily about him, his eyes narrowed. Then, all at once, in the middle of a step, he faltered, and his face was puzzled. He shook his head impatiently, as if he doubted his own sight.

There, between two trees, against a background of gaunt black rocks, was a figure from a dream, a strange beast that was horned and drunken-legged, but like something he had never even imagined. It seemed to be ragged. It looked like a small buck that had black ragged tufts of fur standing up irregularly all over it, with patches of raw flesh beneath ... but the patches of rawness were disappearing under moving black and came again elsewhere; and all the time the creature screamed, in small gasping screams, and leaped drunkenly from side to side, as if it were blind.

Then the boy understood: it *was* a buck. He ran closer, and again stood still, stopped by a new fear. Around him the grass was whispering and alive. He looked wildly about, and then down. The ground was black with ants, great energetic ants that took no notice of him, but hurried and scurried towards the fighting shape, like glistening black water flowing through the grass.

And, as he drew in his breath and pity and terror seized him, the beast fell and the screaming stopped. Now he could hear nothing but one bird singing, and the sound of the rustling, whispering ants.

He peered over at the writhing blackness that jerked convulsively with the jerking nerves. It grew quieter. There were small twitches from the mass that still looked vaguely like the shape of a small animal.

It came into his mind that he should shoot it and end its pain; and he raised the gun. Then he lowered it again. The buck could no longer feel; its fighting was a mechanical protest of the nerves. But it was not that which made him put down the gun. It was a swelling feeling of rage and misery and protest that expressed itself in the thought: If I had not come it would have died like this: so why should I interfere? All over the bush things like this happen; they happen all the time; this is how life goes on, by living things dying in anguish. He gripped the gun between his knees and felt in his own limbs the myriad swarming pain of the twitching animal that could no longer feel, and set his teeth, and said over and over again under his breath: I can't stop it. I can't stop it. There is nothing I can do.

He was glad the buck was unconscious and had gone past suffering so that he did not have to make a decision to kill it even when he was feeling with his whole body: this is what happens, this is how things work.

It was right — that was what he was feeling. *It was right and nothing could alter it.*

The knowledge of fatality, of what has to be, had gripped him and for the first time in his life; and he was left unable to make any movement of brain or body, except to say: 'Yes, yes. That is what living is.' It had entered his flesh and his bones and grown into the farthest corners of his brain and would never leave him. And at that moment he could not have performed the smallest action of mercy, knowing as he did, having lived on it all his life, the vast unalterable cruel veld, where at any moment one might stumble over a skull or crush the skeleton of some small creature.

Suffering, sick, and angry, but also grimly satisfied with his new stoicism, he stood there leaning on his rifle, and watched the seething black mound grow smaller. At his feet, now, were ants trickling back with pink fragments in their mouths, and there was a fresh acid smell in his nostrils. He sternly controlled the uselessly convulsing muscles of his empty stomach, and reminded himself: the ants must eat too! At the same time he found that the tears were streaming down his face, and his clothes were soaked with the sweat of that other creature's pain.

The shape had grown small. Now it looked like nothing recognizable. He did not know how long it was before he saw the blackness thin, and bits of white showed through, shining in the sun — yes, there was the sun, just up, glowing over the rocks. Why, the whole thing could not have taken longer than a few minutes.

He began to swear, as if the shortness of the time was in itself unbearable, using the words he had heard his father say. He strode forward, crushing ants with each step, and brushing them off his clothes, till he stood above the skeleton, which lay sprawled under a small bush. It was clean-picked. It might have been lying there years, save that on the white bones were pink fragments of gristle. About the bones ants were ebbing away, their pincers full of meat.

The boy looked at them, big black ugly insects. A few were standing and gazing up at him with small glittering eyes.

'Go away!' he said to the ants, very coldly. 'I am not for you — not just yet, at any rate. Go away.' And he fancied that the ants turned and went away.

He bent over the bones and touched the sockets in the skull; that was where the eyes were, he thought incredulously, remembering the liquid dark eyes of a buck. And then he bent the slim foreleg bone, swinging it horizontally in his palm.

That morning, perhaps an hour ago, this small creature had been stepping proud and free through the bush, feeling the chill on its hide even as he himself had done, exhilarated by it. Proudly stepping the earth, tossing its horns, frisking a pretty white tail, it had sniffed the cold morning air. Walking like kings and conquerors it had moved through this free-held bush, where each blade of grass grew for it alone, and where the river ran pure sparkling water for its slaking.

And then — what had happened? Such a swift surefooted thing could surely not be trapped by a swarm of ants?

The boy bent curiously to the skeleton. Then he saw that the back leg that lay uppermost and strained out in the tension of death was snapped midway in the thigh, so that broken bones jutted over each other uselessly. So that was it! Limping into the ant-masses it could not escape, once it had sensed the danger. Yes, but how had the leg been broken? Had it fallen, perhaps? Impossible, a buck was too light and graceful. Had some jealous rival horned it?

What could possibly have happened? Perhaps some Africans had thrown stones at it, as they do, trying to kill it for meat, and had broken its leg. Yes, that must be it.

Even as he imagined the crowd of running, shouting natives, and the flying stones, and the leaping buck, another picture came into his mind. He saw himself, on any one of these bright ringing mornings, drunk with excitement, taking a snap shot at some half-seen buck. He saw himself with the gun lowered, wondering whether he had missed or not; and thinking at last that it was late, and he wanted his breakfast, and it was not worthwhile to track miles after an animal that would very likely get away from him in any case.

For a moment he would not face it. He was a small boy again, kicking sulkily at the skeleton, hanging his head, refusing to accept the responsibility.

Then he straightened up, and looked down at the bones with an odd expression of dismay, all the anger gone out of him. His mind went quite empty: all around him he could see trickles of ants disappearing into the grass. The whispering noise was faint and dry, like the rustling of a cast snakeskin.

At last he picked up his gun and walked homewards. He was telling himself half defiantly that he wanted his breakfast. He was telling himself that it was getting very hot, much too hot to be out roaming the bush.

Really, he was tired. He walked heavily, not looking where he put his feet. When he came within sight of his home he stopped, knitting his brows. There was something he had to think out. The death of that small animal was a thing that concerned him, and he was by no means finished with it. It lay at the back of his mind uncomfortably.

Soon, the very next morning, he would get clear of everybody and go to the bush and think about it.

The Soldier without an Ear

Paul Zeleza

Many years ago, while I was still a student, I did some research for one of my history lecturers. He was writing a doctoral thesis and he was trying to find out the reaction of the people of the country to the two World Wars. It was after I had been to several villages and seen quite a number of people who had participated in or witnessed one of the wars or both that I came to Biwi village. I first went to the chief and briefed him on the purpose of my visit. He was co-operative and directed me to the house of Baba Fule, the soldier who had fought in both wars.

'He is an interesting man. You'll like him,' said the chief.

When I got to Baba Fule's house, I agreed with the chief. Baba Fule's house was modest and clean. With its corrugated iron sheets, glass windows and four-cornered structure, it had a touch of the town and was almost out of place in the village. There was nobody outside. I knocked. I was told to enter. I found a very aged man sitting on a chair doing nothing. Save for a few black dots of hair, his head was white. His sunken, nearly-blind eyes gazed at me with surprise.

'Who are you?' he asked me. I introduced myself. He sat for a moment, reflecting on where he could have met me or what relationship I had with him.

'Are you Solomon?'

'No, I'm not.' I told him that I did not come from his village.

'Then, what do you want here?' I explained the purpose of my visit.

'So you want to write a book about me. Ma, ma, ma! Nanyoni, come and hear what this young man wants to do. He wants to write a book about me. Ma, ma, ma!'

Presently, a very old woman, walking with a stick, with her back permanently bent and thereby having the height of an average twelve-year-old girl, came into the room. She extended her weak, thin and wrinkled arm to me. Her face was so wrinkled that if anyone from outer space saw her before setting his eyes on anyone else, he would form a mean impression of the beauty of human beings. He would think our faces are a collection of mouths with a nose in between and two small eyes for decoration. Baba Fule looked much younger and energetic when compared with her.

'This young man wants to write a book about me,' Baba Fule excitedly told his wife. The folds on her face extended, indicating that she was smiling or doing something of the kind.

'Are you at school?' Baba Fule asked me.

'Yes, I am,' I replied.

'What standard are you doing?' he asked. Telling him that I was in my third year at the university would not mean much to him, so I told him that I was doing Standard Fifteen.

'Standard Fifteen. Ma, ma, ma, the children of these days. Standard Fifteen. Ma, ma, ma.'

'What is Standard Fifteen?' his wife asked.

'As many as the fingers on your hands and the toes of one foot,' he explained, smiling, showing his partially-filled gums.

'Has he more standards that Josiah and Aleck?' his wife enquired.

'Yes, Josiah and Aleck have twelve standards.' Baba Fule told me who Josiah and Aleck were. They were his grandchildren. He had eleven children, three of whom had died while they were still young. The eight were still alive and were gifted with big families as he had been.

'If I count all my grandchildren, they reach sixty-nine, and some of these have children of their own,' he said, smiling contentedly.

'Where do they all live?' I asked.

'They live in towns. If they all came back, this village would be too small to accommodate them. But they all come here from time to time. I live with two of my great grandchildren here, a boy and a girl.'

'You've been blessed,' I said.

'Oh, yes, very much. Everything we eat and wear comes from our children and grandchildren. All we do is sit down, basking in the sun, waiting for the day.' He then boasted of the cars some of his children and grandchildren had.

'The world has changed,' he said. 'In my youth there were no cars, only bicycles, and even then only the very rich could afford them. In fact, only the Azungu possessed them. But these days, even children have bicycles and as for cars, even women drive them! In my youth many children did not go to school. Anybody who reached Standard Three was considered very educated. But these days, you get almost every child in school. You know, small children this high,' he indicated with his stick, 'are doing Standard Three. I finished my Standard Two at your age.' He paused, smiling at me. I was fascinated.

'If it were possible, would you exchange your life of those days for the life of these days?' I asked.

'The life these days is easier and more comfortable. But still I would not exchange the life I had.'

'Why?'

'There are many reasons. As boys, we had more fun and adventure in our days than the children of these days. You see, all that the children do these days is go to school from an early age and be stuffed with books in foreign languages and mostly about foreign ways so that they lose their own things. Indeed, now things seem to have no direction, no purpose. You see, in the old days, a man of my age and my family would have left this village long ago and founded his own village and would have been chief. But today, my wife and I are left alone to look after ourselves. I don't complain about my children. They help me. I have some friends who are not in such a fortunate position. However, I still feel something is wrong. It's like a basket-weaver exchanging his best baskets for a bag of maize only to find out that it's full of sand.' Baba Fule went on telling me about his youth with deliberate emphasis to show how superior it was to our youth. I was too absorbed with the conversation to realize that I had not begun my interview.

'Baba, I would now like to ask you a few questions about the two World Wars.'

'Oh, yes, the book. I forgot. Forgive me, my son. I'm feeling cold. Let's go and sit in the sun.'

I offered to carry his chair, but he insisted on carrying it alone. The sun was quite high, and the heat was oppressive. I pretended not to mind.

'Come and sit on this side,' he told me. One side of his face had no ear. It was a memorable souvenir of his life as a soldier.

'You want me to tell you about my whole life or my life as a soldier?' he asked.

'Your life as a soldier,' I replied.

'Alright. I joined the army when the Great War broke out between the Germans and the British. I was already a man by then with a family of four. The training did not take long. I first fought in Tanganyika. There, I got the first big excitement of my life. You know what it was?' he asked me, smilingly.

'No, I don't,' I replied, smiling back.

'I killed a Mzungu, a German. It sounds strange, eh? I don't know how I can explain it. But I was wildly excited. Gradually, shooting them became commonplace. Of course, we also killed the Africans on the side of the Germans, but that was not as exciting as killing the Azungu. Then, in 1916, I was sent to Egypt where fierce battles were being fought. Egypt, as you know, is a land of Arabs. I will always remember it for one thing.' He paused as he saw a young boy standing in the *Khonde*.

'That's the boy I was telling you about. Imagine such a young boy in Standard Five. Richard, come and greet your brother here.' The young boy came and greeted me shyly. Then Baba Fule told him to go away. The boy reluctantly left us.

'What was I saying?' Baba Fule asked me.

'You were saying that Egypt is a land of Arabs and you'll always remember it.'

'Oh, yes. You see, the Arabs are the ones who enslaved our fathers and grandfathers, destroying our villages and all that. I'm sure you learn that at school.'

'Yes, we do,' I replied.

'And you know what? Well,' Baba Fule looked around to see if anyone was listening, 'you see, I and some of my friends slept with their women. Well, don't write that in the book.' He gave a small laugh. I felt slightly embarrassed. But I managed to share his laughter.

'Moreover, for the first time I met a lot of Africans from other countries. It was an unforgettable experience. I remember I had a friend from Kenya. He was ... well, we can forget that.'

'No, tell me,' I pleaded.

'It's a very long story,' he objected.

'It doesn't matter.'

'Alright. I'll cut it short. This friend of mine was called Murasa.

One day he was in the bush with a small group of soldiers. In the distance he saw white soldiers. He ordered his men to fire. The other side also opened fire. Before long, half of Murasa's men lay dead. Murasa surrendered. You know what happened?' Baba Fule asked me.

'No, I don't,' I replied.

'The white soldiers were not German but the British.' I gave a sigh. Baba Fule nodded his white head while muttering. 'Yes, yes, they were British. And Murasa was sent for trial and later executed. It was a tragic incident.' For a moment Baba Fule was silent, as if composing what he would say next. I was fascinated by him. He looked frail and yet his voice was strong and his memory unfolded itself vividly before me.

'When the war ended,' Baba Fule resumed, 'we came back here. We arrived in March 1919. But we were in for a lot of disappointments. The government had promised us a lot of things when we joined the army, but when we came back things were as bad as they had been before. Most of my colleagues found that their wives had remarried and their land had been taken away. It was difficult to start again, especially in the face of such unfulfilled promises. Fortunately, I found my wife waiting for me and my land unoccupied by anybody. However, I was not all that lucky. Two of my four children had died during my absence.'

'Oh, I am sorry,' I muttered.

'Well, it's gone now. You know, it's surprising how we forget our troubles. A woman may claim that she will never marry again after her husband is dead, and a short while later she marries and forgets her first husband. Anyway, that's how we're made.'

'It's true,' I said. 'What would you describe as your most important experiences during the war?' I asked him.

'Hm, that's difficult. I enjoyed seeing so many different new places and meeting many different people. Oh, yes, I forgot to tell you this. When I came back here after the war, I and a few other people were called to Zomba. There we were awarded medals by the governor. I was awarded two medals, one for bravery, the other for good conduct. Wait! I'll show you.' Baba Fule rose and went into the house. He came out with a wooden, silver-rimmed box. He opened it with a key. There were five medals, all shining brightly and carefully laid in the box. He picked up two medals with care and showed them to me.

'These are the medals,' he said, hardly concealing the fact that he was pleased with himself. When he thought I had stared at the medals sufficiently, he laid them back in the box.

'What was I saying again?' he said, after he had closed the box.

'I asked about your most important experiences during the war.'

'Oh, yes. Apart from these medals and the other good experiences of the war, there were some things which seriously troubled me and my colleagues. During the war, we became aware that the Azungu, for all their pretences, were just like us. We fought together. We shared the same hopes and fears. We were all vulnerable to the deadly power of bullets. Indeed, we had the pleasure of killing the Azungu who were enemies of our Azungu. At home they had called us savages and baboons, but in the battlefield we were no different from them.

'You really experienced a lot of things,' I commented.

'Oh, yes. We did. The war was tragic, too. I saw many of my friends die. It was horrible. People died like chickens afflicted with *chitopa*. Most of us were disturbed. We were dying for a war which was not ours, which we did not understand.'

'Did you leave the army after the war?'

'Yes, but only for a short time. Military life fascinated me and still does. It's the discipline, the order and the sense of danger and adventure. And you see, my son, when you are a soldier, you gradually acquire the greatest mark of courage, the courage not to fear death. I rejoined the army in 1920. But between that year and 1939 when war flared up again, everything was relatively normal.

'The Second World War was more dangerous, with more people and countries involved and with more dangerous weapons. In that war I fought in Burma and India. I was thrilled to see the Amwenye in their own home. When they are here, these people are respectable. You should see them at home. They are very poor. They live in deplorable conditions. The way they pile on top of one another is amazing. One man can have as many as twenty children.'

At that moment, a girl with a pot of water on her head entered the house. Baba Fule called her.

'Margaret, come and see your brother here.' She came and greeted me with her eyes staring at the ground and some of her fingers in her mouth.

'Put some water on the fire and make us some tea,' he told her.

'Yes, *agogo*,' the young girl said, leaving.

'What was I saying again? I've a bad memory these days. It's the toll of age.'

'You were talking about the Amwenye you saw in Burma and India.'

'Oh, yes. Now, my experiences in that war were essentially the same as those of the first Great War. The only difference was that everything was on a bigger scale. However, there was one thing that was fundamentally different. Do you know what it was?'

'No, I don't.'

'Try and guess.'

'I've no idea.'

'Have you learnt about the Second World War at school?'

'Yes, I have.'

'What did they teach you?'

'It was a war between Britain with her allies and Germany with her allies.'

'Yes, that's right. But, I mean, what did they give you as the reasons for the war?'

'There were many. But, basically, they were fighting against Hitler who wanted to dominate the world.'

'You're clever, young man. That's it. That's what I wanted. This is what disturbed some of us. The British were fighting against domination and yet they dominated us. Was it not only reasonable for us to do the same?' I had read and heard about this contradiction and its implications. What fascinated me was to hear it fresh from one who had actually fought in the war.

'Should I bring the tea outside?' asked the girl.

'Yes, bring it here,' answered Baba Fule. The girl brought a tea-pot and two cups. She poured the tea for us. It was almost midday and the heat was unbearable. However, I forced myself to drink the tea.

'Was I telling you about the Amwenye in India and Burma?' asked Baba Fule after a couple of sips.

'No, you were telling me about what troubled you about the war.'

'Oh, yes. In that war, I almost died. A bomb blew up near where we were hiding. A few of my colleagues died, and I was blinded. I was taken to hospital. I stayed there for five months. After that, I was able to see again, and almost immediately I went to the battlefield.'

'Hm,' I sighed.

'Yes, my son, I've tasted death over and over again so that the idea of dying does not frighten me, not even a little bit.'

'So, your experiences were almost the same in this war as in the first?'

'Yes. I was struck by the senselessness of the whole thing in the guise of peace and civilization. The indiscriminate slaughter of human life, destruction of property and social life. I came to the conclusion that it would have been incomparably better if the Azungu had not come here. Our frequent small wars were not so disruptive by any means. You know what, my son?' He looked at me. His eyes shone excitedly.

'No, I don't,' I replied, anxious to hear what he wanted to say.

'I don't have your standards. But I've more years and therefore more wisdom. The Azungu have a passion for grand things, be they good or evil.' He paused and smiled at me with both his lips and eyes. The girl brought some food.

'No, put it inside. I can see your brother here is perspiring. Let's go inside.' I was relieved. It was cool inside. We washed hands and he said a prayer before we began to eat. There were two dishes of relish. He hardly dipped his hand into the dish of vegetables. I wondered how on earth he managed to munch the meat with virtually no teeth in his mouth.

'I forgot to ask you where your home is.'

'I come from Lilongwe,' I said.

'Which side of Lilongwe?'

'Nathenje.'

'You know this man Mchenga?'

'No, I don't.'

'You're too young. You wouldn't know him. But I'm sure your parents know him. He is a friend of mine. He also fought in both wars. In the second war he fought in Egypt. And you know what? He saw Churchill himself when he came for inspection of the British soldiers. You should hear him talk about it. It's so amazing. We all envy him.'

For a while we ate in silence. When we had finished, he resumed his story.

'The war ended in 1945 and we came back here at the beginning of 1946. Just as after the first Great War, I was awarded two medals for exceptional bravery and good conduct.'

Baba Fule opened the box again and took the two medals and showed them to me. I admired him. When I told him so, he was visibly moved and pleased.

'And this medal,' he picked up the remaining medal, 'is the one I was awarded in 1957 on retirement for a long and meritorious service. My life is in these medals, my son, my whole life.' He was serious.

'I'm very grateful for the assistance you've given me, Baba,' I thanked him.

'When is the book coming?'

'It depends. One, two or three years from now.'

'I'll be dead by then.'

'I don't think so.'

'No, my son. I'm a very old man. I don't know when I was born, but when the first missionaries came into the country, I was a boy.'

'I would like to say goodbye to *agogo*.'

Baba Fule called his wife. She limped into the room. I bade them farewell. I promised that I would come again someday. Baba Fule accompanied me for a few yards. I felt there was one thing he hadn't told me.

'Baba, did you get your ear cut during the wars?' I asked.

'Oh this. Ha! Ha! Ha! No, my son. It was my wife who cut if off one day in my sleep for being unfaithful to her. But don't write that in the book. Go well, my boy.'

I have not kept my promise that I would go to see Baba Fule again. But I think it's too late now. I am sure he has departed for the other world together with his wife.

Riva

Richard Rive

A cold, misty July afternoon about twenty years ago. I first met Riva Lipschitz under the most unusual circumstances. At that time I was a first-year student majoring in English at university, one of the rare coloured students then enrolled at Cape Town. When I first saw her Riva's age seemed indefinable. Late thirties? Forty perhaps? Certainly more than twenty years older than I was. The place we met in was as unusual as her appearance. The Rangers' hut at the top of Table Mountain near the Hely Hutchinson Reservoir, three-thousand feet above Cape Town.

George, Leonard and I had been climbing all day. George was talkative, an extrovert, given to clowning. Leonard was his exact opposite, shy and introspective. We had gone through high school together but after matriculating they had gone to work while I had won a scholarship which enabled me to proceed to university. We had been climbing without rest all afternoon, scrambling over rugged rocks damp with bracken and heavy with mist. Twice we were lost on the path from India Ravine through Echo Valley. Now soaking wet and tired we were finally in the vicinity of the Rangers' hut where we knew we would find shelter and warmth. Some ranger or other would be off duty and keep the fire warm and going. Someone with a sense of humour had called the hut *At Last*. It couldn't be the rangers for they never spoke English. On the way we passed the hut belonging to the white Mountain Club, and slightly below that was another hut reserved for members of the coloured club. I made some remark about the white club house and the fact that prejudice had permeated even to the top of Table Mountain.

'For that matter we would not even be allowed into the coloured Mountain Club hut,' George remarked, serious for once.

'And why not?'

'Because, dear brother Paul, to get in you can't only be coloured, but you must also be not too coloured. You must have the right complexion, the right sort of hair, the right address and speak the right sort of Walmer Estate English.'

'You mean I might not make it?'

'I mean exactly that.'

I made rapid mental calculations. I was rather dark, had short, curly hair, came from Caledon Street in District Six, but spoke English reasonably well. After all, I was majoring in it at a white university. What more could one want?

'I'm sure that at a pinch I could make it,' I teased George. 'I speak English beautifully and am educated well beyond my intelligence.'

'My dear Paul, it won't help. You are far too coloured, University of Cape Town and all. You are far, far too brown. And in addition you have a lousy address.'

I collapsed in mock horror. 'You can't hold all that against me.'

Leonard grinned. He was not one for saying much.

We trudged on, instinctively skirting both club huts as widely as possible, until we reached *At Last*, which was ten minutes slogging away, just over the next ridge. A large main room with a very welcome fire going in the cast-iron stove. How the hell did they get that stove up there when our haversacks felt like lead? Running off the main room were two tiny bedrooms belonging to each of the rangers. We removed damp haversacks and sleeping bags then took off damp boots and stockings. Both rangers were off duty and made room for us at the fire. They were small, wiry Plattelanders; a hard breed of men with wide-eyed, yellow faces, short hair and high cheekbones. They spoke a pleasant, soft, gutteral Afrikaans with a distinct Malmesbury brogue, and broke into easy laughter especially when they tried to speak English. The smell of warming bodies filled the room and steam rose from our wet shirts and shorts. It became uncomfortably hot and I felt sleepy, so decided to retire to one of the bedrooms, crawl into my bag and read myself to sleep. I lit a lantern and quietly left the group. George was teasing the rangers and insisting that they speak English. I was reading a novel about the massacre in the ravines of Babi Yar, gripping and revolting; a bit out of place in the unnatural calm at the top of a cold, wet mountain. I was beginning to doze off comfortably when the main door of the hut burst open and a blast of cold air swept through the entire place, almost extinguishing the lantern. Before I could shout anything there were loud protests from the main room. The door slammed shut again and then followed what sounded like a muffled apology. A long pause, then I made out George saying something. There was a short snort which was followed by peals of loud, uncontrolled laughter. I felt it was uncanny. The snort, then the rumbling laughter growing in intensity, then stopping abruptly.

By now I was wide awake and curious to know to whom the laugh belonged, though far too self-conscious to join the group immediately. I strained to hear scraps of conversation. Now and then I could make out George's voice and the low, soft Afrikaans of the rangers. There was also another voice which sounded feminine, but nevertheless harsh and screechy. My curiosity was getting the better of me. I climbed out of the sleeping bag and as unobtrusively as possible joined the group around the fire. The newcomer was a gaunt, angular white woman, extremely unattractive, looking incongruous in heavy, ill-fitting mountaineering clothes. She was the centre of the discussion and enjoying it. She was in the middle of making a point when she spotted me. Her finger remained poised in mid-air.

'And who may I ask is that?' She stared at me. I looked back into her hard, expressionless grey eyes.

'Will someone answer me?'

'Who?' George asked grinning at my obvious discomfort.

'Him. That's who.'

'Oh him?' George laughed. 'He's Paul. He's the greatest literary genius the coloured people have produced this decade. He's written a poem.'

'How exciting,' she dismissed me. The others laughed. They were obviously under her spell.

'Let me introduce you. This is Professor Paul. First year B.A., University of Cape Town.'

'Cut it out,' I said very annoyed at him. George ignored my remark.

'And you are? I have already forgotten.'

She made a mock, ludicrous bow. 'Riva Lipschitz. Madame Riva Lipschitz. The greatest Jewish watch-repairer and mountaineer in Cape Town. Display shop, 352 Long Street.'

'Alright, you've made your point. Professor Paul — Madame Riva Lipschitz.'

I mumbled a greeting, keeping well in the background. I was determined not to participate in any conversation. I found George's flattering her loathsome. The bantering continued to the amusement of the two rangers. Leonard smiled sympathetically at me. I remained poker-faced waiting for an opportunity when I could slip away. George made some amusing remark (I was not listening) and Riva snorted and started to laugh. So that was where it came from. She saw the look of surprise on my face and stopped abruptly.

'What's wrong, Professor? Don't you like the way I laugh?'

'I'm sorry, I wasn't even thinking of it.'

'It makes no difference whether you were or not. Nevertheless I hate being ignored. If the others can treat me with the respect due to me, why can't you? I'm like a queen, am I not George?' I wasn't sure whether she was serious or not.

'You certainly are like a queen.'

'Everyone loves me except the Professor. Maybe he thinks too much.'

'Maybe he thinks too much of himself,' George added.

She snorted and started to laugh at his witticism. George glowed with pride. I took in her ridiculous figure and dress. She was wearing a little knitted skullcap, far too small for her, from which wisps of mousey hair was sticking. A thin face, hard around the mouth and grey eyes, with a large nose I had seen in caricatures of Jews. She seemed flat-chested under her thick jersey which ran down to incredible stick-thin legs stuck into heavy woollen stockings and heavily studded climbing boots.

'Come on, Paul, be nice to Riva,' George encouraged.

'Madame Riva Lipschitz, thank you. Don't you think I look like a queen, Professor?'

I maintained my frigid silence.

'Your Professor obviously does not seem over-friendly. Don't you like whites, Professor? I like everyone. I came over specially to be friendly with you people.'

'Whom are you referring to as *you people*?' I was getting angry. She seemed temporarily thrown off her guard at my reaction, but immediately controlled herself and broke into a snort.

'The Professor is extremely sensitive. You should have warned me. He doesn't like me but we shall remain friends all the same; won't we, Professor?'

She shot out her hand for me to kiss. I ignored it. She turned back to George and for the rest of her stay pretended I was not present. When everyone was busy talking I slipped out quietly and returned to the bedroom.

Although falling asleep, I could pick up scraps of conversation. George seemed to be explaining away my reaction, playing the clown to her queen. Then they forgot all about me. I must have dozed off for I awoke suddenly to find someone shaking my shoulder. It was Leonard.

'Would you like to come with us?'

'Where to?'

'Riva's Mountain Club hut. She's invited us over for coffee, and to meet Simon, whoever he is.'

'No, I don't think I'll go.'

'You mustn't take her too seriously.'

'I don't. Only I don't like her type and the way George is playing up to her. Who the hell does she think she is, after all? What does she want with us?'

'I really don't know. You heard she said she was a watch-repairer somewhere in Long Street. Be reasonable, Paul. She's just trying to be friendly.'

'While playing the bloody queen? Whom does she think she is because she's white.'

'Don't be like that. Come along with us. She's just another person.'

George appeared grinning widely. He attempted an imitation of Riva's snort.

'You coming or not?' he asked laughing. For that moment I disliked him intensely.

'I'm certainly not.' I rolled over in my bag to sleep.

'Alright, if that's how you feel.'

I heard Riva calling for him, then after a time she shouted 'Goodbye, Professor, see you again some time.' Then she snorted and they went laughing out at the door. The rangers were speaking softly and I joined them around the fire then fell asleep there. I dreamt of Riva striding with heavy, impatient boots and thin-stick legs over mountains of dead bodies in the ravines of Babi Yar. She was snorting and laughing while pushing bodies aside, climbing ever upwards over dead arms and legs.

It must have been much later when I awoke to the door's opening and a stream of cold air rushing into the room. The fire had died down and the rangers were sleeping in their rooms. George and Leonard were stomping and beating the cold out of their bodies.

'You awake, Paul?' George shouted. Leonard shook me gently.

'What scared you?' George asked. 'Why didn't you come and have coffee with the queen of Table Mountain?'

'I can't stand her type. I wonder how you can.'

'Come off it, Paul. She's great fun.' George attempted a snort and then collapsed with laughter.

'Shut up, you fool. You'll wake up the rangers. What the hell did she want here?'

George sat up, tears running down his cheeks. He spluttered and it produced more laughter. 'She was just being friendly, dear brother Paul, just being friendly. Fraternal greetings from her Mountain Club.'

'Her white Mountain Club?'

'Well yes, if you put it that way, her white Mountain Club. She could hardly join the coloured one, now, could she? Wrong hair, wrong address, wrong laugh.'

'I don't care where she goes as long as you keep her away from me. I have no need to play up to Jews and whites.'

'Now really, Paul,' George seemed hurt. 'Are you anti-Semitic as well as being anti-white?' My remark must have hit home.

'No, I'm only anti-Riva Lipschitz.'

'Well anyhow, I like the way she laughs.' He attempted another imitation, but when he started to snort he choked and collapsed to the floor coughing and spluttering. I rolled over in my bag to sleep.

Three months later I was in the vicinity of Upper Long Street. George worked as a clerk at a furniture store in Bree Street. I had been busy with an assignment in the Hiddingh Hall library and had finished earlier than expected. I had not seen him since we had last gone mountaineering, so strolled across to the place where he worked. I wanted to ask about himself, what he had been doing since last we met, about Riva. A senior clerk told me that he had not come in that day. I wandered around aimlessly, at a loss what to do next. I peered into second-hand shops without any real interest.

It was late afternoon on a dull, overcast day and it was rapidly getting darker with the promise of rain in the air. Upper Long Street and its surrounding lanes seemed more depressing, more beaten up than the rest of the city. Even more so than District Six. Victorian double-storeyed buildings containing mean shops on the ground-floors spilled over into mean side streets and lanes. To catch a bus home meant walking all the way down to the bottom of Adderley Street. I might as well walk all the way back. Caledon Street, the noise, dirt and squalor. My mood was as depressing as my immediate surroundings. I did not wish to stay where I was and at the same time did not wish to go home immediately. What was the number she had said? 352 or 325? I peered through the windows of second-hand bookshops without any wish to go inside and browse. 352, yes that was it. Or 325? In any case I had no money to buy books even if I had the inclination to do so. Had George been at work he might have been able to shake me out of this mood, raise my spirits.

I was now past the swimming baths. A dirty fly-spotted delicatessen store. There was no number on the door, but the name was boldly displayed. *Madeira Fruiterers*. Must be owned by some homesick Portuguese. Next to it what seemed like a dark and dingy watchmaker's. *Lipschitz — Master Jewellers*. This must be it. I decided to enter. A shabby, squat, balding man adjusted an eyepiece he was wearing and looked up from a work-bench cluttered with assorted, broken watches.

'Excuse me, are you Mr Lipschitz?' I wondered whether I should add 'Master Jeweller'.

'What exactly do you want?' He had not answered my question. 'What can I do for you?' His accent was guttural and foreign. I thought of Babi Yar. I was about to apologize and say that I had made some mistake when from the far side of the shop came an unmistakable snort.

'My goodness, if it isn't the Professor!' and then the familiar laugh. Riva came from behind a counter. My eyes had become accustomed to the gloomy interior. The squat man was working from the light filtering in through a dirty window. Rickety showcases and counters cluttered with watches and cheap trinkets. A cat-bin, still wet and smelling pungently, stood against the far counter.

'What brings the Professor here? Coming to visit me?' She

nodded to the squat man indicating that all was in order. He had
already shoved back his eyepiece and was immersed in his work.

'Come to visit the queen?'

This was absurd. I could not imagine anything less regal, more
incongruous. Riva, a queen. As gaunt as she had looked in the
Rangers' hut. Now wearing an unattractive blouse and old-
fashioned skirt. Her face as narrow, strained and unattractive as
ever. I had to say something, explain my presence.

'I was just passing.'

'That's what they all say. George said so last time.'

What the hell did that mean? I started to feel uncomfortable. She
looked at me almost coyly. Then she turned to the squat man.

'Simon, I think I'll pack up now. I have a visitor.' He showed no
sign that he had heard her. She took a shabby coat from a hook.

'Will you be late tonight?' she asked him. Simon grumbled some
unintelligible reply. Was this Simon whom George and Leonard
had met? Simon the mountaineer? He looked most unlike a mountaineer. Who the hell was he then? Her boss? Husband? Lover?
Lipschitz — the Master Jeweller? Or was she Lipschitz, the Master
Jeweller? That seemed most unlikely. Riva nodded to me to follow.
I did so as there was no alternative. Outside it was dark already.

'I live two blocks down. Come along and have some tea.' She did
not wait for a reply but began walking briskly, taking long strides. I
followed as best I could half a pace behind.

'Walk next to me,' she almost commanded. I did so. Why was I
going with her? The last thing I wanted was tea.

'Nasty weather,' she said. 'Bad for climbing.' Table Mountain
was wrapped in a dark mist. It was obviously ridiculous for anyone
to climb at five o'clock on a weekday afternoon in heavy weather
like this. Nobody would be crazy enough. Except George perhaps.

'George,' she said as if reading my thoughts. 'George. What was
the other one's name?'

'Leonard.'

'Oh yes, Leonard, I haven't seen him since the mountain. How
is he getting on?' I was panting to keep up with her. 'I don't see
much of them except when we go climbing together. Leonard
works in Epping and George is in Bree Street.'

'I know about George.' How the hell did she?

'I've come from his work. I wanted to see him but he hasn't come
in today.'

'Yes, I knew he wouldn't be in. So you came to see me instead? I somehow knew that one day you would put in an appearance.'

How the hell did she know? Was she in contact with George? I remained quiet, out of breath with the effort of keeping up with her. What on earth made me go into the shop of Lipschitz — Master Jeweller? Who the hell was Lipschitz — Master Jeweller?

The conversation had stopped. She continued the brisk pace, taking her fast, incongruous strides. Like stepping from rock to rock up Blinkwater Ravine, or Babi Yar.

'Here we are.' She stopped abruptly in front of an old triple-storeyed Victorian building with brown paint peeling off its walls. On the upper floors were wide balconies ringed with wrought-iron gates. The main entrance was cluttered with spilling refuse bins.

'I'm on the first floor.'

We mounted a rickety staircase, then a landing and a long, dark passage lit at intervals by a solitary electric bulb. All the doors, where these could be made out, looked alike. Riva stopped before one and rummaged in her bag for a key. Next to the door was cat litter smelling sharply. The same cat?

'Here we are.' She unlocked the door, entered and switched on a light. I was hesitant about following her inside.

'It's quite safe, I won't rape you,' she snorted. This was a coarse remark. I waited for her to laugh but she did not. I entered, blinking my eyes. Large, high-ceilinged, cavernous bed-sitter with a kitchen and toilet running off it. The room was gloomy and dusty. A double bed, round table, two uncomfortable-looking chairs and a dressing table covered with bric-a-brac. There was a heavy smell of mildew permeating everything. The whole building smelt of mildew. Why a double bed? For her alone or Simon and herself?

'You live here?' It was a silly question and I knew it. I wanted to ask 'You live here alone or does Simon live here also?' Why should I bother about Simon?

'Yes, I live here. Have a seat. The bed's more comfortable to sit on.' I chose one of the chairs. It creaked as I settled into it. All the furniture must have been bought second-hand from junk shops. Or maybe it came with the room. Nothing was modern. Jewish, Victorian, or what I imagined Jewish-Victorian to be. Dickensian in a sort of decaying nineteenth-century way. Riva took off her coat. She was all bustle.

'Let's have some tea. I'll put on the water.' Before I could refuse she disappeared into the kitchen. I must leave now. The surroundings were far too depressing. Riva was far too depressing. I remained as if glued to my seat. She reappeared. Now to make my apologies. I spoke as delicately as I could, but it came out all wrongly.

'I'm very sorry, but I won't be able to stay for tea. You see, I really can't stay. I must get home. I have lots of work to do. An exam tomorrow. Social Anthropology.'

'The trouble with you, Professor, is that you are far too clever, but not clever enough.' She sounded annoyed. 'Maybe you work too hard, far too hard. Have some tea before you go.' There was a twinkle in her eye again. 'Or are you afraid of me?'

I held my breath, expecting her to laugh but she did not. A long pause.

'No,' I said at last, 'No, I'm not afraid of you. I really do have an exam tomorrow. You must believe me. I was on my way home. I was hoping to see George.'

'Yes, I know, and he wasn't at work. You've said so before.'

'I really must leave now.'

'Without first having tea? That would be anti-social. An intellectual like you should know that.'

'But I don't want any tea, thanks.' The conversation was going around in meaningless circles. Why the hell could I not go if I wished to?

'You really are afraid of me. I can see that.'

'I must go.'

'And not have tea with the queen? Is it because I'm white? Or Jewish? Or because I live in a room like this?'

I wanted to say 'It's because you're you. Why can't you leave me alone?' I got up determined to leave.

'Why did you come with me in the first place?'

This was an unfair question. I had not asked to come along. There was a hiss from the kitchen where the water was boiling over onto the plate.

'I don't know why I came. Maybe it was because you asked me.'

'You could have refused.'

'I tried to.'

'But not hard enough.'

'Look, I'm going now. I have overstayed my time.'

'Just a second.' She disappeared into the kitchen. I could hear her switching off the stove then the clinking of cups. I stood at the door waiting for her to appear before leaving.

She entered with a tray containing the tea things and a plate with some assorted biscuits.

'No thank you,' I said, determined that nothing would keep me. 'I said I was leaving and I am.'

She put the tray on the table. 'Alright then, Professor. If you must then you must. Don't let me keep you any longer.' She looked almost pathetic at that moment, staring dejectedly at the tray. This was not the Riva I knew. She was straining to control herself. I felt dirty, sordid, sorry for her.

'Goodbye,' I said hastily and hurried out into the passage. I bumped into someone. Simon looked up surprised, then mumbled some excuse. He looked at me puzzled, then entered the room.

As I swiftly ran down the stairs I heard her snorting. Short pause and then peals of uncontrolled laughter. I stumbled out into Long Street.

Sunlight in Trebizond Street

Alan Paton

Today the lieutenant said to me, *I'm going to do you a favour*. I don't answer him. I don't want his favours. *I'm not supposed to do it*, he said. *If I were caught I'd be in trouble*. He looks at me as though he wanted me to say something, and I could have said, *that'd break my heart*, but I don't say it. I don't speak unless I think it will pay me. That's my one fast rule.

Don't you want me to do you a favour? he asks. *I don't care*, I said, *if you do me a favour or you don't. But if you want to do it, that's your own affair*.

You're a stubborn devil, aren't you? I don't answer that, but I watch him. I have been watching Caspar for a long time, and I have come to the conclusion that he has a grudging respect for me. If the major knew his job, he'd take Caspar away, give me someone more exciting, more dangerous.

Don't you want to get out? I don't answer. There are two kinds of questions I don't answer, and he knows it. One is the kind he needs the answers to. The other is the kind to which he knows the answers already. Of course I want to get out, away from those hard staring eyes, whose look you can bear only if your own are hard and staring too. And I want to eat some tasty food, and drink some wine, in some place with soft music and hidden lights. And I want ... but I do not think of that. I have made a rule.

How many days have you been here? I don't answer that, because I don't know any more. And I don't want Caspar to know that I don't. When they took away the first Bible, it was 81. By an effort of will that exhausted me, I counted up to 105. And I was right, up to 100 at any rate, for on that day they came to inform me, with almost a kind of ceremony, that duly empowered under Act so-and-so, Section so-and-so, they were going to keep me another

100, and would release me when I 'answered satisfactorily'. That shook me, though I tried to hide it from them. But I lost my head a little, and called out quite loudly, 'Hooray for the rule of law.' It was foolish. It achieved exactly nothing. After 105 I nearly went to pieces. The next morning I couldn't remember if it were 106 or 107. After that you can't remember any more. You lose your certitude. You're like a blind man who falls over a stool in the well-known house. There's no birthday, no trip to town, no letter from abroad, by which to remember. If you try going back, it's like going back to look for something you dropped yesterday in the desert, or in the forest, or in the water of the lake. Something is gone from you that you'll never find again.

It took me several days to convince myself that it didn't matter all that much. Only one thing mattered, and that was to give them no access to my private self. Our heroic model was B.B.B. He would not speak, or cry out, or stand up, or do anything they told him to do. He would not even look at them, if such a thing is possible. Solitude did not affect him, for he could withdraw into a solitude of his own, a kind of state of suspended being. He died in one such solitude. Some say he withdrew too far and could not come back. Others say he was tortured to death, that in the end the pain stabbed its way into the solitude. No one knows.

So far they haven't touched me. And if they touched me, what would I do? Pain might open the door to that private self. It's my fear of that that keeps me from being arrogant. I have a kind of superstition that pride gets punished sooner than anything else. It's a relic of my lost religion.

You're thinking deep, said Caspar, *I'll come tomorrow. I expect to bring you interesting news.*

Caspar said to me, *Rafael Swartz has been taken in*. It's all I can do to hide from him that for the first time I stand before him in my private and naked self. I dare not pull the clothes round me, for he would know what he had done. Why doesn't he bring instruments, to measure the sudden uncontrollable kick of the heart, and the sudden tensing of the muscles of the face, and the contraction of the pupils? Or does he think he can tell without them? He doesn't appear to be watching me closely. Perhaps he puts down the bait carelessly, confident that the prey will come. But does he not know that the prey is already a thousand times aware? I am still standing naked, but I try to look as though I am wearing clothes.

Rafael Swartz. Is he brave? Will he keep them waiting 1,000 days, till in anger they let him go? Or will he break as soon as one of them casually picks up the poker that has been left carelessly in the coals?

He's a rat, says Caspar. *He has already ratted on you*. I say foolishly, *How can he rat on me? I'm here already*.

You're here, Caspar agreed. He said complainingly, *But you don't tell us anything. Swartz is going to tell us things that you won't tell. Things you don't want us to know. Tell me, doctor, who's the boss?*

I don't answer him. I begin to feel my clothes stealing back on me. I could now look at Caspar confidently, but that I mustn't do. I must wait till I can do it casually.

I don't know when I'll see you again, he said, quite like conversation. *I'll be spending time with Swartz. I expect to have interesting talks with him. And if there's anything I think you ought to know, I'll be right back. Goodbye, doctor*.

He stops at the door. *There's one thing you might like to know. Swartz thinks you brought him in*.

He looks at me. *He thinks that*, he says, *because we told him so*.

John Forrester always said to me when parting, *Have courage*. Have I any courage? Have I any more courage than Rafael Swartz? And who am I to know the extent of his courage? Perhaps they are lying to me. Perhaps when they told him I had brought him in, he laughed at them and said, *It's an old trick but you can't catch an old dog with it*.

Don't believe them, Rafael. And I shan't believe them either. Have courage, Rafael, and I shall have courage too.

Caspar doesn't come. It's five days now. At least I think it's five. I can't even be sure of that now. Have courage, Rafael.

It must be ten days now. I am not myself. My stomach is upset. I go to and fro the whole day, and it leaves me weak and drained. But though my body is listless, my imagination works incessantly. What is happening there, in some other room, like this, perhaps in this building too? I know it is useless imagining it, but I go on with it. I've stopped saying, *Have courage, Rafael*, on the grounds that if he has lost his courage, it's too late, and if he hasn't lost his courage, it's superfluous. But I'm afraid. It's coming too close.

Who's your boss? asks Caspar, and of course I don't reply. He talks about Rafael Swartz and Lofty Coombe and Helen Columbus, desultory talk, with now and then desultory questions. The talk and the questions are quite pointless. Is the lieutenant a fool or is he not?

He says to me, *You're a dark horse, aren't you, doctor? Leading a double life, and we didn't know.*

I am full of fear. It's coming too close. I can see John Forrester now, white-haired and benevolent, what they call a man of distinction, the most miraculous blend of tenderness and steel that any of us will ever know. He smiles at me as though to say, *Keep up your courage, we're thinking of you every minute of the day.*

What does Caspar mean, my double life? Of course I led a double life, that's why I'm here. Does he mean some other double life? And how would they know? Could Rafael have known?

Can't you get away, my love? I'm afraid of you, I'm afraid for us all. What did I tell you? I can't remember. I swore an oath to tell no one. But with you I can't remember. And I swore an oath that there would never be any woman at all. That was my crime.

When I first came here, I allowed myself to remember you once a day, for about one minute. But now I am thinking of you more and more. Not just love, fear too. Did I tell you who we were?

Love, why don't you go? Tell them you didn't know I was a revolutionary. Tell them anything, but go.

As for myself, my opinion of myself is unspeakable. I thought I was superior, that I could love a woman, and still be remote and unknowable. We take up this work like children. We plot and plan and are full of secrets. Everything is secret except our secrecy.

What is happening now? Today the major comes with the lieutenant, and the mere sight of him sets my heart pounding. The major's not like Caspar. He does not treat me as superior or inferior. He says *Sit down*, and I sit. He says to me, *So you still won't co-operate?* Such is my foolish state that I say to him, *Why should I co-operate? There's no law which says I must co-operate. In fact the law allows for my not co-operating, and gives you the power to detain me until I do.*

The major speaks to me quite evenly. He says, *Yes, I can detain you, but I can do more than that, I can break you. I can send you out of here an old broken man, going about with your head down, mumbling to yourself, like Samuelson.*

He talks to me as though I were an old man already. *You wouldn't like that, doctor. You like being looked up to by others. You like to pity others, it gives you a boost, but it would be hell to be pitied by them. In Fordsville they thought the sun shone out your eyes. Our name stinks down there because we took you away.*

We can break you, doctor, he said. *We don't need to give you shock treatment, or hang you up by the feet, or put a vice on your testicles. There are many other ways. But it isn't convenient. We don't want you drooling round Fordsville.* He adds sardonically, *It would spoil our image.*

He looks at me judicially, but there's a hard note in his voice. *It's inconvenient, but there may be no other way. And if there's no other way, we'll break you. Now listen carefully. I'm going to ask you a question.*

He keeps quiet for a minute, perhaps longer. He wants me to think over his threat earnestly. He says, *Who's your boss?*

After five minutes he stands up. He turns to Caspar. *All right, lieutenant, you can go ahead.*

What can Caspar go ahead with? Torture? for me? or for Rafael Swartz? My mind shies away from the possibility that it might be for you. But what did he mean by the double life? Their cleverness, which might some other time have filled me with admiration, fills me now with despair. They drop a fear into your mind, and then they go away. They're busy with other things, intent on their job of breaking, but you sit alone for days and think about the last thing they said. Ah, I am filled with fear for you. There are 3,000 million people in the world, and I can't get one of them to go to you and say, *Get out, this day, this very minute.*

☆   ☆   ☆   ☆   ☆

Barbara Trevelyan, says Caspar, *it's a smart name. You covered it up well, doctor, so we're angry at you. But there's someone angrier than us. Didn't you promise on oath to have no friendship outside the People's League, more especially with a woman? What is your boss going to say?*

Yes, I promised. But I couldn't go on living like that, cut off from all love, from all persons, from all endearment. I wanted to mean something to somebody, a live person, not a cause. I am filled with shame, not so much that I broke my promise, but because I couldn't make an island where there was only our love, only you and me. But the world had to come in, and the great plan for the transformation of the world, and forbidden knowledge, dangerous knowledge, and ... I don't like to say it, perhaps boasting came in too, dangerous boasting. My head aches with pain, and I try to remember what I told you.

You are having your last chance today, says Caspar. *If you don't talk today, you won't need to talk any more. Take your choice. Do you want her to tell us, or will you?*

I don't know. If I talk, then what was the use of these 100 days? Some will go to prison, some may die. If I don't tell, if I let her tell, then they will suffer just the same. And the shame will be just as terrible.

It doesn't matter, says Caspar, *if you tell or she tells. They'll kill you either way. Because we're going to let you go.*

He launches another bolt at me. *You see, doctor, she doesn't believe in the cause, she believes only in you. Tomorrow she won't even do that. Because we're going to tell her that you brought her in.*

Now he is watching me closely. Something is moving on my face. Is it an insect? or a drop of sweat? Don't tell them, my love. Listen my love, I am sending a message to you. Don't tell them, my love.

Do you remember what Rafael Swartz used to boast at those meetings in the good old days, that he'd follow you to hell? Well, he'd better start soon, hadn't he? Because that's where you are now.

He takes off his watch and puts it on the table. *I give you five minutes*, he said, *and they're the last you'll ever get. Who's your boss?* He puts his hands on the table too, and rests his forehead on them. Tired he is, tired with breaking men. He lifts his head and puts on his watch and stands up. There is a look on his face I haven't seen before, hating and vicious.

You're all the same, aren't you? Subversion most of the time, and women in between. Marriage, children, family, that's for the birds, that's for our decadent society. You want to be free, don't you? You paint FREEDOM *all over the damn town. Well you'll be free soon, and by God it'll be the end of you.*

Lofty and Helen and Le Grange. And now Rafael. Is there anyone they can't break? Does one grow stronger or weaker as the days go by? I say a prayer for you tonight, to whatever God may be ...

Did I say Rafael's name? I'm sorry, Rafael, I'm not myself today. Have courage, Rafael. Don't believe what they say. And I shan't believe either.

5 days? 7 days? More? I can't remember. I hardly sleep now. I think of you and wonder what they are doing to you. I try to remember what I told you. Did I tell you I was deep in? Did I tell you how deep? Did I tell you any of their names? It's a useless question, because I don't know the answer to it. If the answer came suddenly into my mind, I wouldn't know it for what it was.

Ah, never believe that I brought you in. It's an old trick, the cruellest trick of the cruellest profession in the world. Have courage, my love. Look at them out of your grey honest eyes and tell them you don't know anything at all, that you were just a woman in love.

Caspar says to me, *You're free.* What am I supposed to do? Should my face light up with joy? It might have done, only a few days ago. *Do you know why we're letting you go?* Is there point in not answering? I shake my head.

Because we've found your boss, that's why. When he sees I am wary, not knowing whether to believe or disbelieve, he says, *John Forrester's the name. He doesn't know what to believe either, especially when we told him you had brought him in. Doctor, don't come back here any more. You're not made for this game. You've*

only lasted this long because of orders received. Don't ask me why.
Come, I'll take you home.

Outside in the crowded street the sun is shining. The sunlight falls
on the sooty trees in Trebizonds Street, and the black leaves dance
in the breeze. The city is full of noise and life, and laughter too, as
though no one cared what might go on behind those barricaded
walls. There is an illusion of freedom in the air.

The Christmas Reunion

Dambudzo Marechera

I had never killed a goat before. But it was Christmas. And father who had always done it was dead. He had been dead for seven years. My sister, Ruth, could not possibly be expected to kill the goat. It was supposed to be a man's job. And mother was dead too. There were the two of us in the house, Ruth and I. I was on sabbatical from the university and Christmas would, I had hoped, be a break from the book I was writing. But there had to be a goat to spoil everything. Actually it was Christmas Eve, and that was the time of killing and skinning the goat. Everybody in the township would be killing their own family goat. While I tried to find an excuse to get out of having to kill the goat myself, I reminded Ruth that a goat was a passionate creature beloved of Pan and how could I kill that beast in me? I was, I said, myself a hardy, lively, wanton, horned and bearded ruminant quadruped—if not in fact, at least in spirit. I had always been wicked. I was up there in the sky with Capricorn, I said. If all this isn't convincing, I said, what about that all important Tropic of Capricorn which seemed to make those who lived close to it vicious, nasty, spoilt, bloody Boers, and in short to kill the goat would be to disrespect a substantial part of the human extremities and interiorities. Besides, I added, you know I can't eat what I have killed. Also I was mere goat's wool in the general fabric of this great fiction we call life and could not logically be capable of such a monstrosity as murdering a poor old goat. Imagine a large assembly of bloodthirsty Germans shouting GEISS at a terrified little Jewish boy. All this mass-extermination of perfectly harmless but god-created goats seemed to me to be nothing but a distortion of what Christmas was really about. Which was? Which was? Well, we're Africans anyway and all this nonsense about Christmas was merely a sordid distraction. After all, I said, aren't whites and blacks skinning each other now ready for the Christmas pot, lugging each other by the heels into the universal kitchen to dress each one up with chillies and mustard and black pepper and chips and afterwards everybody would pat their stomachs and belch gently and scratch their bellies in which the feeling of Freedom and Christmas was being slowly digested. The whole business of expressing Christian glee by cutting the throats of much-maligned goats was indeed sickening, not to mention the so-called domestication of goats in concentration-camp-style kraals when what could be more majestic and courageous and rugged than pure mountain goats? I could not for the life of me see anything but inhumanity in buying a goat for a few shillings and tethering it to an old barbed-wire fence and having babies watch its throat and guts being cut up. Besides, I was not a real killer at all. Perhaps sometimes I inadvertently stepped on a beetle that was not watching where it was going, and of course I did murder all those damned mosquitoes that were plaguing my rooms at the university, and that nasty fat fly which so maddened me that I took a swipe at it with a hardback Complete Shakespeare. I think I only grazed its compound eyes and chucked it into the waste-paper basket and then the crafty insect played so hard at being dead it actually died. I agree that snake which was skulking around in the apple tree when you were looking longingly at the red-ripest one probably did not deserve to be scared to death by my shotgun. And every self-respecting pimply boy had a rubber sling to stone birds to death. And fighting is not a different business: you raise your fist at somebody and at once you are a potential killer—there is nothing manly in that. This business about 'being a real man' is what is driving all of us crazy. I'll have none of it. There's nothing different between you and me except what's hanging between our legs. And if you want goat meat, kill it yourself. If I'm supposed to become a 'real man' in the twinkling of an eye by cutting the human throats of these human goats, then I don't see why you shouldn't suddenly become a 'real woman' by the same horrible atrocity. How can you ever possibly look any living thing in the eye after becoming a grown-up by cutting the throat of a living being? What I mean is, my mind is in such a mess because every step eats up the step before it and where will this grand staircase of everything eating everything else lead us to? Who wants to be the first step and who will be the last all-eating step? God? I know that goat has probably exterminated a lot of cowering grass, and the grass itself ate up the salt and the water in the earth, and the salt and the water probably came from stinking corpses in the ground, and the corpses probably ate up something else—I mean, what the hell! At least we have got that within us which does not kill when all the bloody world out there is killing. Look, you're my sister, so don't rush me—at least give me a chance. This is not a guerrilla band from which a man cannot desert alive. It isn't Smith's army either. It's me. Me. And I'm just goat's wool that nobody can see. The way the goat is staring at me is making me nervous. But that's natural; how would you stare at people who were, in your presence, openly discussing the subject of doing away with you, skinning you and dressing you up so that you'd not be even a corpse but something good to eat, which would an hour later come out of their arses and be flushed away into a labyrinth of sewers? I know we can't eat air or stone or fire, but we can at any rate drink water. But why do we have to eat and drink at all? Whoever created us had a nasty mind! How would you feel if somebody skinned you and then hung out your skin to dry and made a pair of shoes out of it? I mean, there's people out there who'd boil your very bones to make fertiliser—and if your bones are not good enough, they boil them again and make glue out of them and give it to little schoolkids to paste up their paperdolls and stick them on a time chart that's supposed to explain how human civilisation worked out from the Neanderthal to the man of today who is supposed to see things like a camera lens looks at you just before the shutter falls. I refuse to see things that way! They look at you like you want me to look at that goat. They look at you like you were a potential meal, and they digest your innards and fart you out and call it progress. It terrifies me the way we are capable of imprisoning whole populations of pigs, cattle, poultry, goats and sheep and fatten them up and then herd them into gas-chambers and when they are dead strip them of their flesh and bones and brains and gold teeth and marriage rings and spectacles—strip them of everything and call it what, intensive farming, modern progress. And we call it everything else but exactly what it is. The world was not created to serve for a meal for us. If it was, then God help the likes of me. God? It's his Christmas and in 1915 and 1916 on the western front they took a break from shooting each other up and pushed a football about and then as soon as his holy birthday was over they began blasting the tonsils out of each other again. One of the bloody Germans was a clown with a goldfish. I don't want to be a goldfish in somebody's idea of a cosmic farce. The goat doesn't want to be either. And that poor archbishop in Uganda probably did not want to be a goldfish in Amin's head, either. And probably the goldfish would prefer it if I left its name out of this.

Heavens! It's so late already. What time is supper? What do you mean, I'll have to kill the goat if I want any supper? I want my supper. This is the first time I've been able to come home in seven years, and would you deny me a humble repast? The goat? Him? He is really the humble repast, is he? Then—God help me—I'll . . . Let's give him to those starving Makonis. They probably haven't had anything again today. Hey—look out! It's broken its tether. See how it runs, like Pan himself, or like a scapegoat, or like me when I was younger. It's burst through that crowd! It's in the forest! Well, good luck to you, Pan. Don't look so offended, Ruth, because we are eating out. I've reserved the table already. At that posh place, Brett's. My wife will be joining us there in—let's see—five minutes. You two have got a lot to talk about—it's been seven years, you know. I just hope I won't be booked for speeding.

The King of the Waters

*translated from Xhosa and
retold by A.C. Jordan*

It came about, according to some tale, that Tfulako, renowned hunter and son of a great chief, was returning home with his youthful comrades after a hunt that had lasted many days. On a misty night they lost their way in the forests, and when the next day dawned they found themselves travelling on a wide plain of bare, barren land that they had never seen before. As the days strengthened towards midday, it became very hot. The youths had plenty of baggage—skins and skulls of big game, carcasses of smaller game, as well as their clothes and hunting equipment. They felt hungry and thirsty, but there was no point in camping where there were no trees, no firewood and no water. So they walked on wearily, their baggage becoming heavier and heavier, their stomachs feeling emptier, their lips dry and their throats burning hot with thirst.

At last, just as the sun was beginning to slant towards the west, they suddenly came upon a fertile stretch of low land lying between two mountains. At the foot of the mountains there was a grove of big tall trees surrounding a beautiful fountain of icy-cold water. With shouts of joy the youthful hunters laid down their baggage on the green grass in the shade and made for the fountain. They took turns stooping and drinking in groups. Tfulako was in the last group, together with his immediate subordinates. When he knelt and bent down to drink, the fountain suddenly dried up, as did the stream flowing from the fountain. All the youths fell back, startled. They exchanged glances but said nothing. Tfulako stood a little while gazing at the fountain, and then he motioned to his subordinates to come forward, kneel and bend down again. They obeyed his order, and the fountain filled and the water began to flow as before. Tfulako stepped forward and knelt beside them, but as soon as he bent down to drink the water vanished. He withdrew and the water appeared again, and his comrades drank their fill. Tfulako walked silently back to his place in the shade, and from there he gave a signal that all must draw near.

'Comrades,' he said, 'you all saw what happened just now. I assure you I don't know what it means. You all know me well. I've never practised sorcery. I don't remember doing any evil before or during or after this hunt. Therefore, I've nothing to confess to you, my comrades. It looks as if this matter has its own depth, a depth that cannot be known to any of our age group here. However, I charge you to go about your duties in preparation for our day's feast — wood-gathering, lighting of fires, flaying of carcasses, and roasting — as if nothing has happened. We'll feast and enjoy ourselves, but before I leave this fountain I must drink, for we don't know where and when we'll find water again in this strange land.'

The youths went about their assigned duties, some flaying the wild game, some collecting wood, some kindling the fires, some cutting off titbits from the half-flayed carcasses and roasting them, so that while the main feast was being prepared the company could remove the immediate hunger from their eyes and stop their mouths watering. Tfulako tried to eat some titbits too, but this aggravated his thirst. So he went and stood some distance away from his comrades and watched the fountain. It had filled again, and the water was streaming down the valley as it had been doing when they first came upon this strange place.

When the main feast was ready, Tfulako joined his comrades as he had promised, but found it impossible to eat because of his burning throat. So he just sat there and joined in the chat, trying to share in all the youthful jokes that accompanied the feasting. The meat naturally made all of them thirsty again. So once more they took turns drinking from the fountain. Once more Tfulako came forward with his own group, once more the fountain dried up as soon as he bent down to drink.

There could be no doubt now. It was he and he alone who must not drink, he alone who must die of thirst and hunger, he, son of the great chief. But what power was it that controlled this fountain? He moved away from the fountain and thought deeply. He had heard tales of the King of the Waters who could make rivers flow or dry at will. He concluded that the King of Waters, whoever he was and whatever he looked like, must be in this fountain, that this

King must have recognized him as the son of the great chief, that this King must have resolved that the son of the great chief must either pay a great price for the water from this fountain or die of thirst. What price was he expected to pay? Then suddenly he turned about, walked up to the brink of the fountain and, in sheer desperation, called out aloud:

'King of the Waters! I die of thirst. Allow me to drink and I will give you the most beautiful of my sisters to be your wife.'

At once the fountain filled, and Tfulako bent down and quenched his thirst while all his comrades looked on in silence. Then he had his share of meat.

After this, the whole company felt relaxed, and the youths stripped and bathed in the cool stream to refresh themselves for the long journey before them. Tfulako took part in all this and enjoyed himself as if he had forgotten what had just happened. Towards sunset, they filled their gourds with water from the fountain, picked up their baggage and resumed their journey home. On the afternoon of the fourth day they were within the domain of their great chief and, to announce their approach, they chanted their favourite hunting-song:

> Ye ha he! e ha he!
> A mighty whirlwind, the buffalo!
> Make for your homes, ye who fear him.
> They chase them far! They chase them near!
> As for us, we smite the lively ones
> And we leave the wounded alone.
> Ye ha he! e ha he!
> A mighty whirlwind, the buffalo!

So Tfulako and his comrades entered the gates of the Royal Place, amid the praises of the bards and the cheering of the women.

Tfulako took the first opportunity, when the excitement over the return of the hunters had died down, to report to his people what had happened at the fountain. No one, not even the oldest councillors, had any idea what the King of the Waters looked like. Most of them thought that since he lived in the water, he might look like a giant otter or giant reptile, while others expressed the hope that he was a man-like spirit. But everybody, including the beautiful princess, felt that this was the only offer Tfulako could have made in the circumstances. So they awaited the coming of the King of the Waters.

One afternoon, after many moons had died, a terrible cyclone approached the Royal Place. On seeing it, the people ran quickly into their huts and fastened the doors. As it drew nearer, the cyclone narrowed itself and made straight for the girls' hut where the beautiful princess and the other girls were. But instead of sweeping the hut before it, as cyclones usually do, this one folded itself and vanished at the door.

When calm was restored, the girls discovered that they were in the company of a snake of enormous length. Its girth was greater than the thigh of a very big man. They had never seen a snake of such size before. This then, they concluded, must be *Nkanyamba*, King of the Waters, come to claim his bride. One by one the girls left the hut, until the princess was left alone with the bridegroom. She decided to follow the other girls, but as soon as she rose to go the King of the Waters unfolded quickly, coiled himself round her body, rested his head on her breasts and gazed hungrily into her eyes.

The princess ran out of the hut with her burden round her body and, without stopping to speak to anybody at the Royal Place, set out on a long, long journey to her mother's people, far over the mountains. As she went, she sang in a high-pitched, wailing voice:

Ndingatsi ndihumntfan' abo Tfulako,	Can I, a daughter of Tfulako's people,
Ndingatsi ndihumntfan' abo Tfulako,	Can I, a daughter of Tfulako's people,
Ndilale nesibitwa ngokut- siwa hinyoka, nyoka?	Sleep with that which is called a snake, snake?

In reply, the King of the Waters sang in a deep voice:

Ndingatsi ndimlelelele ndinje, ndinje,	Long and graceful that I am, so graceful,
Ndingatsi ndimlelelele ndinje, ndinje,	Long and graceful that I am, so graceful,
Ndingalali nesibitwa ngokut- siwa humfati, fati lo?	May I not sleep with that which is called a woman, a mere woman?

And so they travelled through forest and ravine the whole night and the following day, singing pride at each other.

At nightfall they reached the home of the princess's mother's people. But the princess decided to wait in the shadows for a while. When she was sure that there was no one in the girls' hut, she entered there unnoticed and closed the door. Then for the first time she addressed herself directly to her burden:

King of the Waters, mighty one!	Saviour of the lives of thirsty hunters!
Sole possessor of the staff of life!	Thou that comest borne on the wings of mighty storms!
Thou that makest the rivers flow or dry at will!	Thou of many coils, long and graceful!

By this time, the King of the Waters had raised his head from its pillowed position and was listening. So the princess went on:

'I am tired, covered with the dust of the road and ugly. I pray you, undo yourself and rest here while I go and announce the great news of your royal visit to my mother's people. Then I shall also take a little time to wash and dress myself in a manner befitting the hostess of the greatest of kings, *Nkanyamba* the Mighty, *Nkanyamba* the King of the Waters.'

Without a word, the King of the Waters unwound himself and slithered to the far end of the hut where he coiled himself into a great heap that almost reached the thatch roof.

The princess went straight to the Great Hut and there, weeping, she told the whole story to her uncle and his wife. They comforted her and assured her that they would rid her of the *Nkanyamba* the same night, if only she would be brave and intelligent. She brushed away her tears immediately and assured them that she would be brave and determined. Thereupon, her mother's brother told his wife to give orders that large quantities of water be boiled so that the princess could have a bath. While these preparations were going on, he took out some ointment and mixed it with some powders that the princess had never seen before. These he gave to his wife and instructed her to anoint the whole of the princess's body as soon as she had had her bath. Then the princess and her aunt disappeared, leaving the head of the family sitting there alone, grim and determined.

When they returned, the princess looked fresh and lovely in her *nkayo*. She had stripped herself of most of her ornaments. All she had were her glittering brass head-ring, a necklace whose pendant hung delicately between her breasts, a pair of armlets and a pair of anklets.

'Your aunt has told you everything you are to do when you get there?' asked her mother's brother, rising to his feet as they came in.

'Everything, *malume*,' replied the princess, smiling brightly.

'You're sure you will not make any mistake — doing things too hastily and so on?'

'I'm quite cool now, *malume*. You can be sure that I'll do everything at the right moment.'

Then the head of the family produced a beautiful *kaross*, all made of leopardskins, unfolded it and covered his sister's daughter with it. 'Go now, my sister's child. I'm sure you'll be more than a match for this — this snake!'

The princess walked briskly back to the girls' hut. Once inside, she threw off the *kaross* and addressed the King of the Waters:

'King of the Waters! Here I stand, I, daughter of the people of Tfulako, ready for the embrace of *Nkanyamba*, the tall and graceful.'

As she said these words, she stretched out her beautiful arms invitingly to the King of the Waters.

This invitation was accepted eagerly, but when the King of the Waters tried to hold her in his coils, he slipped down and fell with a thud on the floor. Smiling and chiding him, the princess once more stretched out her arms and invited him to have another try. He tried again, but again he fell on the floor with a thud. Once again the princess stretched out her arms encouragingly, but again the King of the Waters found her body so slippery that for all his coils and scales he could not hold her. This time he slipped down and fell with such a heavy thud on the floor that he seemed to have lost all strength. He could hardly move his body. All he could do in response to the princess's invitation was to feast his eyes on her beautiful body.

'It's my mistake, graceful one,' said the princess, lowering her arms. 'In my eagerness to make myself beautiful for the King of the Waters, I put too much ointment on my body. I'll go back to the

Great Hut and remove it immediately, then I shall return and claim the embrace I so desire.'

With these words, she picked up her *kaross*, stepped over the threshold and fastened the door securely from outside. Her uncle and aunt were ready with a blazing firebrand, and as soon as she had fastened the door they handed it to her without saying a word. She grabbed it and ran round the hut, setting the grass thatch alight at many points. Finally she thrust the firebrand into the thatch just above the door. The grass caught fire at once, and the flames lit the entire homestead.

No sound of any struggle was heard on the part of the King of the Waters in the burning hut. He had lost all power. No power to lift his body from the ground. No power to summon the wings of mighty storms to bear him away from the scorching flames. The King of the Waters was burned to death.

Everything happened so quickly that, by the time the neighbours came, nothing was left except the crackling wood.

'What happened? What happened?' asked one neighbour after another.

'It's only one of those things that happen because we are in this world.'

'Is everybody safe in your household?' they asked.

'Everybody is safe. It's a pleasant event, my neighbours. Go and sleep in peace. When the present moon dies, I'll invite you all to a great feast in honour of my sister's beautiful daughter here. Then will I tell you all there is to tell about the evil we've just destroyed.'

The following morning the head of the family rose up early and went to examine the scene of the fire very carefully. He found that although the body of the *Nkanyamba* had been reduced to ashes, bones and all, the skull was intact. He picked it up and examined it. Then he collected some wood, piled it on the ashes and set fire to it. He then picked out the brains of the *Nkanyamba* from every little cranny and let them fall on the fire. Then he scraped the inside of the skull, removing every little projection and making it as smooth as a clay pot. All the matter removed fell onto the fire and burned out completely. He took the skull indoors and washed it thoroughly with boiling-hot water, and then rubbed it thoroughly with the remnants of the grease and powder that had been used by the princess on the previous night.

Meanwhile, the princess was in a deep sleep, nor did she wake up at all until the early afternoon. Her aunt had given orders that no one was to go into the hut where she was sleeping, except herself, for a whole day and night. So, after putting the *Nkanyamba's* skull away, the head of the family went about his daily duties and kept away from his niece's hut. But on the following morning, as soon as he knew that the princess was awake, he went to see her, taking the skull with him. The princess shuddered a little when she saw it.

'Touch it, child of my sister,' said her uncle. 'Touch it, and all fear of it will go.'

The princess touched it, but noticing that she still shuddered, her uncle withdrew it, sat beside her and chatted a little.

Later in the day, the head and mistress of the house discussed the condition of the princess. They agreed that her cousins could enter her hut and sit and chat with her as long as they wished, but that she must remain in bed until all signs of fear had disappeared. So every morning her uncle took the skull to her and made her handle it. When he was quite satisfied that she did not shudder any more, he told his wife that the princess was now ready to get up and live normally with the rest of the family.

One day the head and mistress of the family were sitting and chatting with the princess in the Great Hut when the princess casually rose and walked across the floor, took the *Nkanyamba's* skull down from its place on the wall and turned it over and over in her hands, all the time carrying on with the conversation as if she were not thinking about the skull at all. The two elderly people exchanged glances, nodded to each other and smiled.

'Now I can see she's ready to go back to her parents,' said the head of the family as soon as he and his wife were alone. 'She doesn't fear that skull any more now. It's just like any other vessel in the house. So we can proceed with the preparations.'

Two to three days passed and a great feast was held in honour of the princess. All the neighbours came, and the head of the family told them the whole story of Tfulako's promise to the King of the Waters, and what happened thereafter. The neighbours praised the princess for her bravery and thanked their neighbours on behalf of the parents and brother of the girl. The uncle then pointed out five head of cattle that he was giving to his sister's child to take home. Then one after another his well-to-do friends and neighbours rose to make little speeches, thanking him for the gift to his sister's child, adding their own 'little calves to accompany their neighbour's gift', until there were well over two tens of cattle in all. After each gift of a 'little calf', the princess kissed the right hand of the giver. Then it was the uncle's turn to thank his neighbours for making him a somebody by enriching so much the gift that his sister's child would take home with her.

The village mothers had withdrawn to a separate part of the homestead, and while the men were making gifts in cattle, the women were making a joint present consisting of mats, pots, bowls and ornaments of all kinds. When these had been collected, the head of the family was asked to accompany the princess to come and see them. Some of the elderly mothers made little speeches, presented the 'small gift' to the princess on behalf of the whole motherhood and wished her a happy journey back home. Both the head and the mistress of the family thanked the mothers.

Before the festivities came to an end, the young men of the village sent spokesmen to their fathers, reminding them that the princess would need an escort.

'We know that very well,' said one of the elderly men with a smile. 'But you can't all go. And let me remind you that those of you who are going will not only have to drive the cattle but also to carry all those pots and other things that your mothers have loaded the princess with.'

'We understand, father,' replied the chief spokesman. 'We are ready to carry everything. We have already agreed too that it would be fitting that the princess be escorted by those of the age group of her brother, Tfulako.'

'You've done well,' murmured some of the men.

A few days later, while the princess was being helped by her aunt to pack her belongings, the head of the family brought the beautiful *kaross* that the princess had worn on the night of the killing of the *Nkanyamba*. The princess accepted it very gratefully and embraced her uncle for the wonderful gift. Then he produced the *Nkanyamba's* skull and would hand it over to her.

'What am I to do with this thing, *malume*?' asked the princess, much surprised.

'It's yours,' replied her uncle. 'It was you who carried the King of the Waters all the way from your home-village so that you could destroy him here.'

The princess received the skull with both hands, thanked her uncle, looked at it for a little while and smiled.

'I know what I'll do with this,' she said as she packed it away.

'Aren't we going to be told this great secret?' asked her uncle.

'In truth, it's no secret to you two,' replied the princess. 'Some day, some day when my brother Tfulako becomes the chief of our people, I'll give this to him to use as a vessel for washing.'

'You have a mind, child of my sister,' remarked her uncle.

'Why do you say that, *malume?*'

'Because that was exactly what I hoped you would do with it.'

It was a pleasant journey for the princess and her male cousins and other young men of her brother's age group. They did not take their journey hurriedly, for they had to allow the cattle to graze as they went along. They themselves camped and rested whenever they came to a particularly beautiful place. They sang as they travelled and, among other songs, the princess taught them the songs that she and the King of the Waters had sung to each other in these same forests and ravines. She sang her high-pitched song, and the young men sang the song of the King of the Waters in a chorus.

When they approached the Royal Place on the afternoon of the third day of their journey, they started to sing this song aloud. The song was heard and immediately recognized by all those villagers who had heard it on the day of the cyclone. The princess's voice was recognized as hers, but the many deep voices remained a puzzle.

No one had seen Tfulako run into his hut to grab his spears and shield, but there he was, standing alone near the gate, shading his eyes in order to have the first glimpse of the singers who were about to appear on the horizon.

When the singers and the herd of cattle came in sight, he concluded that his sister was in the company of the *Nkanyamba* she loathed, together with a whole troop of followers driving the customary bride-tribute of cattle.

'What!' he exclaimed, blazing with anger. 'Does this mean that my sister has been burdened with this hateful snake all this time? I'm going to set my sister free!' And he took one leap over the closed gate.

'Wait, Son of the Beautiful!' shouted the councillors. 'You're going into danger. Wait until they get here.'

'I'll never allow those snakes to enter this gate. I don't want any of their cattle in the folds of my fathers. If no one will come with me, I'll fight them alone. Let him bring all the *Nkanyambas* in the world. I'll die fighting for my sister.'

And he ran to meet the singers.

Before he had reached them, however, all the hunters of his age group were with him. For the women of the Royal Place had raised the alarm, and it had been taken up by other women throughout the village, travelling then from one village to another, so that in no time all the youths had grabbed their spears and shields and followed the direction indicated by the cries of the womenfolk.

The singing suddenly stopped, and there were bursts of laughter from the princess's escort.

'Withhold your spears!' shouted one of them. 'The enemy you're looking for is not here. That which was he is now ashes at Tfulako's mother's people. Here's Tfulako's sister, beautiful as the rising sun.'

And the princess stepped forward to meet her brother who had already leapt forward to meet her. They embraced with affection.

'Forgive me, my father's child,' said Tfulako, deeply moved.

But the princess would not allow her brother to shed a tear in the presence of other young men. She laughed, disengaged herself and stepped away from him.

'Forgive you what?' she asked. 'Forgive you for giving me a chance to prove that I am the worthy sister of Tfulako, killer of buffaloes?'

Before Tfulako could reply, she started to sing his favourite hunting-song, altering the words to suit the event. By this time, the youths of the two groups had mingled together in a friendly manner. As soon as they took up the song, she pulled out the *Nkanyamba's* skull and, holding it high, led the march into the village and through the gates of the Royal Place:

Ye ha he! e ha he!
A mighty whirlwind, the *Nkanyamba*!
Fasten your doors, ye who fear him.
They chase them far! They chase them near!
As for us, we scorch the cyclone-borne.
And we carry their skulls aloft.
Ye ha he! e ha he!
A mighty whirlwind, the *Nkanyamba*!

Power

Jack Cope

From the gum tree at the corner he looked out over, well —
nothing. There was nothing more after his father's place, only the
veld, so flat and unchanging that the single shadowy koppie away
off towards the skyline made it look more empty still. It was a
lonely koppie like himself.

The one thing that made a difference was the powerline. High
above the earth on its giant steel lattice towers, the powerline
strode across the veld until it disappeared beyond the koppie. It
passed close to his father's place and one of the great pylons was on
their ground in a square patch fenced off with barbed wire, a
forbidden place. André used to look through the wire at the pylon.
Around the steelwork itself were more screens of barbed wire, and
on all four sides of it enamel warning-plates with a red skull-and-
crossbones said in three languages, DANGER! And there was a
huge figure of volts, millions of volts.

André was ten and he knew volts were electricity and the line
took power by a short cut far across country. It worked gold mines,
it lit towns, and hauled trains and drove machinery somewhere out
beyond. The power station was in the town ten miles on the other
side of his father's place and the great line simply jumped right over
them without stopping.

André filled the empty spaces in his life by imagining things.
Often he was a jet plane and roared around the house and along the
paths with his arms outspread. He saw an Everest film once and for
a long time he was Hillary or Tensing, or both, conquering a
mountain. There were no mountains so he conquered the roof of
the house which wasn't very high and was made of red-painted tin.
But he reached the summit and planted a flag on the lightning
conductor. When he got down his mother hit his legs with a quince

switch for being naughty.

Another time he conquered the koppie. It took him the whole afternoon to get there and back and it was not as exciting as he expected, being less steep than it looked from a distance, so he did not need his rope and pick. Also, he found a cow had beaten him to the summit.

He thought of conquering one of the powerline towers. It had everything, the danger especially, and studying it from all sides he guessed he could make the summit without touching a live wire. But he was not as disobedient as all that, and he knew if he so much as went inside the barbed-wire fence his mother would skin him with the quince, not to mention his father. There were peaks which had to remain unconquered.

He used to lie and listen to the marvellous hum of the powerline, the millions of volts flowing invisible and beyond all one's ideas along the copper wires that hung so smooth and light from ties of crinkled white china looking like chinese lanterns up against the sky. Faint cracklings and murmurs and rushes of sound would sometimes come from the powerline, and at night he was sure he saw soft blue flames lapping and trembling on the wires as if they were only half peeping out of that fierce river of volts. The flames danced and their voices chattered to him of a mystery.

In the early morning when the mist was rising and the first sun's rays were shooting underneath it, the powerline sparkled like a tremendous spiderweb. It took his thoughts away into a magical distance, far — far off among gigantic machines and busy factories. That was where the world opened up. So he loved the powerline dearly. It made a door through the distance for his thoughts. It was like him except that it never slept, and while he was dreaming it went on without stopping, crackling faintly and murmuring. Its electricity hauled up the mine skips from the heart of the earth, hurtled huge green rail units along their shining lines, and thundered day and night in the factories.

Now that the veld's green was darkening and gathering black-and-gold tints from the ripe seeds and withering grass blades, now that clear warm autumn days were coming after the summer thunderstorms, the birds began gathering on the powerline. At evening he would see the wires like necklaces of blue-and-black glass beads when the swallows gathered. It took them days and days, it seemed, to make up their minds. He did not know whether the same swallows collected each evening in growing numbers or whether a batch went off each day to be replaced by others. He did not know enough about them. He loved to hear them making excited twittering sounds, he loved to see how they simply fell off the copper wire into space and their perfect curved wings lifted them on the air.

They were going not merely beyond the skyline like the power, they were flying thousands of miles over land and sea and mountains and forests to countries he had never dreamt of. They would fly over Everest, perhaps, they would see ships below them on blue seas among islands, they would build nests under bridges and on chimneys where other boys in funny clothes would watch them. The birds opened another door for him and he liked them too, very much.

He watched the swallows one morning as they took off from their perch. Suddenly, as if they had a secret signal, a whole stretch of them along a wire would start together. They dropped forward into the air and their blue-and-white wings flicked out. Flying seemed to be the easiest thing in the world. They swooped and flew up, crisscrossing in flight and chirping crazily, so pleased to be awake in the morning. Then another flight of them winged off, and another. There was standing-room only on those wires. Close to the lofty pylon and the gleaming china ties another flight took off. But one of the swallows stayed behind, quite close to the tie. André watched them fall forward, but it alone did not leave the line. It flapped its wings and he saw it was caught by its leg.

He should have been going to school but he stood watching the swallow, his cap pulled over his white hair and eyes wrinkled against the light. After a minute the swallow stopped flapping and hung there. He wondered how it could have got caught, maybe in the wire binding or at a join. Swallows had short legs and small black claws; he had caught one once in its nest and held it in his hands before it struggled free and was gone in a flash. He thought the bird on the powerline would get free soon, but looking at it there he had a tingling kind of pain in his chest and in one leg as if he too were caught by the foot. André wanted to rush back and tell his mother, only she would scold him for being late to school. So he climbed on his bike, and with one more look up at the helpless bird there against the sky and the steel framework of the tower, he rode off to the bus.

At school he thought once or twice about the swallow, but mostly he forgot about it and that made him feel bad. Anyway, he thought, it would be free by the time he got home. Twisting and flapping a few times, it was sure to work its foot out; and there was no need for him to worry about it hanging there.

Coming back from the crossroads he felt anxious, but he did not like to look up until he was quite near. Then he shot one glance at the top of the pylon — the swallow was still there, its wings spread but not moving. It was dead, he guessed, as he stopped and put down one foot. Then he saw it flutter and fold up its wings. He felt awful to think it had hung there all day, trapped. The boy went in and called his mother and they stood off some distance below the powerline and looked at the bird. The mother shaded her eyes with her hand. It was a pity, she said, but really she was sure it would free itself somehow. Nothing could be done about it.

'Couldn't —?' he began.

'Couldn't nothing, dear,' she said quite firmly so that he knew she meant business. 'Now stop thinking about it, and tomorrow you'll see.'

His father came home at six and had tea, and afterwards there was a little time to work in his patch of vegetables out at the back. André followed him and he soon got round to the swallow on the powerline.

'I know,' his father said. 'Mama told me.'

'It's still there.'

'Well —' his father tilted up his old working-hat and looked at him hard with his sharp blue eyes '— well, we can't do anything about it, can we, now?'

'No, Papa, but —'

'But what?'

He kicked at a stone and said nothing more. He could see his father was kind of stiff about it; that meant he did not want to hear anything more. They had been talking about it, and maybe — yes, that was it. They were afraid he would try to climb up the pylon.

At supper none of them talked about the swallow, but André felt it all right. He felt as if it was hanging above their heads and his mother and father felt it and they all had a load on them. Going to bed his mother said to him he must not worry himself about the poor bird. 'Not a sparrow falls without our Good Lord knowing.'

'It's not a sparrow, it's a swallow,' he said. 'It's going to hang there all night, by its foot.' His mother sighed and put out the light. She was worried.

The next day was a Saturday and he did not have to go to school. First thing he looked out and the bird was still there. The other swallows were with it, and when they took off it fluttered and made little thin calls but could not get free.

He would rather have been at school instead of knowing all day that it was hanging up there on the cruel wire. It was strange how the electricity did nothing to it. He knew, of course, that the wires were quite safe as long as you did not touch anything else. The morning was very long, though he did forget about the swallow quite often. He was building a mud fort under the gum tree, and he had to carry water and dig up the red earth and mix it into a stiff clay. When he was coming in at midday with his khaki hat flapping round his face he had one more look, and what he saw kept him standing there a long time with his mouth open. Other swallows were fluttering and hovering around the trapped bird, trying to help it. He rushed inside and dragged his mother out by her hand and she stood too, shading her eyes again and looking up.

'Yes, they're feeding it. Isn't that strange,' she said.

'Sssh! Don't frighten them,' he whispered.

In the afternoon he lay in the grass and twice again he saw the other swallows fluttering round the fastened bird with short quivering strokes of their wings and opening their beaks wide. Swallows had pouches in their throats where they made small mud bricks to build their nests, and that was how they brought food to it. They knew how to feed their fledglings and when the trapped bird squeaked and cried out they brought it food. André felt choked thinking how they helped it and nobody else would do anything. His parents would not even talk about it.

With his keen eyes he traced the way a climber could get up the tower. Most difficult would be to get round the barbed-wire screens about a quarter of the way up. After that there were footholds in the steel lattice supports. He had studied it before. But if you did get up, what then? How could you touch the swallow? Just putting your hand near the wire, wouldn't those millions of volts flame out and jump at you? The only thing was to get somebody to turn off the power for a minute, then he could whip up the tower like a monkey. At supper that night he suggested it, and his father was as grim and angry as he'd ever been.

'Crumbs,' André said to himself. 'Crumbs! They are both het up about it.'

'Listen, son,' his father had said. He never said 'son' unless he was really mad over something. 'Listen, I don't want you to get all worked up about that bird. I'll see what can be done. But you leave it alone. Don't get any ideas into your head, and don't go near that damned pylon.'

'What ideas, Papa?' he asked, trembling inside himself.

'Any ideas at all.'

'The other birds are feeding it, but it may die.'

'Well, I'm sorry; try not to think about it.'

When his mother came to say goodnight to him he turned his face over into his pillow and would not kiss her. It was something he had never done before and it was because he was angry with them both. They let the swallow swing there in the night and did nothing.

His mother patted his back and ruffled his white hair and said, 'Goodnight, darling.' But he gritted his teeth and did not answer.

Ages seemed to him to have passed. On Sunday the bird was still hanging on the lofty powerline, fluttering feebly. He could not bear to look up at it. After breakfast he went out and tried to carry on building his fort under the gum tree. The birds were chattering in the tree above him and in the wattles at the back of the house. Through the corner of his eye he saw a handsome black-and-white bird fly out in swinging loops from the tree and it settled on the powerline some distance from the tower. It was a butcher-bird, a Jackey-hangman, a terrible greedy pirate of a bird. His heart fell like a stone — he just guessed what it was up to. It sat there on the wire impudently copying the calls of other birds. It could imitate a toppie or a robin or a finch as it liked. It stole their naked little kickers from their nests and spiked them on the barbed wire to eat at pleasure, as it stole their songs too. The butcher-bird flew off and settled higher up the wire near the pylon.

André rushed up the path and then took a swing from the house to come under the powerline. Stopping, he saw the other birds were making a whirl and flutter round the cannibal. Swallows darted and skimmed and made him duck his head, but he went on sitting there. Then some starlings came screaming out of the gum tree and flew in a menacing bunch at the butcher-bird. They all hated him. He made the mistake of losing his balance and fluttered out into the air and all the birds were round him at once, darting and pecking and screaming.

The butcher-bird pulled off one of his typical tricks: he fell plumb down and when near the ground spread his wings, sailed low over the shrubs, and came up at the house where he settled on the lightning conductor. André stood panting and felt his heart beating fast. He wanted to throw a stone at the butcher-bird but he reckoned the stone would land on the roof and get him in trouble. So he ran towards the house waving his arms and shouting. The bird cocked its head and watched him.

His mother came out. 'Darling, what's the matter?'

'That Jackey, he's on the roof. He wanted to kill the swallow.'

'Oh, darling!' the mother said softly.

It was Sunday night and he said to his mother, 'It's only the other birds keeping him alive. They were feeding him again today.'

'I saw them.'

'He can't live much longer, Mama. And now the Jackey knows he's there. Why can't Papa get them to switch off the electricity?'

'They wouldn't do it for a bird, darling. Now try and go to sleep.'

Leaving for school on Monday, he tried not to look up. But he couldn't help it and there was the swallow spreading and closing its wings. He quickly got on his bike and rode as fast as he could. He could not think of anything but the trapped bird on the powerline.

After school, André did not catch the bus home. Instead he took a bus the other way, into town. He got out in a busy street and threading down through the factory area he kept his bearings on the four huge smokestacks of the power station. Out of two of the smokestacks white plumes were rising calmly into the clear sky. When he got to the power station he was faced with an enormous high fence of iron staves with spiked tops and a tall steel gate, locked fast. He peered through the gate and saw some black men off duty, sitting in the sun on upturned boxes playing some kind of draughts game. He called them, and a big slow-moving man in brown overalls and a wide leather belt came over to talk.

André explained very carefully what he wanted. If they would switch off the current then he or somebody good at climbing could go up and save the swallow. The man smiled broadly and clicked his tongue. He shouted something at the others and they laughed. His name, he said, was Gas — Gas Makabeni. He was just a maintenance boy and he couldn't switch off the current. But he unlocked a steel frame-door in the gate and let André in.

'Ask them in there,' he said, grinning. André liked Gas very much. He had ESCOM in big cloth letters on his back and he was friendly, opening the door like that. André went with Gas through a high arched entrance and at once he seemed to be surrounded with the vast awesome hum of the power station. It made him feel jumpy. Gas took him to a door and pushed him in. A white engineer in overalls questioned him and he smiled too.

'Well,' he said. 'Let's see what can be done.'

He led him down a long corridor and up a short cut of steel zigzag steps. Another corridor came to an enormous panelled hall with banks of dials and glowing lights and men in long white coats sitting in raised chairs or moving about silently. André's heart was pounding good and fast. He could hear the humming sound strongly and it seemed to come from everywhere, not so much a sound as a feeling under his feet.

The engineer in overalls handed him over to one of the men at the control panels and he was so nervous by this time he took a long while trying to explain about the swallow. The man had to ask him a lot of questions and he got tongue-tied and could not give clear answers. The man did not smile at all. He went off and a minute later came and fetched André to a big office. A black-haired man with glasses was sitting at a desk. On both sides of the desk were telephones and panels of push-buttons. There was a carpet on the floor and huge leather easy chairs. The whole of one wall was a large and exciting circuit map with flickering coloured lights showing where the power was going all over the country.

André did not say five words before his lip began trembling and two tears rolled out of his eyes. The man told him, 'Sit down, son, and don't be scared.'

Then the man tried to explain. How could they cut off the power when thousands and thousands of machines were running on electricity? He pointed with the back of his pencil at the circuit map. If there were a shutdown the power would have to be rerouted, and that meant calling in other power stations and putting a heavy load on the lines. Without current for one minute the trains would stop, hospitals would go dark in the middle of an operation, the mine skips would suddenly halt twelve thousand feet down. He knew André was worried about the swallow, only things like that just happened and that was life.

'Life?' André said, thinking it was more like death.

The big man smiled. He took down the boy's name and address, and he said, 'You've done your best, André. I'm sorry I can't promise you anything.'

Downstairs again, Gas Makabeni let him out at the gate. 'Are they switching off the power?' Gas asked.

'No.'

'*Mayi babo!*' Gas shook his head and clicked. But he did not smile this time. He could see the boy was very unhappy.

André got home hours late and his mother was frantic. He lied to her too, saying he had been detained after school. He kept his eyes away from the powerline and did not have the stomach to look for the swallow. He felt so bad about it because they were all letting it die. Except for the other swallows that brought it food it would be dead already.

And that was life, the man said. ...

It must have been the middle of the night when he woke up. His mother was in the room and the light was on.

'There's a man come to see you,' she said. 'Did you ask anyone to come here?'

'No, Mama,' he said, dazed.

'Get up and come.' She sounded cross and he was scared stiff. He went out on to the stoep and there he saw his father in his pyjamas and the back of a big man in brown overalls with ESCOM on them: a black man. It was Gas Makabeni!

'Gas!' he shouted. 'Are they going to do it?'

'They're doing it,' Gas said.

A linesman and a truck driver came up the steps on the stoep. The linesman explained to André fatther a maintenance switch-down had been ordered at minimum-load hour. He wanted to be shown where the bird was. André glanced, frightened, at his father who nodded and said, 'Show him.'

He went in the maintenance truck with the man and the driver and Gas. It took them only five minutes to get the truck in position under the tower. The maintenance man checked the time and they began running up the extension ladder. Gas hooked a chain in his broad belt and pulled on his flashlight helmet. He swung out on the ladder and began running up it as if he had no weight at all. Up level with the pylon insulators, his flashlight picked out the swallow hanging on the dead wire. He leaned over and carefully worked the bird's tiny claw loose from the wire binding and then he put the swallow in the breast pocket of his overalls.

In a minute he was down again and he took the bird out and handed it to the boy. André could see even in the light of the flashlamp that the swallow had faint grey fringes round the edges of its shining blue-black feathers and that meant it was a young bird. This was its first year. He was almost speechless, holding the swallow in his hands and feeling its slight quiver.

'Thanks,' he said. 'Thanks, Gas. Thanks, sir.'

His father took the swallow from him at the house and went off to find a box to keep it out of reach of the cats.

'Off you go to bed now,' the mother said. 'You've had quite enough excitement for one day.'

The swallow drank thirstily but would not eat anything, so the parents thought it best to let it go as soon as it would fly. André took the box to his fort near the gum tree and looked towards the koppie and the powerline. It was early morning and dew sparkled on the overhead wires and made the whole level veld gleam like a magic inland sea. He held the swallow in his cupped hands and it lay there quiet with the tips of its wings crossed. Suddenly it took two little jumps with its tiny claws and spread its slender wings. Frantically they beat the air. The bird seemed to be dropping to the ground. Then it skimmed forward only a foot above the grass.

He remembered long afterwards how, when it really took wing and began to gain height, it gave a little shiver of happiness, as if it knew it was free.

In Corner B

Es'kia (Zeke) Mphahlele

How can boys just stick a knife into someone's man like that?
Talita mused. Leap out of the dark and start beating up a man and
then drive a knife into him. What do the parents of such boys think
of them? What does it matter now? I'm sitting in this room weeping
till my heart wants to burst....

Talita's man was at the government mortuary, and she sat
waiting, waiting and thinking in her house. A number of stab
wounds had done the job, but it wasn't till he had lain in hospital
for a few hours that the system caved in and he turned his back on
his people, as they say. This was a Thursday. But if one dies in the
middle of the week, the customary thing is for him to wait for a
week and be buried on the first weekend after the seven days. A
burial must be on a weekend to give as many people as possible an
opportunity to attend it. At least a week must be allowed for the
next-of-kin to come from the farthest parts of the country.

There are a number of things city folk can afford to do
precipitately: a couple may marry by special licence and listen to
enquiries from their next-of-kin after the fact; they can be
precipitate in making children and marry after the event; children
will break with their parents and lose themselves in other townships; some parents do not hold coming-out parties to celebrate the
last day of a new-born baby's month-long confinement in the
house. But death humbles the most unconventional, the hardest
rebel. The dead person cannot simply be packed off to the
cemetery. You are a person because of other human beings, you are
told. The aunt from a distant province will never forgive you if she
arrives and finds the deceased buried before she has seen his lifeless
face for the last time. Between the death and the funeral, while the
body lies in the mortuary (which had to be paid for), there is a wake

each night. Day and night relatives and friends and their relatives and *their* friends come and go, saying words of consolation to the bereaved. And all the time some next-of-kin must act as spokesman to relate the circumstances of death to all who are arriving for the first time. Petty intrigues and dramatic scenes among the relatives as they prepare for the funeral are innumerable. Without them, a funeral doesn't look like one.

Talita slept where she sat, on a mattress spread out on the floor in a corner, thinking and saying little, and then only when asked questions like: 'What will you eat now?' or 'Has your headache stopped today?' or 'Are your bowels moving properly?' or 'The burial society wants your marriage certificate, where do you keep it?' Apart from this, she sat or lay down and thought.

Her man was tall, not very handsome, but lovable; an insurance agent who moved about in a car. Most others in the business walked from house to house and used buses and electric trains between townships. But her man's firm was prosperous and after his fifteen years' good service it put a new car at his disposal. Her man had soft gentle eyes and was not at all as vivacious as she. Talita often teased him about his shyness and what she called the weariness in his tongue because he spoke little. But she always prattled on and on, hardly ever short of topics to talk about.

'Ah, you met your match last night, mother-of-Luka,' her man would say, teasingly.

'My what — who?'

'The woman we met at the dance talked as if you were not there.'

'How was she my match?'

'Don't pretend to be foolish — *hau*, here's a woman! She talked you to a standstill and left you almost wide-mouthed when I rescued you. Anyone who can do that takes the flag.'

'Ach, get away! And anyhow if I don't talk enough my tongue will rot and grow mouldy.'

They had lived through nineteen years of married life that yielded three children and countless bright and cloudy days. It was blissful generally, in spite of the physical and mental violence around them; the privation, police raids, political strikes and attendant clashes between the police and boycotters, death, ten years of low wages during which she experienced a long spell of ill health. But like everybody else, Talita and her man stuck it through. They were in an urban township and like everybody else they made their home there. In the midst of all these living conditions, at once in spite and because of them, the people of Corner B alternately clung together desperately and fell away from the centre — like birds that scatter when the tree on which they have gathered is shaken. And yet for each individual life, a new day dawned and set, and each acted out his own drama which the others might never know of or might only get a glimpse of or guess at.

For Talita, there was that little drama which almost blackened things for herself and her man and children. But because they loved each other so intensely, the ugliest bend was well negotiated, and the cloud passed on, the sun shone again. This was when a love-letter fell into her hands owing to one of those clumsy things that often happen when lovers become stupid enough to write to each other. Talita wondered about something, as she sat huddled in the corner of her dining-sitting room and looked at the flame of a candle nearby, now quivering, now swaying this way and that and now coming into an erect position as if it lived a separate life from the stick of wax. She wondered how or why it happened that a mistress should entrust a confidential letter to a stupid messenger, who in turn sends someone else without telling him to return the letter if the man should be out; and why the second messenger should give the letter to her youngest child who then opens it and calls his mother from the bedroom to read it. Accident? Just downright brazen cheek on the part of the mistress ...!

A hymn was struck and the wake began in earnest. There was singing, praying, singing, preaching, in which the deceased was mentioned several times, often in vehement praise of him and his kindness. The room filled rapidly, until the air was one thick choking lump of grief. Once during the evening someone fainted. 'An aunt of the deceased, the one who loved him most,' a whisper escaped from someone who seemed to know and it was relayed from mouth to mouth right out into the yard where some people stood or sat. 'Shame! Shame!' one could hear the comment from active sympathizers. More than once during the evening a woman screamed at high pitch. 'The sister of the deceased,' a further whisper escaped, and it was relayed. 'Shame! Shame!' was the murmured comment. '*Ao*, God's people!' an old man exclaimed. During the prayers inside the people outside continued to speak in low tones.

'Have the police caught the boys?'

'No — what, when has a black corpse been important?'

'But they have been asking questions in Corner B today.'

'Hm.'

'When's a black corpse been important?'

'Das' right, just ask him.'

'It is Saturday today and if it was a white man lying there in the mortuary the newspapers would be screaming about a manhunt morning and evening since Thursday, the city would be upside down, God's truth.'

'Now look here you men these boys don't mean to kill nobody. Their empty stomachs and no work to do turns their heads on evil things.'

'Ach you and your politics let one of them break into your house or ra —'

The speaker broke off short and wiped his mouth with his hand as if to remove pieces of a foul word hanging carelessly from his lip.

'Das' not the point,' squeaked someone else.

Just then the notes of a moving hymn rolled out of the room and the men left the subject hanging and joined enthusiastically in the singing, taking different parts.

Some women were serving tea and sandwiches. A middle-aged man was sitting at a table in a corner of the room. He had an exercise book in front of him, in which he entered the names of those who donated money and the amounts they gave. Such collections were meant to help meet funeral expenses. In fact they went into buying tea, coffee, bread and even groceries for meals served to guests who came from afar.

'Who put him there?' asked an uncle of the deceased in an anxious tone, pointing at the money collector.

'Do I know?' an aunt said.

The question was relayed in whispers in different forms. Every one of the next-of-kin denied responsibility. It was soon discovered that the collector had mounted the stool on his own initiative.

'But don't you know that he has long fingers?' the same uncle flung the question in a general direction, just as if it were a loud thought.

'I'm going to tell him to stop taking money. *Hei*, cousin Stoffel, take that exercise book at once, otherwise we shall never know what has happened to the money.' Cousin Stoffel was not fast, but he had a reputation for honesty.

It was generally known that the deposed young man appeared at every death house where he could easily be suspected of being related to the deceased, and invariably used his initiative to take collections and dispose of some of the revenue. But of course several of the folk who came to console Talita could be seen at other vigils and funerals by those who themselves were regular customers. The communal spirit? Largely. But also they were known to like their drinks very much. So a small fund was usually raised from the collections to buy liquor from a shebeen nearby for the wake.

Bang in the middle of a hymn a man came into the room and hissed while he made a beckoning sign to someone. Another hiss, yet another. An interested person who was meanly being left out immediately sensed conspiracy and followed those who answered the call. As they went out, they seemed to peel off a layer of the hymn and carry it out with them as they sang while moving out. In some corner of the yard or in the bedroom, a group of men, and sometimes a woman or two, conducted a familiar ritual.

'God's people,' an uncle said solemnly, screwing his face at the time in an attempt to identify those who had been called. If he saw a stray one or two, he merely frowned but could do nothing about it on such a solemn occasion. The gate-crashers just stood, half-shy and half-sure of themselves, now rubbing a nose, now changing postures.

'God's people, as I was about to say, here is an ox for slaughter.' At this point he introduced a bottle of brandy. One did not simply plant a whole number of bottles on the floor: that was imprudent. 'Cousin Felang came driving it to this house of sorrow. I have been given the honour of slaughtering it, as the uncle of this clan.' With this he uncorked the bottle and served the brandy, taking care to measure with his fingers.

'This will kill the heart for a time so that it does not break from grief. Do not the English say *drown de sorry?*' he belched from deep down in his stomach.

And then tongues began to wag. Anecdotes flew as freely as the drinks. And when they could not contain their mirth they laughed. 'Yes, God's people,' one observed, 'the great death is often funny.'

They did not continually take from the collections. If they felt they were still thirsty, someone went round among those suspected of feeling the thirst too, and collected money from them to buy more drinks for another bout.

At midnight the people dispersed. The next-of-kin and close friends would alternate in sleeping in Talita's house. They simply huddled against the wall in the same room and covered themselves with blankets.

Talita sat and waited at her corner like a fixture in the house. The children were staying with a relative and would come back on Sunday to see their father for the last time in his coffin. The corpse would be brought home on Saturday afternoon.

Thoughts continued to mill round in Talita's mind. A line of thought continued from where it had been cut off. One might imagine disjointed lines running around in circles. But always she wanted to keep the image of her man in front of her. Just as though it were an insult to the memory of him when the image escaped her even once.

Her man had confessed without making any scene at all. Perhaps it was due to the soft and timid manner in which Talita had asked him about the letter. She said she was sorry she had taken the letter from the child and, even when she had seen that instead of beginning 'Dear Talita' it was 'My everything,' she had yielded to the temptation to read it. She was very sorry, she said, and added something to the effect that if she hadn't known, and he continued to carry on with the mistress, it wouldn't have been so bad. But the knowing it. ... Her man had promised not to see his mistress again. Not that his affair had detracted in any way from the relationship between man and wife, or made the man neglect the welfare of his family. Talita remembered how loyal he had been. The matter was regarded as closed and life had proceeded unhaltingly.

A few months later, however, she had noticed things almost imperceptible, had heard stray words outside the house almost inaudible or insignificant, which showed that her man was still seeing his mistress. Talita had gone out of her way to track 'the other woman' down. No one was going to share her man with her, full stop, she said to herself. She had found her: Marta, also a married woman. One evening Talita, when she was sure she could not be wrong in her suspicions, had followed Marta from the railway station to the latter's house in another part of Corner B. She entered shortly after her unsuspecting hostess. Marta's husband was in. Talita greeted both and sat down.

'I am glad you are in, *Morena* — sir. I have just come to ask you to chain your bitch. That is my man and mine alone.' She stood up to leave.

'Wait, my sister,' Marta's husband said. 'Marta!' he called to his wife who had walked off saying, laughingly and defyingly, 'Aha, ooh,' perhaps to suppress any feeling of embarrassment, as Talita thought. She wouldn't come out.

'You know, my sister,' the man said with disturbing calm, 'you know a bitch often answers to the sniffing of a male. And I think we both have to do some fastening.' He gave Talita a piercing look which made her drop her eyes. She left the house. So he knows too! she thought. That look he gave her told her they shared the same apprehensions. Her man had never talked about the incident, although she was sure that Marta must have told him of it. Or would she have the courage to?

Often there were moments of deep silence as Talita and her man sat together or lay side by side. But he seldom stiffened up. He would take her into his arms and love her furiously and she would respond generously and tenderly, because she loved him and the pathos in his eyes.

'You know, my man,' she ventured to say one evening in bed, 'if there is anything I can help you with, if there is anything you would like to tell me, you mustn't be afraid to tell me. There may be certain things a woman can do for her man which he never suspected she could do.'

'Oh don't worry about me. There is nothing you need do for me.' And, like someone who had at last found a refuge after a rough and dangerous journey, her man would fold her in his arms and love her.

Was this it, she wondered? But how? Did it begin during her long period of ill health — this Marta thing? Or did it begin with a school episode? How could she tell? Her man never talked about his former boy-girl attachments, except in an oblique or vague way which yielded not a clue. Marta was pretty, no doubt. She was robust, had a firm waist and seemed to possess in physical appearance all that could attract a man. But if she, Talita, failed to give her man something Marta had to offer, she could not trace it.

How could she? Her man was not the complaining type, and she often found out things that displeased him herself and set to put them out of his way if she could. In the morning, while he was asleep, she would stare into his broad face, into his tender eyes, to see if she could read something. But all she saw was the face she loved. Funny that you saw your man's face every day almost and yet you couldn't look at it while he slept without the sensation of some guilt or something timid or tense or something held in suspension; so that if the man stirred, your heart gave a leap as you turned your face away. One thing she was sure of amidst all the wild and agonizing speculation: her man loved her and their children ...

'They're always doing this to me I do not matter I cannot allow plans to be made over the body of my cousin without my being told about it and why do they talk behind my back I don't stand for dusty nonsense me. And someone's daughter has the cheek to say I am nobody in the family of my cousin's and says me, I am always going ahead of others yes I am always running ahead of the others because I think other people are fools what right has she to talk behind my back why does she not tell me face to face what she thinks of me she is afraid I can make her see her mother if once I ...'

'Sh!' The senior uncle of the dead man cut it to try and keep the peace. And he was firm. 'What do you want to turn this house into? There is a widow in there in grief and here you are you haven't got what the English call respection. Do you want all the people around to laugh at us, think little of us? All of us bury our quarrels when we come together to weep over a dear one who has left; what *nawsons* is this?'

The cousin who felt outraged stood against the wall with her hands hidden behind her apron like a child caught in an act of mischief. She had not been addressing herself to anyone in particular and hoped someone would pick up the challenge. And although she felt rebuked, she said, 'But uncle-of-the-clan, these people are always whispering dirty things behind my back what should I say? And then they go and order three buses instead of four these God's people have collected money for us to hire enough buses for them I shall not be surprised if someone helped himself to some of the money —'

'Sh!' the senior uncle interrupted. 'We do not throw urine out of the chamber for everybody to see.'

Someone whispered, '*Mapodisa!* Police! With two boys!' Everyone in the yard stood still, as if to some command. An African constable came in, preceded by two dirty-looking youngsters in handcuffs.

'Stop,' he barked, when they neared the door.

'Where is the widow?' the constable asked, addressing no one in particular.

Silence.

'*Hela!* Are these people dumb?' Silence. One of the boys blew his nose on to the ground with his free hand and wiped off the stuff from his upper lip and ran the hand down the flank of his trousers.

The constable went into the room with a firm stride, almost lifting the boys clear off the ground in the process. Inside, he came face to face with Talita, who was sitting in her usual corner. She seemed to look through him, and this unsettled him slightly. He braced himself visibly.

'Face the mother there you fakabond!' he barked at the boys.

'I say look at the mother there, you dirty tsotsi.' He angrily lifted the drooping head of one of them.

'You know this mother?' The boys shook their heads and mumbled adolescently.

'Mother, look at these tsotsis. Have you ever seen them before? Look at them carefully, take your time.'

Talita looked at them wearily. She shook her head.

'Sure-sure?' Again she shook her head.

'I know what you do at night you fakabond.' The whole house was now full of him, the rustle of his khaki uniform and his voice and his official importance. 'You kill you steal you rape and give other people no peace. Fakabond! You saw boys attack a man the other night, did you? Dung, let me tell you! You talk dung. Pure dung! You took out your knives for the man, fakabond! You see that bucket in front of your cells? You will fill it in quick time tonight when the baas is finished with you. This big white sergeant doesn't play around with black boys like you as I do. Dung! You didn't mean to kill him, you say, just wanted to beat him up and he fought back. Dung!'

The constable had hardly said the last word when an elderly woman came out of another room, holding a stick for support.

'What is all this?' she asked. 'First you come and shake this poor child out of her peace when she has lost her man and then you use foul words at a time like this. Cannot this business wait until after the burial? Tell me who are you? Who is your father? Where were you born?'

He mumbled a few words, but the woman cut him short.

'Is this how you would like your mother or your wife to be treated, I mean your own own mother?'

'I am doing the government's work.'

'Go and tell that government of yours that he is full of dung to send you to do such things. *Sies! Kgoboromente kgoboromente!* You and him can go to hell where you belong. Get out!'

She made a lunge and landed her stick on him. Once, then twice, and the third time she missed because the constable dashed noisily out of the house, hauling the boys by the handcuffs. The woman pursued him with a limp, right up to the car in which was a white man in plain clothes — directly in front of the gate. The white man was obviously at pains to suppress a laugh. The constable entered with the boys in a most disorderly, undignified manner. ... The vehicle started off amidst the clatter of words that continued to come from the woman's mouth.

Talita wondered: Were the boys merely the arms of some monster sitting in the dark somewhere, wreaking vengeance on her man ...?

Evening came. One caucus after another was held to make sure all arrangements were intact; for this was Saturday and the corpse had arrived. The double-decker buses from the city transport garages, were they booked? You son of Kobe did you get the death certificate and permit for the cemetery? And the number plate? They want to see the dead man's pass first. Ask for it in the house. ... Pass pass be damned, cannot a man go to his grave in peace without dragging his chains after him ...! Is the pastor coming tonight? Those three goats, have they been slaughtered? Right, this is how men work. ... You have worked well. The caucus meetings went on ...

Word went round that the grandmother of the deceased had come. She loved Talita, so everyone who mattered testified. Heads nodded. Relatives who had not seen one another for a long long time were there and family bonds were in place again. Some who were enemies tolerated each other, shooting side-glances at each other. Those who loved each other tended to exaggerate and exhibit the fact.

The people came in to keep vigil for the last night. The brown coffin — nothing ostentatious enough to cause a ripple of tell-tale excitement — stood against a wall. A white sheet was thrown across to partition the room so that in the smaller portion the corpse lay on a mattress under a white sheet. Tatila sat next to it, leaning against her man's grandmother. The days and nights of waiting had told on her face; the black head-tie that was fastened like a hood cast a shade over it. Her hair had already been reduced by a pair of scissors to look like a schoolgirl's. Singing began. The elderly ladies washed the corpse. The tune sailed out of the room, floated in the air and was caught by those outside.

'Tomorrow after the funeral eh? O.K.?'

'Yes, tomorrow after the funeral. Where?'

'At the party.'

'Oh-ja, I forgot Cy's party. I'll go home first and change, eh? But I'm scared of my Pa.'

'Let the old beard go fly a kite.'

'He's my Pa all the same.' She pushed him slightly as a reproach.

'O.K. He is, so let's not fight 'bout it. Still don't want me to come to your house?'

'You know he don't like you and he'd kill me if he saw me with you.'

'Because you work and I don't I'm sure. I'm getting a job Monday that'll fix the old beard.'

'No it's not just a job and it's not you Pa hates.'

'That's funny talk. What then?'

'Just because I'm twenty-three and I shouldn't have a boy yet.'

'Jesus! Where's the old man been living all these years? Jesus!'

'Doesn't matter, Bee. You're my boy.' She giggled.

'What's funny?'

'Just remembered my Pa asked me the other day who's that he saw me with. I say your name — Bee, I say.'

'And then?'

'And then his face becomes sour and he says Who? I say Bee. He says Where have you heard someone called Bee — *Bee* did you say?

I say anybody can call his son what he likes. He say you must be mad or a tsotsi without even a decent name.'

A deep sigh and then: 'That's not funny.' He trembled slightly.

'Don't be cross Bee, you know it means nothing to me what you're called.'

'Sh — they're praying now.'

Two mouths and two tongues suck each other as he presses her against the wall of the shed that served as a fowl-run.

'Hm, they're praying,' but her words are lost in the other's mouth. He feels her all over and she wriggles against him. She allows herself to be floored ...

A hymn strikes again.

Two figures heave themselves up from the ground, panting. It has been a dark, delicious, fugitive time. They go back and join the singers, almost unnoticed.

The hymn continues. A hymn of hope, of release by death, of refuge for the weary and tormented: a surrender to death once it has been let loose among a flock of sheep. Underlying the poetry of this surrender is the one long and huge irony of endurance.

In another corner of the yard an elderly man was uncorking a bottle of whisky and pouring it into glasses. The sound of it, like water flowing down a rocky crevice, was pleasing to the ear as the company squatted in front of the 'priest'. 'Here my children, kill the heart and as the Englishman says, *drown de sorry*. Ah you see now ...' Someone, for lack of something important or relevant to say, but out of sheer blissful expectation, sighed: '*Ja Madoda* — yes, men, death is a strange thing. If he came to my house he would ask my woman to give him food any time and he could come any time of night and say I've come to see if you're all right and then we would talk and talk and talk. We were so close. And now he's late, just like that.' And he sobbed and sniffled.

'*Ja,*' the other sighed in chorus.

A woman screamed in the room and broke into sobs. The others carried her out.

'Quiet child,' a middle-age woman coaxed. 'Quiet, quiet, quiet.' Talita held out. When Sunday dawned she said in her heart, God let it pass this time. The final act came and passed ...

They were all walking away from the grave towards the tarmac path leading to the exit. Suddenly a woman, seemingly from nowhere, went and flung herself on the soft, red damp mound of the new grave. It was Marta. She screamed like one calling a person across a river in flood, knowing the futility of it all. 'Why did you leave me alone?' Marta yelled, her arms thrown over her head. Her legs kicked as she cried unashamedly, like a child whose toy had been wrenched out of its hand. Soon there was one long horizontal gasp as whispered words escaped the crowd, underlining the grotesqueness of the scene. Some stood stolidly, others amused, others outraged. Two men went and dragged Marta away, while she still cried, 'Come back come back why did you leave me alone?'

Talita stopped short. She wanted badly to leap clear of the hands that supported her, but she was too weak. The urge strained every nerve, every muscle of her body. The women who supported her whispered to her to ignore the female's theatrics. 'Let us go, child,' they said. 'She wants you to talk.' They propelled Talita towards the black 'family car'.

A few days later, a letter arrived addressed to Talita. She was walking about in the yard, but was not allowed to go to work or anywhere beyond her gate. The letter was in a bad but legible scrawl and read:

Dear Missis Molamo, I am dropping this few lines for to hoping that you are living good now i want to teling you my hart is sore sore. i hold myselfe bad on the day of youre mans funeral my hart was ful of pane too much and i see myselfe already o Missie Molamo alreaddy doing mad doings i think the gods are beatting me now for holding myselfe as wyle animall forgeef forgeef i pray with all my hart child of the people.

Talita paused. These wild women who can't even write must needs try to do so in English. She felt the tide of anger and despite mounting up, flushing her whole body, and wondered if she should continue to read. She planted her elbow on the table and supported her head with her hand. She felt drawn to the letter, so she obeyed the impulse to continue.

now i must tel you something you must noe quik quik thees that i can see that when you come to my hause and then whenn you see me kriing neer the grafe i can see you think i am sweet chokolet of your man i can see you think in your hart my man love that wooman no no i want to tel you that he neva love me nevaneva he livd same haus my femily rented in Fitas and i lovd him mad i tel you i lovd him mad i wanted him with red eyes he was nise leetl bit nise to me but i see he sham for me as i hav got no big ejucashin he got too much book i make nise tea and cake for him and he like my muther and he is so nise i want to foss him to love me but he just nise i am shoor he come to meet me in toun even now we are 2 merryd peeple bicos he remember me and muther looked aftar him like bruther for me he was stil nise to me but al wooman can see whenn there is no loveness in a man and they can see lovfulness. now he is gonn i feel i want to rite with my al ten fingas becos i hav too muche to say aboute your sorriness and my sorriness i will help you to kry you help me to kry and leev that man in peas with his gods. so i stop press here my deer i beg to pen off the gods look aftar us

i remain your sinserity
Missis Marta Shuping.

When Talita finished reading, a great dawn was breaking upon her, and she stood up and made tea for herself. She felt like a foot-traveller after a good refreshing bath.